D0387174

THIS
IS MY
BRAIN ON
BOYS

THIS IS MY BRAIN ON BOYS

by SARAH STROHMEYER

An Imprint of HarperCollins Publishers

Balzer + Bray is an imprint of HarperCollins Publishers.

This Is My Brain on Boys
Copyright © 2016 by Sarah Strohmeyer
All rights reserved. Printed in the United States of America.
No part of this book may be used or reproduced in any manner whatsoever without written permission except in the case of brief quotations embodied in critical articles and reviews. For information address HarperCollins Children's Books, a division of HarperCollins Publishers, 195 Broadway, New York, NY 10007.
www.epicreads.com

Library of Congress Control Number: 2015961010
ISBN 978-0-06-225962-2 (trade bdg.)

Typography by Michelle Gengaro-Kokmen
16 17 18 19 20   PC/RRDH   10 9 8 7 6 5 4 3 2 1
❖
First Edition

For Sasha Kennedy, one of the smartest girls I know.
For reading between motorcycle trips

Love is the absence of judgment. —Dalai Lama

ONE

It is an accepted scientific fact that the brain of the average adolescent male thinks about girls every seven heartbeats. Which, when placed in perspective, leaves very little time for the brain of the average adolescent male to seriously think about anything else—including, quite possibly, imminent death.

Addie figured this was the only explanation for why the boy wedged in the seat next to her wasn't freaking out like everyone else on Flight 1160 from New York to Boston.

A violent summer storm tossed the plane like a Frisbee; it climbed, then fell, banking to the left, then to the right, only to do it all again. The electricity flickered.

Drinks spilled. Luggage actually broke through a couple of the overhead compartments. People alternately gasped, groaned, and clutched their stomachs.

Intellectually, Addie understood that their fear was illogical. With at least thirty thousand feet of space between the ground and the plane, which was specifically designed to withstand the external stress of high winds and the occasional lightning strike, the chances of a free-falling crash were ridiculously minuscule.

But try telling that to her amygdala. That troublesome almond-shaped segment of her brain too often overruled the cortex's calm reasoning when it came to fear, anxiety, and, much to her embarrassment, love. So despite mentally recalling the statistical improbability of midflight crashes (eleven million to one) and trying to distract herself with the latest edition of *Neuroscience Today*, she was inwardly roiling in heart-pounding, palm-sweating, pulse-racing panic.

Unlike 11B, as Addie had mentally nicknamed him. He was blissed out to the music from his earphones, totally oblivious under his black curls, a silly half smile on his face, seat back, eyes closed.

Suddenly, the lights went off and the plane dropped, belly down, like a rock, which was so unexpected that the cabin went completely silent.

"I think we might have lost an engine," said a man in

row eleven, loud enough to be heard all the way to first class. He pointed out the right window. "It's on fire!"

"We're going to die!" screamed the woman in the window seat next to him, gripping the armrest. "Die!"

This was the third such outburst from 11A and Addie was growing mildly annoyed. For one thing, screaming was a primal reflex meant to alert others to flee approaching danger and was, therefore, completely useless on a plane. (Which was ironic when you thought about it—while they were in flight, they couldn't *engage* in flight.)

Moreover, due to her frequent outbursts, 11A was increasing the cabin's CO_2 to dangerous levels.

"Excuse me," Addie said, leaning across the long legs of 11B to get the woman's attention. "Is that really necessary?"

She regarded Addie through thick lenses. "*What?*"

"Your pointless emissions."

"I beg your pardon," the woman exclaimed, reddening. "I don't mean to criticize . . ."

(This was Addie's go-to opening line, suggested by her best friend, Tess, who had once gently noted that even though Addie might possess the noblest of intentions, occasionally, in an effort to be informative, she came across as, well, bossy. "But only because you're *so* smart and right ninety percent of the time," Tess had added quickly so Addie's feelings wouldn't be hurt.)

". . . but considering the diminishing levels of oxygen in the cabin, it would be ever so helpful if you could keep your carbon dioxide production to a minimum."

"Who cares about carbon dioxide?" the woman snapped. "Can't you see? We're about to die!"

A little boy sitting on his mother's lap across the aisle began bawling.

Addie estimated his age to be approximately six to eight—old enough, surely, to not be treated like a baby. Her twin stepsisters were that age and already they were acquainted with the mysterious art of cosmetics and the climate-change themes in *Frozen*.

"Hey, what's the problem, buddy?" Addie inquired.

The mother smoothed his hair. "Tommy gets upset when other people are upset. He's very sensitive."

Immature cerebellum, Addie deduced. Common among boys of that age group and, well, older ones, too.

"Perhaps this will allay your fears: flying has a 99.999 percent survival rate, and no American plane in modern history has fallen to the ground due to turbulence. Not once."

He sniffed and rubbed snot from his nose. "Really?"

Addie nodded. "Really. You're one-hundred-percent safe. Planes fly with one engine all the time."

"See, Tommy?" his mother said. "No reason to cry."

"I didn't know that." He sniffed again.

"It's the first three minutes after takeoff and the last eight minutes until landing where you run into trouble," she continued, hoping to nurture his nascent interest in aviation. "That's why landing is nothing more than a controlled crash." To illustrate, Addie plunged her hand through the air between them. "One gust of wind shear and we're toast!"

And Tommy started crying all over again.

11B pulled out an earbud and murmured, "Nice going."

"You can do better?" she asked.

"Probably anyone could." He tapped Tommy on the shoulder. "Hey, little dude, you want to see something neat?" He pulled out a set of keys attached to an unusual object—a large brown scorpion encased in acrylic.

Repulsive, Addie thought. Taking a creature of nature and turning it into a tchotchke.

"What is that?" Tommy asked.

11B said, "You tell me."

"A spider?"

"Nope. Close, though."

"A tarantula?"

"A tarantula is a spider," Addie said. "*Obvi.*"

11B flashed her a quizzical half grin. "Thank you, Bill Nye the Science Guy. However, next time let's remember to raise our hands." Turning back to the boy, he said,

"Here's a hint. It lives in the desert and there's a stinger at the end of its tail."

Addie raised her hand. 11B paid no attention, even when she flapped it and said, "I know, I know."

Tommy took the key chain, being mindful to pinch the one corner absent a leg. "Is it a . . . scorpion?"

11B shot him a finger. "Bingo. This one's a Manchurian scorpion I brought back from China. They eat them there, you know. On a stick!"

Mesobuthus martensii, Addie thought, fighting the temptation to inform them of the venom's fascinating use by Eastern physicians to treat neurological disorders such as paralysis and chronic pain and its untapped potential to cure forms of cancer.

The boy gazed at the dead bug with fresh awe. "I've never seen one up close before."

"You can keep it," 11B said kindly, smiling at the boy's stunned expression.

"No way!"

"Sure. It's good luck, you know."

"It is?"

Even though Addie was impressed, even touched, by 11B's easy generosity, she had to scoff at the silly notion of a lucky charm. Like "luck" was even a thing. She was about to put paid to this silly superstition when she felt a distinct pressure on her toe and looked down to see 11B's black sneakered foot pressing on hers—hard.

"What do you say?" the mother prompted.

"Thank you!" the boy gushed.

"Yes, thank you," the mother repeated with relief, handing the keys to 11B. "That was extremely thoughtful. He's totally forgotten . . . everything." She pointedly looked at Addie, as if somehow her mentioning the chances of dying at the beginning and end of flights had been inappropriate, when she'd only been stating facts.

"No problem," 11B said, handing back the freed scorpion. "To be honest, I'm not big on carrying around dead animals, even if they are scorpions, but I bet it'll keep Tommy busy." The two of them stared adoringly at Tommy, who was busy flipping the key chain over and over, inspecting every detail.

Addie sighed. It was extremely awkward to be stuck in the middle of a conversation when you were trying to comprehend *Neuroscience Today*'s exclusive on the untold secrets of dopamine.

"Do you want to switch seats?" she asked 11B.

He shook his head. "Nah. My work here is done." He sat back and untangled his earbuds, which wasn't easy as, in attempting to begin its early descent, the plane had begun listing from side to side.

She resumed reading and managed to get through one whole paragraph before she heard shallow panting, a telltale sign of hyperventilation. Her diagnosis was further confirmed by a cursory visual examination of 11B's hand.

"That twitch," she asked, gingerly touching the muscle at the base of his thumb, scientifically referred to as the opponens pollicis, "did that just start?"

"Huh?" He pulled out the right earbud.

She brushed her finger along the fleshy mound. It pulsed. "See?"

He rotated his wrist, examining the situation. "Not sure."

The plane plummeted yet again, eliciting another round of gasps from the passengers. 11A grabbed the white barf bag from the middle seat and heaved.

Kinetosis. When the inner ear and optic nerve send mixed signals to the brain, prompting the brain to assume, weirdly enough, that the body is being poisoned . . . whereupon it orders the stomach to empty its contents. *Fascinating.*

11B flinched at the muscle spasm. "Should I be worried?"

He sounded concerned. Addie assessed his other symptoms. Faint perspiration on his upper lip and above his heavy dark brows. Dilated pupils in his large brown eyes. A bluish tinge at the base of his nails. Well, that ruled out her two prior assumptions about him being unfazed by the turbulence.

"Are you dizzy?" she asked, circling his wrist to take his pulse.

"I don't know." He massaged his temple. "I think I might be getting a headache."

"You've been panting out too much carbon dioxide. You need to reabsorb some by breathing into a paper bag."

Which was in the process of being filled by 11A.

"That's the last one around so . . . not an option," he murmured.

The plane pivoted a sharp ninety degrees as smoke began to fill the cabin. 11B blanched, and even Addie, minutes after explaining to Tommy that the odds were solidly in their favor, found herself wondering if this was the end.

A crackling from the speakers overhead signaled an incoming announcement from the cockpit. "Well, folks, I'm going to do my best to get us into Logan without too many bumps," the captain drawled, "but it might be a rough landing. Therefore, I need you to put up your tray tables, seatbacks up, and, just to be extra cautious, to place your heads between your knees."

"And kiss your butts good-bye," 11B said under his breath.

The last eight minutes are the most dangerous. Addie braced herself for the worst.

11A shoved the soiled barf bag into the seat pocket and bent forward. 11B keeled slightly. If Addie didn't act fast, he was going to lose consciousness, possibly hit his head or . . .

She grabbed his chin and gave him a shake. "Wake up!"

He blinked slowly. "I don't feel good. There's this strange tingling . . ."

"Around the edges of your mouth. I know." He was farther along than she'd thought. This was bad. "Listen, do you trust me?"

"To do what?"

"To follow my advice, no questions."

"What kind of advice?"

"Put your lips on mine."

His eyes widened as if she'd asked him to kiss a toilet seat. "What for?"

Typical boy, she thought. "Oh, please. I'm not interested in you that way! This is purely a medical intervention. Without a bag handy, the only way to avoid stage five hyperventilation is for you to put your lips to mine and breathe. Otherwise, there is a very good chance that you will pass out. Or, in the extreme case, lose enough oxygen that you actually suffer a stroke, possible brain damage, and/or death."

"You're joking."

"See me laughing?"

"Do you ever? Somehow, you don't strike me as the giggling type."

She narrowed her eyes. "It's your choice. Live or die."

He hesitated and then, just when the plane took another free fall, leaned in. Addie pursed her lips, ready to perform her public service, but as he moved closer, there was something about him that made her do a double take.

Those eyes.

And then it clicked.

TWO

"I know you!" she exclaimed. "You go to the Academy."

He flinched, backing off. "355?"

She nodded, trying to place him, which was often a challenge. People who weren't in her advanced science classes, who didn't spend all their free time in the library or the lab or live in her all-girls dorm were, even in their small school, strangers.

"Heads down, please." A flight attendant placed slight pressure on Addie's head. She and 11B did as they were told.

"This actually helps with the dizziness," he said, inhaling deeply. "Probably not as much as a kiss, but . . ."

"This was going to be my second option, though it's

more effective with a bag." She peeked at 11A, whose lips were moving rapidly in a silent prayer. "So, how come we've never met before?"

"I'm fairly new," he said, palming sweat off his brow. "I used to go to Andover, but I transferred in January after I came back from Nepal."

Something crashed in the overhead bins. "What were you doing there?"

"Volunteered with Projects Abroad to help rebuild after the earthquake. Most amazing experience of my life. You can't imagine the devastation in Kathmandu. No running water. Some people walking around like ghosts, having lost their entire families, others opening what was left of their homes to you, just grateful to be alive. It was surreal.

"On top of that, I went to China on the way back and saw the Great Wall, which totally blew my mind. Made everything else I'd ever seen seem meaningless in comparison."

"And that's where you got the scorpion key chain."

He nodded. "Along with a whole new perspective on the world. Just that."

"Just that," she repeated.

"Which was why I couldn't go back to school. I barely lasted a month. Guys who'd been my best friends seemed like such dirtbags. They'd go, 'Dude, wish I thought of that, padding the college résumé with some humanitarian crap. Yale eats up that kind of stuff.'"

Addie cringed. "So cynical." She wanted to keep him talking. Distraction was an excellent antidote for anxiety-induced hyperventilation.

"I know, right? I mean, by the time I left, my family in Nepal was like my own. They weren't just a thing on my college to-do list. So, I dropped out of Andover in October and switched to the Academy for the next term. And I'm a semester behind."

Which explained why he wasn't in her classes, she thought, noticing that his thumb had quit twitching even though the turbulence was so rough the seats squeaked as they plowed through the clouds.

"Cognitive changes," she said.

"Pardon?"

The plane lurched and she closed her eyes briefly, willing her stomach to quit churning. "Dealing with unfamiliar surroundings stimulates the creation of new neural pathways, thereby leading to a greater range of cogitation. Similarly, mastering Liszt's famously complex Hungarian Rhapsody no. 2 might broaden a pianist's skill at playing subsequent pieces."

He rubbed the back of his neck. "Greater range of cogitation, huh? If I knew what that meant I'd say you're right, maybe."

Maybe? She was *always* right, but she didn't quibble. "My theory is that even transferring to the Academy didn't solve your existential crisis. No doubt, having witnessed human suffering firsthand along with the Great Wall of China's majestic grandeur, you found it nearly impossible to rejoin the game. Striving for a perfect 4.0 and a perfect score on the SAT became irrelevant."

"Exactly! Where were you when I was trying to explain that to my parents when I dropped out of Andover?"

Addie checked her mental calendar. "If it was during Christmas break, then probably back home in the suburb where my parents live outside of Philly."

He chuckled. "Good one."

She didn't get what was so funny. She *had* been at home; the prospect of a ski vacation or a winter trip to the Caribbean would have been prohibitively expensive for the Emersons' shoestring budget. Unlike Tess, who spent every Christmas in Wales.

Tess was forever doing cool stuff on her vacations: surfing off the coast of Australia, basking on a beach in Thailand, riding elephants in Zimbabwe, where her mothers sponsored a school for girls. Last summer, she skied in Norway. In June. At midnight. In the sun.

Meanwhile, Addie was at home in Perkiomen, Pennsylvania, babysitting the twins. For free.

"Of course I won't pay you to watch your sisters," her father said indignantly when she politely asked to be compensated for sacrificing her free time to entertain two demanding little girls with endless games of Pretty, Pretty Princess. "I'm surprised by your selfishness, Adelaide. We all chip in here as a family, and even though you go to boarding school, when you're in this house, you're expected to be a team player."

Unfortunately, pleading to her mother was useless, since her mother was usually off researching venomous arachnids in some remote outback without cell service.

The upshot was that with all of her father's attention focused on his second family and all of her mother's energy devoted to the Karakurt spider, Addie's interests fell through the cracks. So she'd learned to look out for herself, even finding a way to pay for college—the reason she was on the plane to begin with.

Final submissions were due in two weeks for the Athenian Award—the highest honor granted to high school seniors who planned to pursue careers in neuroscience. She and her lab partner, Dex, planned to turn in their step-by-step Brain Adrenaline, Dopamine, and Amine Synthesis System, otherwise known as B.A.D.A.S.S.

Winners received a full scholarship to the college of their choice for four years. This meant nothing to Dex, whose parents annually dashed off $50,000 checks the way some people hand out Halloween candy. But for Addie, who relied on the good graces of Academy bene-factors to cover her schooling, every penny counted. Dex had already promised that he would donate his half of the money to her if they won.

That was a big *if.*

Even their project advisor, Dr. Brooks, doubted that the Athenian Committee would vote for the controversial premise that she and Dex could make anyone fall in love with anyone by implementing a few simple methods.

"I fear a glorified love potion is too silly to win an Athenian," Dr. Brooks told them last semester when they pleaded for her faculty endorsement, a key requirement for all high-school submissions. "I will keep an open mind, however, and wait for your trial presentation this sum-mer. By then you should have finished your experiments and honed your thesis. At that point, the headmaster and I decide whether to endorse this project."

The trial presentation was scheduled for that after-noon, and the truth was, they weren't even close to finished. They still had one more experiment to run, the make-or-break test that would determine whether they could duplicate the results of previous experiments. It was totally nail biting.

Dex had been at the Academy all summer refining the project, but Addie had been allowed to return now only because her father and his new wife, Jillian, were taking the twins on a one-month tour of Europe. Not that they'd even considered asking her to come along—even as a free au pair.

"At least your parents are involved in your life," she told 11B. "If I didn't take care of my twin sisters, my father probably wouldn't notice if I fell off the face of the earth. Not that such a thing would be possible, seeing as how the earth doesn't have a face and, of course, because of gravity."

He laughed again. "You're pretty funny, you know that?" He took advantage of his position to tie his sneaker laces. "Wish I met you last semester instead of . . ."

She waited.

He said nothing, just switched to the other shoe to redo those laces, too.

"Instead of what?" she asked.

He sat up and looked around. "Instead of . . ." He paused. "I didn't know anyone and I was a junior-year transfer student. . . ."

"You should resume the crash position," Addie said, as the smoke grew thicker. "We're about to make contact."

He lowered his head, his dark curls falling over his face and obscuring his features so she couldn't see his expression. Not that this was an obstacle. When it came to reading body language, Addie was the first to admit that she sucked.

"Anyway," he said, "I ended up doing things I shouldn't have done, so I'm going back for summer school. To atone for past sins."

Sin was such an odd word. Academy 355 was strictly secular, not Catholic like Gonzaga or Episcopalian like St. Paul's. Those "things he shouldn't have done" must have been really, really bad. "Did you kill someone?"

He turned to her and furrowed his brows. "No."

"Steal an item valued at over three thousand dollars, such as a late-model car?"

"Grand theft auto? Yeah, I don't think so."

"Torture an animal?"

"*Me?* I'd be the last person to hurt an animal. That's why I gave away that key chain."

He opened his brown eyes wide. Addie noted that his lashes were freakishly long and curled up at the edges.

"Then," she said, "I hardly see why you have to make amends."

"Let's put it this way: if I don't, there's a place reserved for me at a certain all-boys military school in Colorado." He exhaled. "All. Boys. How frightening is that?"

"Depends on who's going. My best friend, Tess, would love it."

For some reason, that, too, made him laugh. Though it was true. Despite—or perhaps because of—her vegan actor liberal parents, Tess was instantly attracted to boys with an overabundance of militarized patriotism and a penchant for buzz cuts. Case in point, her ROTC boy-friend, Ed.

"How about you?" 11B said. "Ever have an existential crisis?"

"Not per se," she said slowly, playing with the strap on her sandal. "But that's because I realized that existence was overrated. Like reality, it is nothing more than the result of our brain's ability to process stimuli."

"In other words, you think existence is only what you perceive?" He had to shout to be heard above the flaps that were being lowered with a loud groan.

There was no way to answer this without launching into a long and detailed explanation—complete with diagrams—illustrating how sight, smell, sounds, taste, and touch, i.e., the sum total of existence, were unfixed and fluid depending on one's brain. But since Tess had often cautioned her against "nerding out," all she said was "Yes."

There was a deafening thud and a jolt followed by a roaring screech. Involuntarily, she hugged her legs and braced her body, preparing for final impact. Seconds passed where the entire plane held its collective breath. . . .

"Hey!" 11B was sitting up and pointing past 11A out the window to the scenery passing by: other planes, the runway lights, the flashing of awaiting fire trucks.

It was over. The cabin broke out into thunderous

applause. Addie sat up and clapped, too.

"We made it!" 11B exclaimed, breaking into a huge grin.

And that's when he did it.

He was so fast, she didn't have time to process his movements and react appropriately. Hand reaching out, sliding behind her ear, the sensation of warm fingers along her jawbone, on her hairline. The way he hesitated for a half of a half second and then brought his lips to hers.

She let out a muffled gasp of, "Oh!" But he didn't recoil in shock at his impulsivity. He let his lips linger, soft and firm, like he was trying to leave a message.

Addie could count on one hand the times she'd been kissed by a boy. There was the necessary exploratory testing of lip-on-lip contact with Michael Utard in kindergarten. (She remembered he tasted disgustingly of peanut butter and sour milk.) In seventh grade, Nick Elias had tried to sneak a quick peck during a school dance and she promptly squished his toes in retribution. Park, the son of one of her mother's boyfriends, had made out with her down at the Jersey Shore a few times, and then there was that moment of weakness with Dex. An incident of which they never spoke.

Ever.

But this was a completely different experience. Michael, Nick, Park, and Dex had been her friends or classmates. 11B, however, was a stranger she referred to by a JetBlue seat number.

They broke apart. 11B held up his hand. "You were right. That did it. My thumb isn't twitching anymore."

"I don't even know your name," she whispered, still half in shock.

"Kris." A corner of his mouth curled upward. "And you?"

"Adelaide Emerson. Addie."

His lower jaw dropped. "*You're* Addie Emerson?"

He acted like she'd just introduced herself as Kate Middleton.

Or Godzilla.

"Yes, Addie Emerson," she said. "Is that good or bad?"

He collapsed in his seat. "I have no idea."

THREE

So, that was Addie Emerson.

Holy crap.

Addie Emerson was the reason he was headed to summer school, the cause of his spring demerits and near expulsion, though that wasn't exactly fair. It wasn't *her* fault that he'd landed in hot water with the administration. You couldn't blame the victim.

Still . . . *Addie. Freaking. Emerson.*

They were taxiing to the gate. People started gathering their things, desperate to get off the plane that had nearly spelled their doom.

"Thank you so much for sharing your experiences with me." Addie turned to him with a smile that was far too wide and artificial, as if she was imitating a model from the cover of a teen magazine.

Her eyes were gray, almost colorless, and completely devoid of makeup. Her hair was a mousy brown gathered in a careless ponytail. And in a plain white cropped T-shirt and blue-checked skirt, she looked more like a kid than a rising high school senior.

"Nice talking to you, too," he said.

To his own surprise, he realized he meant it. It *had* been nice. During their brief conversation, he found her to be smart, insightful, even funny—right up until he found out who she was.

Now all he wanted to do was get the heck away from her as fast as humanly possible.

He switched on his phone and checked his messages. Three popped up, all from Kara.

Hey, KC, glad to have you back in civilization. Text me when you land so we can meet up.

She was home for the summer at (one of) her parents' homes in Boston's Back Bay, a short bus and T ride from the Academy. Kara had informed him in not so many words that she considered his return to the Boston area to be a chance for them to rekindle their fizzled romance.

Kris did not.

Landed, he replied. He did not add a "can't wait to see you, too," because it wasn't true.

Kara was a big part of the semester he wanted to forget. He often wondered how last spring might have ended if they hadn't met in the cafeteria line waiting for the cooks to heat up veggie burgers and if he hadn't mentioned how the Academy was surprisingly backward in its paltry vegan offerings. That was all it took to set her off on a tirade about the school's whole screwed-up attitude about animal rights.

Then again, if he was being totally honest, he'd have to confess that he'd let her rant just to watch her eyes flash with outrage. And, okay, so maybe he hadn't been as concerned about the "paltry vegan offerings" as he was eager to get to know the tall girl with the long straight black hair and cool, intricate silver earrings he would later learn she'd hammered herself.

Despite all her faults—and there were many—Kara was fueled by fierce passions. For jewelry and art. For animals. For him. Maybe that was why it was so hard to break it off with her once and for all. Or maybe they were doomed to be permanently bonded by being partners in crime.

God. He hoped not.

Come here first, she texted. *My parents are in Europe.*

Sorry. Got an appt w/Foy.

Screw it. You don't need the Academy. After the way they treated you???

Gotta go. Call you later, he replied, and put his phone on silent, hoping that would hold her for a while.

There was a commotion overhead, and he looked up to see Addie standing on tiptoe struggling with opening the bin. "It's jammed." She fiddled with the latch. "It must have locked during turbulence."

Clearly written above the latch in black letters on the white plastic was the word PUSH, and there she was . . . pulling.

"Here." He stood and pushed the metal latch. The bin flung open.

"Oh," she said sheepishly, pink rising to her cheeks. "The instructions should have clearly specified a forward action."

He opened his mouth to crack a joke and decided she wouldn't appreciate the humor. "This it?" He yanked out a black suitcase adorned with a fluorescent-green . . . *was that a chemical test strip?*

"Thanks for your assistance," she said, removing it from his arms. "I assume we will see each other on campus."

Not if I can help it. Because sooner or later she'd find out who he was, and then she'd hate him . . . and rightly so. "Sure."

"Okay." She stepped in line with everyone else clamoring to get off the plane, her posture ramrod straight, chin lifted.

Strange girl, Kris thought, falling back into his old

seat to wait for the crush of humanity to pass. The more distance he could put between him and Addie, the better.

The plane was almost empty by the time he swung out of his seat, got his duffel bag from the bin, threw his backpack over his shoulder, thanked the flight attendants, and strolled out the door to the blue-carpeted gangplank.

He got a rush passing through this part of the airport, still in international territory, not technically on American soil. Outside the banks of windows, planes from all over the world were waiting to take passengers to China, Australia, Ireland, and Israel. All he had to do was step through one of those doors and he'd be in Patagonia. Or Iceland.

Someday I will take every single one of these flights and travel all over the world.

Not today, however. Today, he was headed straight to the doghouse.

According to the letter folded in his pocket, once he arrived on campus, he was to proceed directly to Chisolm Hall, the administration building, for a meeting with Tim Foy, the headmaster, who would specify the details of the "Agreement of Reinstatement" hammered out by the Academy and Kris's parents.

Kris had no idea what the agreement involved, though he imagined a series of menial tasks ranging from writing a thoughtful essay to performing community service (the

Academy was big on stocking the local food pantry) and, perhaps, repainting the lab walls they'd defaced. Although Buildings and Grounds had taken care of that the morning after, sandblasting off all the graffiti before noon.

He was lucky. The other two had been sent packing in May, the week before finals, which meant they earned zip for the semester. A cool $15,000 of tuition down the drain. Then again . . .

His phone buzzed. *Dude. You back in prison?*

Mack. Kris stifled a wave of resentment. Now here was someone to blame, the guy who ruined everything.

Yeah, he replied tersely.

Sux 2 b u.

A nanosecond later, Mack texted a photo of a white beach, blue skies, and his tanned self on a towel soaking up the sun next to two girls in bikinis. Mack at his parents' beachfront condo in Florida.

That was an aggravating aspect about karma. It didn't always bite the butts of those who deserved it most.

He decided just to ignore that last shot. Shoving his phone back in his pocket, he shifted his backpack and skirted the line of family and friends leaning over the Plexiglas barricades searching for the familiar faces among the arriving passengers. He only wanted to pass through baggage claim on his way to the shuttle without being seen by . . .

"Kris!"

He kept moving forward, pretending not to notice Addie shouting at him from the other side of the barrier.

"You need a ride?"

Too late. He'd been spotted. To pretend otherwise would be beyond the bounds of rude.

"Oh, hey, Addie!" He acted startled, as if seeing her was some pleasant surprise.

She waved him toward her. "If you're going back to the Academy, come with us. Tess's boyfriend has a car."

He scanned the crowd until his gaze fell on a tall, outrageously redheaded girl in a filmy pink dress. Tess McGrew. He knew her. Or, rather, knew *of* her and her super-famous mothers—major Hollywood actors with a couple of Academy Awards.

In a million years, the last person he'd have figured to be friends with Addie Emerson was Tess McGrew.

"Come on," she was saying, "we have to hurry. Ed's parked illegally."

Kris halted. Something about the vibe Tess was giving off made him uneasy. It might have been her green eyes, narrowed with suspicion. Or that her hands had balled into fists. Maybe Addie hadn't put two and two together, but judging from Tess's body language, it was likely her best friend had. The girl looked about ready to clock him.

"I better not. I can take the T," he said, backing away. "It's just as fast."

Addie frowned. "No, it's not. The shuttle to the T runs every fifteen minutes and it will take twelve minutes more to get to Wonderland at the end of the Blue Line. The 411 bus won't pick you up until"—she checked the watch that she wore on her right wrist upside down—"nine forty-five. Which means you will reach the Academy at ten thirty at the earliest. We'll be there by nine fifty!"

"Did you memorize the schedule?"

"I just know it. Don't you?"

He glanced over to Tess, who appeared to have relented somewhat. "Addie's right," she said, coming over and introducing herself. "And you better do as she says. She rarely takes no for an answer."

"That's not true. There are many instances where the negative is appropriate," Addie replied, jumping onto the down escalator.

Kris relented. A quick ride to school wouldn't do any harm. A lot better than taking the bus and the T, he thought with a shrug.

"Hold on, genius." Tess snagged his backpack at the top of the escalator. "I need to talk to you."

Uh-oh. He looked down at Addie, who stared up at them, confused.

"You can wipe that grin off your face," Tess whispered sweetly, holding up a finger to signal that Addie should wait just out of earshot. "I don't know what you're up to, hanging out with her, but if this is just more of the crap you and your whack-case friends pulled last semester, I will personally burn your ass. Got that?"

His throat tightened. "Absolutely, but . . ."

"But nothing." More sweetness. She could have been cooing to a kitten. "Addie is my best friend in the whole wide world. And she can be a little innocent, you know what I mean? She doesn't have much experience with people like you and Kara and that total douchebag, Mack Jeffries."

Tess called that one. If there was any word for Mack, it was douchebag. "Actually . . ."

"Shut up. I'm talking." Tess exhaled, composing herself, then pasted on another smile. "What I'm trying to say is that I will give you one chance. One. Blow it and you're toast. *Comprende?*"

"*Comprende,*" he responded dumbly.

"You will never set foot in the Academy again. I will personally see to it that your college dreams are crushed and that you never find happiness as long as you live. Seriously. I have people."

"People?"

"People."

"Okay," he said as Tess pushed past him to catch up with her friend.

He had no idea what she meant by one chance or how he might blow it. But he did know this: after getting reamed out by Tess McGrew, the prospect of another lecture from the headmaster would be a piece of cake.

FOUR

Addie couldn't fathom why Tess wasn't happier about Kris, especially since Tess was forever advising her to "meet new people," which, in Addie's opinion, was entirely unnecessary, as she already had three close friends: Tess, Ed, and Dex.

"Dex is your lab partner," Tess would correct.

"With benefits," Addie would add.

"Not the kind of benefits people think about when you say lab partner with benefits."

What other benefits could there be? Dex was super-smart and organized. He calibrated every measurement to the last millimeter and took meticulous notes on their observations. As a result, their reports were always 100 percent complete and they earned stellar grades for tidiness as well as procedure.

Added bonus: he had his own 3D printer and permission to work at the lab unsupervised.

Okay, so now she'd made a new friend per Tess's advice. Kris was personable, outgoing, and, even according to Tess's ridiculously high standards, cute. That is if by cute, you meant tall, dark, and handsome, with a mischievous gleam in his eyes and unruly black hair that added a touch of wildness to his otherwise standard seventeen-year-old-boy demeanor. He attended the Academy, which was convenient. He had traveled to Asia and had retrieved her bag from the overhead compartment, thereby proving he could be worldly and polite. What could be more perfect?

And yet Tess had seemed reluctant to give Kris a ride. Or maybe Addie had misread the situation. After all, they had stopped to chat at the top of the escalator, so clearly they got along. Maybe Tess knew him from drama.

Why couldn't she be better at reading body language? Tess could tell right off when someone was simmering with resentment or harboring a grudge. She could even pick out who had a crush on whom—from half a classroom away! Addie never could, which was odd since, having extensively studied the biology of infatuation, she should have been able to pinpoint who was in the midst of it.

It was too complicated. She wished people would be more direct.

For example, Ed's reaction when Kris slid into the backseat. What was up with that? He seemed completely put off that Tess had offered him a ride even though there was plenty of room for everyone.

"Um, *Kris Condos*?" he'd said, as if he was a wanted criminal.

"We met on the plane," Addie informed him. "He's spending the summer at the Academy to atone for past sins."

Kris winced, and Ed looked to Tess, who said, "We've had a talk. Just go with it."

Which was unusual, because Tess knew Ed was not a "go with it" kind of person. He came from a long line of army generals who were big on discipline, rules, order, and military time. He was short, squat, muscular, and might otherwise have been impossible to tolerate had it not been for a wayward love of practical jokes.

Before he and Tess had reached the endorphin level of their relationship, he'd snagged her phone and temporarily switched all her contacts to *Lord of the Rings* characters. Gollum was on speed dial.

In contrast, Tess was one of seven children adopted by the Famous Actor Mothers who, when not starring in period dramas about English high society or medieval fantasies, were protesting US invasions abroad and chaining themselves to nuclear facilities.

Ed and Tess were Addie's first successful experiment, living proof that it was possible to induce attraction and even "love" between the unlikeliest of partners.

Not that Tess was aware they were the first B.A.D.A.S.S. pair, of course. To this day, she remained convinced her "chance" meeting with Ed and subsequent romance had been nothing but pure kismet.

As if.

Weeks of planning had gone into ensuring that when she and Tess climbed Mount Washington in New Hampshire last fall—a feat in itself, since Tess loathed hiking—that Ed would be on the mountain to rush to her rescue with his Eagle Scout training.

"It wasn't fate," Addie once tried explaining to her best friend. "You sprained your ankle during a random nor'easter and Ed happened to be hiking in the area with a first-aid kit."

"Yes, but he saved me."

"Because he knew how to wrap an ankle."

"He made a bier!" Whenever Tess arrived at this point in the story, she would sigh and get all dreamy. "He carried me down the mountain."

It was true that the bier was an impressive feat. Even Addie, who was with Tess when she hurt her ankle, had to admit that Ed's ability to fashion a stretcher out of interwoven twigs was inspired.

They were scaling the infamously slick rock face of Huntington Ravine when Tess lost her footing and slid a good twenty feet, landing on a ledge not much wider than a park bench. By the time Addie crawled to her, Tess's ankle was swollen like a butternut squash and growing purple.

So were the clouds overhead. Mount Washington had its own weather system that could switch on a whim from hot to cold, calm to stormy like it was doing that Saturday afternoon. There was no way they'd be able to reach the safety of the Lake of the Clouds shelter at the summit with Tess barely able to move.

"We'll find an outcropping of rock," Addie had said, lifting an arm under her friend's shoulders so she could at least hobble. "And then I'll call for help."

Tess let out a little cry with each step. Meanwhile, the wind grew intense and big drops of rain started to fall as lightning flashed nearby. "We're doomed," she declared, sparing none of the drama that had made her the Academy's reigning diva. "Oh my god. I've never been so scared."

Even Addie, who was well aware of the nor'easter predictions when she took to the hill, was rattled by the storm's ferocity, the bending trees, the drastic plunge in temperatures, and the heart-stopping thunderclaps. It was much more than she'd bargained for. Plus, getting Tess injured hadn't been part of the plan. The plan had been for them to get caught in the storm and call for Ed's help. Now they were in deep, deep trouble.

Fortunately, Ed seemed almost charged that not only was his crush in need of protection, but also medical treatment. "Be right there. I'm a half mile away," he told Addie on his cell. "Stay put."

"Ed Wiziak?" Tess grimaced in disappointment when Addie explained that he just happened to be leading a Scout troop in the area and was coming to their rescue. "He's such a dork."

It was true that Ed preferred white cotton knee highs and liked to tuck his shirts into the waistband of his pants. The buzz cut was not the most flattering hairstyle and his attitude of lead, follow, or get out of the way didn't exactly jibe with Tess's West Coast philosophy of live and let live. He was also a year older than they were, which presented its own set of challenges.

But Addie had observed Ed sneaking furtive looks at Tess while they were outside sketching charcoal images during their drawing elective class. She took no notice of him, even when he went out of his way to compliment her use of shading, which, to be honest, wasn't anything special. The boy was smitten, that much was obvious, even to Addie.

To Tess, not so much.

"Whatever," she said. "If he can get us out of here, then he's my hero." Though her tone was totally blasé.

It was dark when Ed finally found them cold, wet, and hungry. He arrived with a backpack of fresh water, hot chocolate, granola bars, blankets, a first-aid kit, and a hearty upbeat attitude.

"Two points," he joked, examining Tess's ankle with an expert eye. "Four if it's broken."

He assured her that he knew all about breaks and sprains, seeing as how he'd been volunteering as a local EMT since he was fifteen. During his winters back in Colorado, he was on the ski patrol, where he handled injuries way worse than this, and in the snow, too. He'd have her fixed up in a jiffy. No worries.

Addie watched in fascination as Tess melted in his capable hands. After he securely wrapped her ankle and assured her repeatedly that lightning could not enter their little cave, she let him fold a blanket in his lap so she could rest her head and sleep off the pain. Ed sat up all night, happily holding her in his arms.

By morning, she was madly, passionately, and seemingly permanently in love, as was Ed, their two hearts fused by trauma, adrenaline, and the primeval urge to survive.

That was the day she knew her thesis was solid. Love could be induced, as long as you had the right conditions.

Addie's phone dinged and she jumped in her seat. Dexter!

I see by my GPS that you have deplaned and are en route. Will you be coming to the lab? P.S. You are late.

She imagined him peering into a microscope, blond head angled intently. Most likely, he was attired in summer casual—salmon-colored shorts, teal polo shirt (collar popped), Lacoste flip-flops. He bought all his clothes online from a store in Martha's Vineyard where his mother had a standing line of credit. Many of his accessories were decorated with whales, which she found incongruous since whales did not wear belts.

Bad weather, she texted back. *Nearly died.*

For shame, A. It's not like you to succumb to hyperbole. Is your presentation ready?

She inhaled and quickly texted a reply. Dex's forthright manner never failed to leave her slightly dizzy. Of course she hadn't "nearly died." Why had she written that?

The PowerPoint is cued up. I will meet you at the lab once I unpack and wash my face.

He would appreciate this. They'd had many conversations about their fear of the nearly invisible Demodex mites burrowing and procreating in skin pores.

"Security check," Ed announced, slowing down at the guard house at the base of the bridge to the Academy.

Tess, Ed, and Addie pulled out their IDs. Kris sat, hands between his knees. "My, um, ID was taken from me last spring."

Ed cleared his throat and murmured something that sounded like "too bad they didn't take it sooner."

"If you don't have an Academy ID, they won't let you pass," Addie said, removing hers from her wallet. If the school had yanked his ID, then Kris really must have been expelled. And the only people who were expelled that she knew about were the group that vandalized the lab.

Of course, Kris wouldn't have had a part in that.

"Maybe my driver's license will work," he said, getting his out.

Ed handed over the four cards.

The guard passed them over a scanner and then stuck his head in the window, zeroing in on Kris. "This isn't an official 355 ID."

"I know," Kris said. "I'm on a list."

The guard checked his computer. Then he swiped a temporary ID and handed it to him. "This expires in five days. After that, you won't be allowed in without special permission. There's a note here that you should check with Administration ASAP."

Kris slid his license back into his wallet. "Don't worry. It's my first stop."

Addie was about to propose that Kris could have manufactured a fake driver's license and hacked into the school's computer system to add his name to a list, but Tess shot her one of those looks that she thought might possibly mean "not now."

"You're lucky they're letting you back on campus at all," Ed said cryptically.

After that, an awkward silence settled over the car and the three passengers suddenly developed an intense interest in the scenery as Ed drove up the causeway.

The bay was still churning from the morning's storm, white-capped waves lashing the rocks along the shoreline ahead. Ed stopped at the iron gates, punched in his code, and they swung open.

Home, Addie thought happily, admiring the grand willow trees, their graceful branches swaying in the wind, the banks of colorful red, pink, purple, and yellow petunias so carefully maintained by the landscapers, the bright green lawn of the quad, the stone administration hall with its antique clock, the white-clapboard residential buildings, and, her favorite, the nearly hidden laboratory perched at the edge of the cliff.

As its unusual name indicated, the Academy was not the average New England prep school, though with its historic brick buildings, ivy-covered walls, and massive oak trees, it could have passed for one in a lineup.

It was named in honor of Agent 355, a still-unidentified female spy from the American Revolution who was thought to have exposed the American traitor Benedict Arnold. Unfortunately for Agent 355, she was captured by the British, gave birth to a son she conceived with another American spy, and died on board an enemy ship.

Almost two hundred years later, a group of spies who were also mothers worried that their children would not be safe from the Soviet Union's KGB if they attended normal schools. So they founded Academy 355. Its reputation for educational excellence—along with state-of-the-art security—quickly became a draw for others who felt a need to protect their kids.

The Academy didn't admit just anyone. Tess was invited to apply, because her Famous Actor parents were hounded constantly by paparazzi and desperately wanted to protect their daughter from the limelight.

Dex was admitted because his mother directed a private assassination-for-hire agency contracted by the US government to discreetly eliminate terrorists. Her son, therefore, required added surveillance.

Addie, among all of her friends, was the lone scholarship student. She was accepted after her seventh-grade math teacher sent her stellar scores to the Academy's administration, along with a plea to take her as a student because their little Pennsylvania public school didn't have the resources to provide her with an education befitting her intelligence.

To offset the cost of providing free tuition to her and a few others, the Academy opened its doors each summer to rising high school juniors from around the world for intensive SAT preparation and New England college tours. So, for four weeks, the campus was overrun with offspring of sheikhs, minor European royalty, and California real estate moguls, who arrived with designer bags, glittering diamond tennis bracelets, Cartier sunglasses, and a whole heap of attitude.

Addie hadn't witnessed this phenomenon herself; she was relying on descriptions provided by Tess, who, like Ed, was working as a PC—Peer Counselor. This was a bit of a sore spot in their friendship, as Addie had also applied to be a PC and was rejected, despite her significantly higher grades and numerous teacher recommendations.

It was confusing. Never before had she been rejected for anything, except varsity field hockey. (Though that was to be expected, she supposed, after she accidentally dislodged three of the coach's front teeth with an illegal scoop.)

"What did I do wrong?" she'd asked Dex while they were cramming for their chemistry final after she got her letter of rejection last spring. "I've got the scores and the recommendations. Why did they take Tess and not me?"

"You're socially awkward," he said without hesitation as he scribbled a formula for oxidation reduction.

"I am?"

He laid down his pencil. "This revelation shouldn't come as a surprise. People like us—well, people like you—have poor communication skills. We—I mean, you—often unknowingly say things that are interpreted as rude."

She sat back, gob-smacked. "No, I don't."

He peered over his frameless glasses. "Isn't Tess often correcting you on proper behavior?"

"Yeeesss," she said slowly. "And I help her with Calculus."

"Exactly. That's the upside." He went back to finishing the formula. "People like us have Mensa-level IQs. At least, according to my test results, I certainly do. I can't speak to your intelligence level. This is why we find it impossible to associate with the normal. Compared with us, they are intellectually inadequate."

This only made her feel worse. Okay. So she was slightly smarter, maybe, and particularly fixated on the brain, sure. But that didn't make her a freak. . . .

Did it?

"No, no. You're fine, Adelaide," the headmaster, Mr. Foy, had informed her when she showed up in his office the next day, having lain awake the night before mulling over Dexter's analysis. "Think nothing of the committee's decision."

"They didn't reject me because I'm socially awkward, did they?" She studied his glass paperweight to avoid his penetrating gaze. "I've read plenty of books on the social behavioral patterns of adolescents. I know to keep at least forty-six centimeters between myself and others to ensure enough personal space." She pushed back her chair. "And Tess taught me that observations such as 'You're short,' or in your case, Mr. Foy, 'You're bald,' are not appreciated even though they are stated facts."

He cleared his throat. "That's excellent, Adelaide, but being a Peer Counselor requires a unique skill set. For example, a good PC is able to detect when her students are homesick or being bullied, suffering from anorexia, or even understanding their sexuality. How would you deal with those issues?"

"I would ask them about their issues directly. That's what I told the committee in my interview, and still I was denied! Now can you see why I'm upset?"

Mr. Foy sighed and switched topics. "What about the Athenian Award? Dr. Brooks tells me that you and Dexter are finishing up your research and are almost prepared to submit. That will give you plenty to do this summer."

"That's true. But I really want to help people."

This must have resonated, because he nodded thoughtfully. "I understand. Hey, how about a compromise?

Since you and Tess are such good friends, perhaps you can help her on an as-needed basis. A kind of Assistant PC. After all, you'll be staying in the same dorm, and Tess might need a helping hand now and then."

"I do know a lot about the adolescent brain!" she exclaimed, feeling better. "Thank you, Mr. Foy. I knew you'd find a solution."

So far, however, Tess had not come to her for assistance, only to complain.

"I've had to deal with two sets of bickering roommates, three cases of homesickness, one case of love sickness, an accusation of yogurt theft, and a queen bee who thinks I'm supposed to arrange her mani-pedis," Tess groaned over the phone. "I am so sick and tired of the drama!"

Addie found this statement illogical, since Tess had volunteered to direct the summer play, *Little Shop of Horrors*. She was born for the stage.

Ed's car rounded the quad with its lush green lawn pockmarked with brown patches that no amount of seeding could cure. At the center was a white wooden gazebo, a favorite meeting spot, especially on rainy days like this. A cluster of students huddled under its roof while the sky unleashed a sudden downpour.

"Let us out," Tess announced abruptly.

"Here? But it's raining. Can't he drop us off at the dorm?" Addie asked.

"Yeah, it's no problem for me to take you to Wren,"

Ed said. "I have to go past the admin building for Kris anyway."

"No!" Tess said shrilly. "Now! I have to meet the exchange students in Thwing and I'm already late."

"Okay, okay." Ed slammed on the brakes. Tess was half out the door before they came to a complete stop.

Addie got out and gathered her things from the trunk, eager to get to the lab and start working, but also slightly disappointed to be leaving Kris so soon, before they'd cemented their friendship. She could already hear Tess nagging her about blowing a chance to broaden her social circle.

She had to devise a way to make sure they saw each other again. This presented a challenge, as Kris wasn't in her classes, showed no interest in science and/or the lab, and also was a boy, so he wouldn't be living at Wren, the girls' dorm. However, when Tess dated guys B.E. (Before Ed), she would always leave something behind in their rooms that would give them an excuse to contact her. Perhaps that might work.

Addie zipped open her computer case, found a USB cord, and tossed it through the back window so it landed on the seat next to him.

"What's this for?" Kris asked, holding the cord.

Darn. He found it too soon. "Thank you," she said. "I must have dropped it."

"You just threw it in."

Then she had another idea. An invitation. "You should visit us in the lab. You might enjoy Dexter's crabs."

Kris's lips twitched. "The lab is probably the last place I should visit."

"Nonsense. We have a moray eel. And a centrifuge! It's state of the art, you know."

"He knows," Ed said, and for some reason Tess poked him in the shoulder. There was an awkward silence, and then Kris got out of the car and took his own pack from the trunk.

"I'm gonna split, too. Thanks for the ride, man." He gave Ed a wave, but Ed just lifted his chin in bare acknowledgment. With that, he slung his pack over his shoulder, shoved a hand in his pocket, and trudged across the soggy quad toward Chisolm Hall.

His exit was highly unsatisfactory. No "See you around," or "Hey, we should hang out," or "You know, I might just visit Dexter's crabs." It was as if those last fifteen minutes on the tossing and turning plane where he bared his soul had meant nothing. She couldn't help feeling as if she'd failed, yet again, in the social department.

"We have to talk." Tess was standing alone with a scarf over her head to keep off the rain. Addie hadn't even noticed that Ed had driven off.

"Why do people say they have to talk when they are

already talking?" Addie snapped, suddenly aware that she was extremely grumpy. No wonder. Her normal sleep cycle had been disturbed to catch an early flight and she'd consumed way too much caffeine.

Her skin itched and her heart thudded, warning signs that one of "her moods" was about to descend. If she didn't eat something, soon, she was going to be super-*hangry*. Just then, she remembered the shiny vending machine in the lobby of Wren bursting with indestructible cookies, candy bars, and chips. Normally, she avoided that machine like a sewer hole, but at that moment, it was the mecca of junk food, the source of all salvation.

"I've gotta get a Snickers ASAP. See ya." She began marching to their dorm, a girl on a mission.

"Wait!" Tess slipped off her sandals and went after her, barefoot. "I have to tell you about Kris Condos. Do you remember last spring when . . . ?"

"Please, Tess. Not now."

"He did something bad!"

"I don't care. We all make mistakes."

"But this is different. He did this to you!"

Addie spun around, her rising agitation growing with such intensity that if she wasn't precisely aware of the chemical processes in her brain, she would fear that her head was about to explode.

"If you're referring to last semester, he told me he

screwed up. We analyzed what led to his errant behavior. I explained about his new neural pathways. He agreed that made sense. So I don't care what he did last spring. What I care about is being his friend."

Tess's jaw dropped. "Hold on. You *like* him?"

"What's the big deal? You're always on my case to make new friends and here I am doing my best, but for some crazy reason you're all negative."

"I can't believe it." Tess's feet were apart, fists on hips. She was either stunned or ready to fight. "I thought you weren't going to have anything to do with boys until you got your doctorate from Oxford. What about when you said that they'd be too much of a distraction?"

Addie shrugged and resumed walking to the dorm. "The brain is constantly evolving and my current state is not in the same configuration as this morning when I got on the plane. Between the adrenaline of the turbulence and an invigorating discussion with Kris, my cerebellum created new pathways, too."

"Or, to put it in normal speak, a girl has a right to change her mind." Tess was laughing now.

Addie kept marching forward. "I don't know why you're making such a big deal about this," she said hotly. "Kris is going to be my friend like you and Ed and Dex. That's all. It's not as though I'm planning to drop out of school and run away with him. I just want to go for coffee, maybe hang out and watch Netflix on a Sunday night."

Tess snapped her mouth shut. "Sorry, Addie. It's just unlike you to care about this kind of stuff."

Addie bent her head against the rain and the cold and a sudden wave of self-pity. "It's not. With you and Ed wrapped up in each other 24-7 and Dex wrapped up in himself, sometimes I'm kind of . . . lonely. Can you blame me for wanting another person when you're not there for me?"

"Oh, honey. I'm always here for you."

"That's not true. Not always."

"I am." Tess stopped. "Besides, Ed's going off to college next month and who knows what will happen? He could meet someone freshman year and break up with me at Thanksgiving. So you're not the only one who feels alone these days."

Addie turned and regarded her friend, the soaked scarf plastered on her head, raindrops dripping off the tip of her thin nose, looking strangely vulnerable and small despite her regal height. A lot of kids at school sucked up to Tess with the hope that she'd invite them home to LA to meet her mothers and the celebrities who apparently hung around her backyard pool.

None of that had ever mattered to Addie. She didn't even know about Tess's mothers until halfway through their first semester as roomies in ninth grade, when Jake

Gyllenhaal stopped by to take her out to lunch and invited Addie along, too. He was very polite and super-smart, so he and Addie got along swimmingly.

Maybe that's why Tess liked her, because she loved Tess for herself, not her access to the red carpet. Or maybe it was because Addie had saved her butt in Calculus. For whatever reason, Addie couldn't imagine life without her flamboyant, crazy, impulsive best friend, her complete and total polar opposite.

Tess stretched her arms. "Hug?"

"Hug," Addie agreed, letting herself be folded into Tess's wet embrace.

Even if Kris never spoke to her again, Tess was right. They'd always be there for each other. No boy could tear them apart. Their bond was like the lithium iodide of friendship—powerfully electrifying and permanently unbreakable.

FIVE

"Do you play tennis, Mr. Condos?" Mr. Foy creamed an invisible ball with a perfect backhand.

"A little. Running's more my thing." Kris stood awkwardly, crossing and uncrossing his arms in the well-appointed office, more nervous than he wanted to be.

Since the headmaster was standing, he felt like he should stand, too. But he didn't quite know how to deal with the imaginary tennis match this man appeared to be playing, or the fact that he was taking his own sweet time delivering the death sentence to Kris's summer.

Tess's warnings about ruining his life still rang in his ears.

"Running, eh? Good for the heart. Great for long-term

health." Mr. Foy tossed the phantom ball high for a serve. "Distance or sprinting?"

"Distance. Cross-country in the fall. I'm closing in at fifteen in a 5K." It struck him, then, the stupidity of this statement. "But I guess you wouldn't know that, seeing as how I . . ."

"Transferred in January." Foy slammed the invisible ball with his pretend racket. "On my recommendation."

Kris followed the fantasy serve and applauded lightly, wishing with all his might that Foy would just get the lecture over and done with.

The headmaster tossed the imaginary racket onto a leather couch and wiped his brow. "Did you know that?" he asked, placing his hands on his hips and regarding Kris coldly.

"That it was your recommendation that got me in? No, sir."

"You had a 4.0 at the end of your sophomore year at Andover. Went to Nepal on a humanitarian mission on your own volition. Published an insightful and moving piece about Sherpa children dealing with grief after losing their fathers on Everest and single-handedly raised over twenty thousand dollars for them when you returned."

The achievements were true, though hearing them out loud was like getting shot with darts.

Foy returned to his antique mahogany desk and sat,

linking his fingers on the large green blotter. "I bought your line about not fitting in back at Andover—"

"It wasn't a line, sir."

"Excuse me. Let me finish."

Kris stiffened, unsure whether he should say "Yes, sir" or if that would be considered an interruption, too.

The headmaster smiled weakly. "I convinced our admissions department that a bright, thoughtful, driven boy like you would be an asset to the Academy 355 community. You would bring a fresh perspective. Third-world experience. You would be open-minded, dynamic, inspiring!"

Kris knew what was coming and it was almost too much to bear. The physical temptation to cut and run was overwhelming.

"Instead, you chose to pursue a radical path that resulted in destruction of school property, not to mention harassment of fellow students, in clear violation of the Academy Handbook."

God, this was awful. Worse than when he was found with the spray can on that chilly morning.

"What happened, Mr. Condos?"

He was caught in a quandary. He wanted to tell the truth about what he'd really been doing in the lab at three a.m., which was not what the administration assumed. But he was afraid that any explanation might come across as a cover-up, and nothing would get him booted off campus faster than a lie. So he said, "I don't know, sir. I'm sorry."

"Sorry is meaningless. Who cares about whether you're sorry? Anyone can say he's sorry."

At the tip of his tongue was the word "Sorry."

Foy swiveled back in his large chair. "Now, some of the faculty believe that your honesty immediately after the crime should be weighed as a mitigating factor. They also like you because you're an engaging student with promise."

There was a "but" coming. Kris could feel it.

"*Buuuuut,* I believe that unless you can explain why you did what you did, giving you a second chance would be a waste of my time and the Academy's resources. So, Mr. Condos, can you answer this simple question?"

"Why?"

Kris felt a twitch. The muscle at the base of his thumb was flexing. Did that mean he was hyperventilating?

Hyperventilation. The plane. The sound of the engines. The smell of jet fuel being dumped in case of a crash. The crying kid. The scorpion key chain. (Did he really give that away?) Addie. Heads between their knees. Talking. *Addie.*

"Neural pathways," he heard himself say in sudden clarity. "I laid down new ones in Nepal and wasn't prepared to deal with the implications."

Foy looked up. "Did you say *neural pathways?*"

Did he just say neural pathways? "Yes, I did," he answered with shaky confidence. "Immersing yourself in another culture often creates hundreds, if not thousands"—this part he might have been making up—"of neural pathways, especially in teenagers. Addie Emerson taught me that."

"Addie Emerson? When did you talk to Addie Emerson?"

"On the plane here. We actually had a pretty good conversation."

Foy reeled, as if Kris had smacked him with a shovel. "I must say, that is wonderful news. I'm quite fond of Adelaide. She's a cut above the norm."

"I can see that. She's very smart."

"More than smart." Foy tapped his temple. "A genius, especially when it comes to the brain. A passion of hers."

A girl with a passion for brains. Okay.

Foy leaned closer. "Does she, er, know what you did?"

He shook his head. "I hope not."

"Do you *hope*? Or do you *know*?"

Kris corrected himself. "What I mean is I don't think so, sir. She didn't seem to know who I was, except that she'd seen me around campus."

"Aha." Foy was silent for a minute as he contemplated his clasped hands. "Well, then, the restitution program

I've devised for your summer might just work after all. Are you ready?" He got up and went to the door. "Did you bring your work boots?"

"Excuse me?"

"Physical labor, boy, a tried-and-true method for rehabilitation. That and community service."

The food pantry.

"Come now." Foy snatched an umbrella. "We need to hurry. I assured Dr. Brooks we'd be at the lab by noon." With that, he threw open the door and marched out, past his secretary, Mrs. Plunkett, who raised a finger as he passed.

"Headmaster. Your eleven thirty appointment with the . . ." Too late. He was already down the marble stairway, Kris on his heels.

"Why are we going to the lab, sir?"

"You'll see." Foy took the steps two at a time. "This is the community service component. Great character building."

Never good when adults mentioned "character building." Another not-good thing? The lab. It was THE one place he'd planned on avoiding this summer. Probably, Foy had him lined up to scrape paint, scrub floors, clean out gutters and animal tanks. Yes, definitely the animal tanks.

The headmaster pushed open the large front doors of Chisolm Hall and stood stock-still. "Oh, crikey. I completely forgot about the exchange students."

A group of students stood in a cluster away from the drizzle under the gazebo.

"I bet that's what Mrs. Plunkett was trying to tell you," Kris said.

"Every summer we have the privilege of hosting several students from Beijing for a week." Foy squinted toward the quad. "They're part of a tour that starts in New York, goes to Chicago, California, and back to China. Along the way, they stop in Boston to tour colleges. We always try to take at least two boys and two girls. You speak Mandarin, don't you?"

"A little," Kris said. "Enough to get by. Languages come easy to me." He didn't mean to brag, but it was true.

"Good. I must introduce myself. And you." Foy deployed his umbrella and plowed toward the gazebo, free hand outstretched. "Welcome, welcome!"

It wasn't until the students parted that Kris saw the wet red hair. Tess smiled broadly at the headmaster, who exchanged greetings while Kris hung back in the rain, out of his new enemy's peripheral vision.

Tess had made it clear she didn't like him. She practically had it stamped on her forehead: I HATE KRIS. Now that he knew she was best friends with Addie, he understood why she'd led the protest on campus demanding zero tolerance for bullying. She was sticking up for her friend, not, as Kara claimed, riding a power trip.

"Tess McGrew can't resist exploiting a cause," Kara had said, twirling her black hair while the two of them watched the protest from her second-floor dorm room in Wren. "That's her mothers' jam, too, yanking orphans from their homes in Africa and bringing them back to London and LA. They only do it for the publicity."

"I read somewhere that a lot of those kids needed medical treatment," he'd offered. "Tess's moms paid for surgery that straightened their legs and even saved their lives."

Kara rolled her eyes. "Oh my god, Condor. You are so gullible. That's why I love you." Then she kissed him. Hard.

Condor. Kara found it impossible to call anyone by their real names. For the first few weeks after she met Mack, she called him "Slack" before Kris suggested, ever so politely, that she knock it off.

What he didn't mention was that he'd actually written to Tess's mothers when he returned from Nepal asking them for donations to help the orphans there. Their publicist had responded with a nice handwritten note thanking him for his interest and promising to forward his request to the couple. A month later, his organization received a huge check. Really huge.

He should have set Kara straight about Tess's mothers from the get-go. He should have told her about the check they wrote and the supportive emails that followed. While he was at it, he might have stopped Kara and Mack's plans to vandalize the lab.

Vandalism had never been part of the plan. In fact, neither Mack nor Kara had ever mentioned destroying anything. The idea was to free the animals. That was it. Clean. Simple. Innocent. Release the mice from their cages and the frogs from their tanks so they could scamper to freedom. And after listening to Kara's horror stories, how could he not be on board?

"Do you know what they do to the frogs?" she explained as they sat cross-legged on her dorm room floor, strategizing. "It's almost too awful to describe."

Kara was still furious over what she'd witnessed the semester before when she took anatomy and physiology. She claimed she couldn't sleep or eat until she stood up for those poor, defenseless animals.

"In anat and phys you need real muscles to test sodium and potassium reactions, okay? That means you have to kill the frog in the lab. First, you stun it." She mimicked slamming the frog's head on a table. "And it lets out a little croak."

Kris's heart flipped. As a kid growing up in rural Connecticut, he'd loved to watch tadpoles swim around vernal pools as the miracle of evolution revealed itself stage by stage. Fins turned into legs. Gills closed. The tadpole became a frog and crawled out of the water onto the mud. And he fell asleep at night with the windows open, listening to the cacophony of the bulls singing their mating chorus. "They take them to a guillotine," Kara continued. "No joke. Like Marie Antoinette. You put the frog underneath it and push down the blade and . . ." She drew a line across her throat. "That's what they do to frogs. Don't even get me started on the cats."

The cats came preserved. Bags and bags of them to be dissected by the upperclassmen. Fetal pigs—"yanked from their mothers' wombs at the slaughterhouse"—were also splayed on dissecting boards, pickled in formaldehyde.

"The Academy is so backward," Mack said angrily. "Other schools have stopped torturing animals. Kara's right. If we don't do something major, nothing will change."

It wasn't until Kris witnessed Mack going berserk, spray-painting random, violent images, smashing beakers in a rain of glass, swinging a baseball bat into terrariums, and almost—until Kris stopped him—tossing a laptop into the moray eel tank, that he realized it had never been about frogs or gerbils for Mack. It was something else.

But Kris didn't find out about that until it was too late. And now, here he was being condemned to a summer of hard labor and community service to pay for what had started out as a seemingly worthy cause.

"Mr. Condos!" Foy called.

Kris snapped to attention. "Yes, sir."

"Come here. I want you to meet our visiting students."

Tess pivoted slowly. *"Kris?* What are you doing here?"

"Mr. Condos has been to China and speaks fluent Mandarin. Isn't that true?" The headmaster waved him into the gazebo.

"I don't know about fluent," Kris said, nodding to the exchange students.

They nodded in return.

Tess introduced the girls. "This is Mindy and Fiona." The girls smiled.

"Hi," Mindy said shyly.

"You guys learned English really young, right?" Tess said. "I wish I'd learned another language."

Fiona butted in. "Yeah, I'm planning on majoring in hospitality so I can travel the world and run international hotels."

"Ooh, like the one I stayed at on Moofushi Island in the Maldives. The water is gorgeous," Tess chimed in.

"It's awesome," Fiona said. "We stayed in a grass hut at the same place, a . . ." She searched for the right word.

"Villa," Tess prompted.

". . . that was over water with fish and sharks underneath. And the diving and . . ."

". . . snorkeling?" Tess suggested.

"Yes. It was another world. Ever since then, all I want is to run a hotel in the Maldives with its endless white beaches and crystal-blue water. It would be like working in paradise."

"I hear that," Tess said. "You've been around the world. You, too, Kris, right?"

Kris remembered Mack bragging that it cost his parents $30,000 for a week at a Maldives resort before plane fare, which tacked on another $10,000 since his mother refused to fly that distance in anything but first class.

"I want to be a doctor," Mindy said.

Tess jumped in with mock dismissal. "As if that's anything to shoot for." She and Fiona laughed, but Mindy looked confused.

"It's a compliment," Kris said.

When she still didn't respond, he tried again in Mandarin, adding something about how being a doctor was far more noble.

"Oh!" She covered her smile. "Thank you. Yes. I've always wanted to help people."

Tess gestured to the two boys. "And this is Sam and Jack."

They bobbed their heads curtly. Sam pulled up the zipper of his blue Windbreaker and said, "It's noon, we should go."

"*Riiight.*" Tess glanced at Mr. Foy, who was talking to Jack. "We're supposed to have lunch with the headmaster in his private quarters. Are you coming, Kris?"

He was about to answer when Mindy said, "What about Harvard?"

"Harvard's on Friday, remember?" Tess said.

"But I have to go to Harvard today."

Fiona put a reassuring hand on her arm. "It can wait," she said in Mandarin. "He'll still be there."

"I hope so." Mindy pouted. "There's no point to this trip if we can't see each other."

That was odd, Kris thought. Just when it crossed his mind that, perhaps, he should let someone know what the girls said, Mr. Foy clapped him on the shoulder. "I'm afraid I can't accompany you to the lab this afternoon. Go see Dr. Brooks. She has your assignments."

Tess whipped around, red hair flying. "*You're* going to the lab?"

"I guess so." He felt a thin film of sweat on his upper lip, a Pavlovian response to her last lashing. "And I better be going." He checked a wristwatch that wasn't there.

"Yeah. You're almost two freckles past a hair," she quipped. "Wait. I need to talk to you. Alone."

Again? "I got the message already," he said as Foy led the students across the squishy lawn.

"This is a new and improved message," she said. "Look, I'm sorry for being hard on you back at the airport. I was just being protective of Addie after what you and your girlfriend did to her last spring."

He ran a hand through his wet hair. The rain had mostly stopped, but it was still drizzling. "It's okay."

"No, it's not. I get too involved in other people's business. Ed's always telling me to butt out."

Honestly, he was wet and cold and he just wanted to get someplace dry, even if was in Dr. Brooks's office being read the riot act. "We can talk later." He thumbed behind him. "I have an appointment with Dr. Brooks. And if I don't make it . . ."

"Addie's not very good at reading people," Tess interrupted, as if he wasn't speaking. "She takes things at face value."

"Yup. I got that." He tried stepping backward.

But Tess grabbed the sleeve of his sweatshirt and pulled him toward her. "I think she really likes you and wants you two to hang out . . . which is unusual. She's not normally that way."

"Well, we kind of went through hell and back on that flight." He tried wrenching free, but Tess McGrew had the talons of an eagle. "Imminent mortality has a way of bringing strangers together."

She released him abruptly. "Yes, I know. Interesting. So you were scared?"

"Um, the plane lost an engine, there was smoke in the cabin, we dropped fifty feet in a matter of seconds, the woman next to me was giving herself last rites, and I started hyperventilating." He pulled the hood of his sweatshirt over his head as an ominous black cloud drifted by. "You might say I was more than uncomfortable." What was Tess after? He felt like he was on the witness stand and she was the prosecutor.

"And how did Addie react?"

He shifted feet, trying to remember. "She read. And we talked about the brain. That's what got me through the turbulence, actually. There was something about the way she speaks that's so logical it was kind of . . ."

"Calming," Tess finished for him. He got the impression she did that a lot. "Yeah. I've had the same experience. She's the yin to my yang or the yang to my yin. Which is it?"

"It doesn't matter. Yin balances out yang and vice versa."

"Uh-huh." Tess seemed lost in thought. Kris wondered if he could go without her sinking her claws into him.

Nope.

"One last thing," she said, grabbing his sweatshirt again. "What were Mindy and Fiona talking about in Chinese?"

"Mandarin," he corrected. "I don't know exactly. Going to Harvard, I think. There's some guy . . ."

"Oh, no. I knew it. David?"

"David? Um." Kris scratched his head, feeling slightly uncomfortable, as if he was snitching. "They didn't mention a name."

"The tour group leader said that under no circumstances are we to allow Mindy to meet up with David at the Harvard summer session. Their parents have both forbidden it."

"And this is relevant to me because . . . ?"

Tess wagged a finger. "Because you better make sure that if you hear anything of a meeting with David that you tell Mr. Foy immediately. If Mindy runs off with David or whatever, it could cause an international incident. For real. Her dad's a diplomat. Like, the president would have to get involved."

Kris almost burst out laughing, it was such an absurd concept. "Isn't she fifteen? That's a little young."

"Sixteen next week. Haven't you read *Romeo and Juliet*?" Tess frowned when he started laughing at that. "It's not funny, Condos. You're in hot enough water as it is. If you add aiding and abetting an international kidnapping, forget ever coming back to school. Foy will throw you in prison."

She hoisted her bag over her shoulder, flashed him one more stern look, and trudged to the administration building, leaving Kris to wonder if the entire world had gone crazy—or just him.

SIX

The Agnes B. Whitchurch Marine Biology Laboratory—
aka the Whit—was tucked into the cliff overlooking
the roiling Atlantic Ocean and happened to be exactly
a 10.5-minute walk from Addie's dorm room in Wren,
provided her forward progress was not impeded by unexpected, if well-intentioned, interlopers.

Tess said it was more polite to refer to them as "friends."

An hour alone in her room, sorting, organizing, and
cleaning, had done wonders to settle Addie's brain. First,
she had unzipped each item of clothing from its individ-
ual Ziploc bag and placed them in drawers or hung them
in the closet.

Then she arranged her toiletries by necessity and size

in her plastic caddy and took them down the hall for a quick shower to rinse off the grime of the airport. After blow-drying her hair, she combed it smooth into a ponytail and applied special sunblock to her face.

Once again, she contemplated makeup. Tess said she should at least try a little mascara and subtle eyeliner. Even just a swipe of lip gloss. Addie understood the technical advantages of these enhancements, the way they tricked the viewer's caudate nucleus into imagining that the eyes were a perfect 63.5 millimeters apart, that glossy lips created a perception of health and, therefore, reproductive potential.

Would Kris find her more attractive if she enhanced her features as a parasite-free partner? That, after all, was the purpose of blush, though perhaps not a selling point Clinique would choose in marketing its Cheek Pop line. Still, she would have to research extensively in order to select the best products, a prospect that left her feeling slightly overwhelmed.

Addie caught herself. What did she *care* whether Kris found her attractive? She hardly knew him and she definitely didn't want him as that kind of friend. Maybe in fifteen years after finishing her PhD at Oxford, but not now. Boyfriends demanded too much time and energy, every last bit of which needed to be devoted to earning a full scholarship to Harvard—or a school of similar quality. (MIT would do in a pinch.)

Hmm. If she was developing feelings for Kris, then perhaps her amygdala had been temporarily damaged during the adrenaline rush of turbulence. She would have to review the literature. Somewhere there was an answer to her sudden interest in mascara, and if there wasn't . . . she would devise an experiment to find one.

She brushed her teeth and changed into a royal-blue tank top and white skirt. Blue was her calming color and she rarely deviated into the more alarming reds and oranges so adored by Tess, who also preferred greens, despite their tendency to trigger feelings of jealousy and envy in the subconscious of others. Addie had warned her of this, to which Tess's response had been an illogical "Excellent!"

After making up her bed, tucking the corners in tightly, she ran a tube of ChapStick over her lips, hooked her computer case over her shoulder, slipped her feet into a pair of ballet flats, and was about to head out when she spied the tiny bottle of perfume Tess had bought for her in Paris. Why not? she thought, spritzing a little on her wrist and taking a sniff.

Instantly she was transported to a flower garden of lilies of the valley. Smell was the most interesting and primal of the senses—instantly recalling the most vivid experiences: freshly cut grass on a summer day, wood smoke in winter.

She debated formulating an experiment measuring brain waves as they reacted to various scents, especially unusual smells to which those brains had never been exposed. Then again, the Whit didn't have the necessary equipment. That would be another benefit of winning the Athenian, the chance to get to use a CT scanner.

Pushing open Wren's heavy wooden front door, she crossed the quad to the stone wall that edged the cliffs and bordered the path down to the Whit. The morning's storm had swept away all the humidity and made everything green, sparkly, and invigorating.

Fierce waves crashed against the rocks below as seagulls swooped and dove into the blue-gray water. Addie inhaled the fresh sea air deeply into her lungs, since it might be hours before she was outside again. She tended to lose all sense of time when she was working in the lab and was often surprised to find when she left that day had somehow become night.

Footsteps pounded down the path. Lauren Lowes, one of the school's best field hockey players, ran past in blazing neon-green sneakers, her face bathed in sweat.

"Hey," she said, doing a double take and backing up. "I wanna talk to you."

"We are talking," Addie said. "Are you okay?"

Lauren was squeezing her side and grimacing. "I've got a stitch, dammit. Sucks."

She reminded Addie of a Russian ballerina. Slim with

blond, almost white, hair pulled into a bun, she ran with the grace of a gazelle—but displayed the manners of a long-haul trucker.

"You should exhale when your left foot lands," Addie said. "For some reason, it prevents ERTAP."

"What's that?" Lauren leaned against the wall.

"Exercise-related transient abdominal pain. Is that why you wanted to talk?"

"No. I wanted to ask what *you* were doing giving Kris Condos a ride?"

Addie stiffened. "You saw?"

"I was in the gazebo when you guys got out of the car this morning. I was like, what the . . ."

"Honestly, it's no big deal." Addie flipped her ponytail in an effort to come across as unfazed. "We sat next to each other on the plane and Ed and Tess were picking me up, so . . . Yeah." She adjusted the computer bag on her shoulder. "Are you ready for our experiments?"

At the end of last semester, Lauren had answered an advertisement Addie posted on the Academy's virtual bulletin board looking for volunteers to participate in "behavioral science studies" for extra credit. Having bombed AP Bio, Lauren was doing everything possible to bring up her GPA, including retaking the class over the summer and participating in Addie and Dex's experiment.

"I guess." She began walking, still clutching her side. "Not quite sure what I'm supposed to do other than show up. We start tomorrow, right?"

"It depends," Addie said, keeping pace. "We still need one more guy. That's what we're meeting with Dr. Brooks about in a few minutes. She apparently found another"— Addie reconsidered the euphemism *lab rat*—"participant. Once he agrees, we're good to go."

"Who else is there?"

"Alex."

"Do I know him?"

I hope not, Addie thought. "Doubtful. He's just here for the summer. I haven't met him, but Dexter has."

Dexter had solicited (roped in) Alex Tavarez, a rising junior back at his prep school in California who was working at the Academy as a summer PC and assistant boys' lacrosse coach. He, too, was looking for extra credit. Between their athletics and difficulties with science, Alex and Lauren would make an ideal pair, a factor the Athenian Committee should appreciate when they analyzed the experiment's equanimity.

If all went according to plan, Lauren would be as equally attracted to Alex as she would be to the other volunteer at the start. Then the fascinating part would begin. Which guy she ultimately chose would depend entirely on the B.A.D.A.S.S. system. While it had worked flawlessly on Tess and Ed, the Athenian guidelines mandated that the same result had to be replicated. If it wasn't, they were screwed.

Lauren said, "So if this guy is good to go, when should I be at the lab?"

"Let's see." Addie took out her phone and called up her calendar. "Considering classes start at eight thirty and you most likely have some sort of athletic practice before that, I'm thinking maybe five."

"At night? But that's dinner."

Addie shook her head. "No. Five a.m."

Lauren snorted. "Oh my god. You do not want to be within a ten-mile radius of me that early in the morning. I will bite your head off."

"Well, we don't want that," Addie said, scrolling to a different time. "How about noon?"

"That'll work. Is there going to be food? Because if I don't get something to eat by twelve thirty, I'll . . ."

"Bite my head off. Yes, I know." Just then, Addie had a brilliant idea. "Actually, we'll give you lunch. No problem."

"Excellent. Because I only have an hour between AP Bio and field hockey practice. If I'm doing this experiment, no way can I get to the cafeteria."

"Your caloric intake is assured."

With this settled, they broke apart, Addie quick-stepping to the lab and Lauren finishing her run, exhaling purposefully with every left step.

Addie waved her key card over the scanner and a buzz signaled she had one minute to enter. After the vandalism spree, the administration had installed a state-of-the-art security system, and she was still getting used to the intimidating alarm and watchful camera eyes. It was very disconcerting.

Inside, however, the lab's foyer—with its familiar blue concrete floor and artificial tide pools—filled her with a sense of peace. She'd whiled away many happy hours in this building, peering through microscopes at ever-evolving plankton, measuring the electrical charge of frog muscles, comparing pH test strips to their charts, or simply gazing into the tank of her beloved moray eel. The Whit was her sanctuary, which was what made the break-in last spring such a violation. It was as if the lab was a church and she was a priest heartbroken over a smashed stained-glass window.

"There you are." Dexter appeared in a pink polo shirt and madras shorts, the white-blond hairs on his legs prominent over his summer tan, which set off a sparkling new rope bracelet. "An hour behind schedule and you're procrastinating."

"I was delayed by an interloper." She did not dare mention the minutes she'd wasted gazing at the ocean, an activity that Dex would have dismissed as foolishly inefficient.

"Hmph." He headed down to Dr. Brooks's office. "You need to learn to anticipate distractions and take them into account when setting your schedule. Otherwise, you'll be late—as you are now—which sends the message to others that you think your time is more valuable than theirs, which it is most definitely not."

He was absolutely right. Even if he did sound exactly like her mother. "I'm sorry," she murmured, hurrying to catch up.

"You'll find that I always add at least ten minutes to my itinerary to avoid this mistake." He sniffed. "Is that . . . *perfume?*"

"A little. From Paris."

"You know I'm allergic." He reached into his pocket and removed a packet of prescription antihistamines, breaking open the blister pack and popping one in his mouth. He swallowed and scowled. "More inconsideration."

"Sorry," she said again, though she wasn't. She loved the perfume.

He uncapped a Vicks decongestant stick and shoved it up his right nostril, then the left. "That's better." He sneezed and wiped his nose with a tissue from one of the tiny packets his mother sent him regularly. "We must hurry. Shouldn't keep Dr. Brooks waiting any longer than you already have."

They passed his tanks of crabs toward Dr. Brooks's door on the left. When they entered, their advisor had one pair of glasses on her head and another on her nose.

"Oh, good. You've arrived, Adelaide," she said warmly. "How was your flight?"

"Bumpy." Addie shot a sideways glance at Dex, who was fiddling with his smart watch impatiently. "Turbulence was terrible."

He sighed.

Dr. Brooks was a slight woman in her sixties who dressed like a college student, preferring jeans to slacks and flowing purple-and-blue batik dresses to the tweed suits so beloved by her colleagues. She wore her graying hair in long braids like an aging hippie in denial and often nibbled from a bag of granola she'd made herself.

She slipped a finger into the closed venetian blinds and peered out. "Understandable. An extremely unstable air mass passed just south of us this morning due to a cold front, causing extreme variations in temperature. Now there are updrafts." She let the blinds fall. "Interesting to study, unless you're in it. Can be disconcerting even for the most rational of us."

"Ahem." Dex cleared his throat, impatiently. "Shall we begin? We're already behind."

"If you're prepared, then yes." Dr. Brooks perched at the edge of her desk. "I'm very eager to see how you've progressed. This is your introduction to the committee, remember, and it bears repeating that first impressions count."

Addie hooked up her computer, opened the pertinent file, and clicked to the first slide. All business.

Dex said, "I thought it might be valuable to begin with a quick overview of our thesis."

Dr. Brooks nodded. "Proceed."

"Addie and I have developed the Brain Adrenaline, Dopamine, and Amine Synthesis System—aka B.A.D.A.S.S.—based on observations that the human brain releases the same series of neurochemicals during high levels of stress as it does in the initial stages of love, i.e., infatuation. Therefore, we posit that it is possible to trick the brain, if you will, into believing it is in love by subjecting a person to trauma."

Addie wanted to point out that, actually, she'd been the one to develop B.A.D.A.S.S. after researching cases where mere acquaintances "fell in love" after surviving tragedies—shipwrecks, the sudden deaths of friends, floods, fire, and war.

Perhaps the most striking example she found online of this phenomenon involved the supermodel Christie Brinkley, who survived a helicopter crash on a Colorado mountain in 1994 while she was married to singer Billy Joel. The helicopter dropped out of the sky and rolled down the mountain more than 200 feet. One of the passengers was Richard Taubman, who, though being just a friend of a friend before the crash, asked Christie to marry him within two months. She accepted. They even held their wedding near the crash site where they "fell in love." When they divorced a year later, she explained that she had mistaken post-traumatic stress syndrome for love.

That's what started Addie thinking: Maybe it didn't take a helicopter crash to trigger a flood of dopamine and epinephrine. Maybe all you needed was a roller coaster. Or a rock wall. Or being trapped on a barren island in a violent electrical storm.

Dexter clicked to the first slide. A pair of gerbils appeared on the screen, each clutching small gerbil treats. "Here we have Will and Kate, two gerbils named not by me, of opposite gender of sufficient maturity. Previously Will showed no interest in Kate and vice versa."

Addie clicked to the next slide and took over the narration: "On the theory that the perception of extreme danger triggers the brain's response by releasing stimulants such as phenylethylamine (PEA), adrenaline, and norepinephrine—the exact same hormones the brain produces in creating instant physical attraction"—she cleared her throat—"Dex and I placed Will and Kate in precarious, though ultimately safe, situations, with the goal of inducing said attraction."

Next slide. Will and Kate in a clear plastic exercise ball. Addie held her breath.

This was the experiment that had caused all the trouble.

Somehow, word had gotten out that she and Dex were traumatizing mice—though they weren't. Without even bothering to get her facts right, a fellow class member and die-hard animal-rights activist, Kara Wilkes, had embarked on a ruthless smear campaign against the lab.

The administration tried to make her stop, but Kara and her lawyer parents counterclaimed that she had a First Amendment right to free speech. It wasn't until Kara and her friends went too far by breaking into the lab, trashing the equipment, and spray-painting all over the walls, that they were finally booted off campus.

Addie still had nightmares about that period and she was still furious. Not Kara, not anyone in her self-righteous clique, had ever bothered to visit the lab to see for themselves if animals were actually being abused. If they had taken the trouble to do the original research, they would have found clean cages, plenty of food and water, and peacefully sleeping rodents.

That's what angered her the most—their assumptions, their quickness to judge, the joy they took in making her depressed. It was so unfair, especially since Addie couldn't undo the damage. Everywhere she went, people stared and whispered. Forget eating hamburger in public. That only proved she was a bloodthirsty murderer.

"Ignore them," Dex urged after she refused to leave her room for three days. "They're beneath you."

But Addie wasn't like him. She didn't divide people into superior or inferior subspecies. Besides, somehow he'd completely escaped Kara's radar outside of the lab.

Her only regret was that she hadn't had a chance to tell off Kara and her boyfriend and that smirking lackey of theirs, Mack or Max or whatever, before they disappeared. Mr. Foy saw to it that they were on a bus to Boston immediately after they were caught out of concern that they'd be targets for bullying if they stuck around.

Ironic much?

Dr. Brooks called Addie back to earth. "Go on. How did the exercise ball fit into your experiment?"

Addie refocused on the presentation. "We rolled the ball down an inclined plane." Shot of Will and Kate rolling down a board.

"As you can see," Dex continued when Addie proceeded to the slide of the two gerbils happily munching on treats, "no attraction. However, when we chose a more treacherous route for a different pair of gerbils, Brad and Angelina"—slide of ball at the top of the back hallway stairs—"the results were more encouraging."

Dr. Brooks let out a small gasp. "You threw them down the stairs?"

"Not threw," Dex said. "More like gently bounced."

"They were perfectly fine," Addie added quickly. "I swear. Look!"

Indeed, the next photo was of Brad and Angelina out of their ball and putting their newfound attraction to full and productive use.

"Oh," Dr. Brooks said quietly. "Oh, my."

Addie felt her cheeks go warm. Dex seemed to have no problem discussing this outcome, which had led to several litters of baby gerbils. And, really, she shouldn't have been embarrassed. This was science, after all. Biology!

Still . . .

Dr. Brooks switched on the lights, appearing rather flustered. "I will admit that your PowerPoint is more effective than the version you showed me in May, though it definitely needs polishing."

Dex groaned. "I think it's fine."

"It'll get there," Dr. Brooks said. "Do you think you can replicate this final part of the experiment with humans safely?"

"We won't put anyone in danger," Addie said, wishing Dex would chime in instead of standing there moping about having to do more polishing. "And since Lauren and Alex will act as controls, all they'll have to do is stare at each other for ten minutes each session and journal their thoughts before and after. That's pretty safe."

"Not for Lauren and the other volunteer," Dex said. "Especially at the end, when we strand them on Owl Island overnight."

Not helping, Addie thought. "Before that, we plan to check their progress by surreptitiously observing their social interactions at the Midsummer Night's Dream Dance on Saturday. We will monitor which boy Lauren chooses, Alex or the other participant. If our thesis is on track, then she will choose the other participant and we will proceed with Owl Island. If not, then . . ."

"Back to the whiteboard," Dex finished.

"I wonder," Dr. Brooks said, getting up and opening the blinds. "Why not use a different girl and boy like you did with the gerbils?"

"We want to show that, all things being equal, given two similarly attractive guys, Lauren will ultimately prefer the one with whom she's endured more . . . *thrilling* . . . experiences," Addie answered. "And, similarly, the same will be true for the boys. That is, if the other guy you've found meets that criteria."

"He absolutely does. He's extremely handsome and intelligent, and that's not merely my opinion." Dr. Brooks flicked on the lights. "Headmaster Foy interviewed him this morning and called me with the green light."

"Excellent!" Addie smiled at Dexter, expecting him to be relieved.

He wasn't. "He's already been approved? But we haven't even met him."

"That's about to be rectified." Dr. Brooks peeked out her door and crooked her finger. "Why don't you stop sweeping for a second, Kris, and step into my office."

Addie felt her legs go numb as Kris entered carrying a broom and decked head to toe in the ugly green uniform of the Academy's Buildings and Grounds employees.

No. Way.

Dr. Brooks said, "Dexter. Adelaide. I'd like you to meet participant number three."

"*Kris Condos?*" Dex slapped his forehead. "You have got to be kidding. Is this a joke?"

Wait, Addie thought, confused. Dex knew him? That was odd. Dex didn't know anyone besides her, the faculty, and the nurses down at the infirmary.

Dr. Brooks knit her brows. "I'm surprised you two are acquainted. I thought for sure . . ."

"Not personally," Dex interjected, "but . . ." He took Dr. Brooks aside and whispered in her ear.

"Yes, yes, that's true," she said, breaking apart. "As long as you don't have a close relationship with him, it shouldn't affect the outcome of the experiment."

Dex scowled. "Close relationship? *With him?* Definitely not."

Addie remained baffled. What was going on? What did Dex know that she didn't? Why was he giving Kris such a dirty look?

Unless . . . ? Oh god. No. The *sins.* The *mistakes.* The *screwed-up neural pathways*!

She looked to Dex, who confirmed her fears by whispering under his breath three simple words: "Kara. Wilkes's. Boyfriend."

The news hit her hard, like a sucker punch to the solar plexus. It knocked the wind out of her and left her dizzy. *Kris was Kara's boyfriend.* He'd been part of the trio that had ransacked her sanctuary, smashing tanks and terrariums, sending the gerbils scurrying in fear and the frogs into dark corners, only to be found days later shriveled and dead.

She'd been so stupid, so incredibly blind. How had it not dawned on her before that of course this was why Kris had been expelled? Ed knew. That's why he was so standoffish in the car. That must have been why Tess stopped Kris at the top of the escalator, to tear him a new one. She was good at tearing new ones.

"And you, Addie?" Dr. Brooks was saying, her voice sounding far off. "Do *you* have a personal relationship with Kris?"

She pivoted, prepared to let him have it. Her fists clenched and the muscles in her jaw ached, she was so angry. "Do I have a personal relationship with Kris? Is that what you're asking?"

Are you kidding? she wanted to scream. *Kris Condos and his jerk of a girlfriend ruined my junior year. They ruined the lab and they almost ruined me. They had no business doing what they did.*

Instead, when she locked on to his deep-chocolate-brown eyes, all she could think of was their conversation on the plane and how remorseful he'd been, how willing to make amends, how sad she was that he was burdened with guilt.

"Yes?" The corners of those eyes crinkled, and despite her swirling fury, something inside her snapped.

Then things got really weird.

Her pulse fluttered and her senses sharpened. She should have understood what was going on in her brain, except she seemed to have inexplicably forgotten every-thing from her research. (Though that, of course, was another symptom of PEA overload, which she would have recognized if Kris hadn't been a few feet away all tall and dark in his butt-ugly uniform.)

Dex scoffed. "Of course Addie doesn't know Condos."

Kris opened his mouth and then closed it, smiling at her slightly. Addie did the same.

What was wrong with her?

"Then we can get started right away." Dr. Brooks clapped once. "Addie, what time are you meeting Lauren tomorrow?"

She licked her oddly dry lips. "Noon."

Kris was still looking at her with that smile.

"How does noon work for you, Kris?" Dr. Brooks asked. "It might eat into your lunch break, no pun intended, but I will add fifteen minutes to your work schedule."

Kris blinked. "What am I doing?"

"A research project for our Athenian Award submission," Dex drawled with disgust. "Addie and I are running an experiment measuring the difference between male and female responses to various stimuli. Do try to keep up."

Even though Kris deserved the cut, she felt bad. "Sorry," she said. "Dex didn't mean it."

"Yes, I did."

"It's okay," Kris said. "It's not like I don't have it coming."

"True that." Dex folded his arms, superior.

Dr. Brooks escorted Kris to the door. "All righty, then. See you at noon, and thank you for volunteering."

When he left, she swung around and placed her hands on her hips. "As scientists, I hope you two would ignore whatever slights we perceive Kris has committed. He is trying to repay his debt to the Academy and for that he should be commended, not ridiculed. Everyone deserves a second chance."

Dex said, "With all due respect, the headmaster should have consulted us first. How can we be objective when . . . ?"

Dr. Brooks wagged a finger. "I'll have none of that. You know how I feel about grudges. Anger and resentment lead to destruction."

Addie had to agree. Anger was only useful to precipitate a rush of adrenaline so one could battle a predator. Therefore, from an evolutionary standpoint, there was no reason to hold on to this purely temporal emotion.

Dr. Brooks said, "You must strictly adhere to the rules of scientific procedure, not your emotions. Are we clear?"

"Yes," Addie and Dex said simultaneously.

"Therefore, can I count on you two to conduct this experiment with professional detachment?"

They nodded, duly shamed.

"Good. Now, if your so-called B.A.D.A.S.S. theory is correct, Lauren and Alex will end up as platonic friends," Dr. Brooks concluded, crossing her fingers, "while Lauren and Kris will be something more. If your system is as effective as you claim, then you should be able to delude anyone into feeling as if they were falling madly in love."

A few minutes later, Dr. Brooks left to go to her next class, and Dex returned to his crabs, while Addie simply stared at nothing on her laptop, replaying those words over and over in her mind.

If your system is as effective as you claim, then you should be able to delude anyone into feeling as if they were falling madly in love.

Did she dare? Was it wrong? Did she have a choice?

Yes. Yes. And, unfortunately, no.

Then she picked up her phone and texted the only person who could possibly help.

Ed.

SEVEN

"That's what I was trying to tell you after Ed dropped us off. Kris is Kara Wilkes's boyfriend." Tess handed Addie the pitcher of limeade. "So how do you feel about him now?"

"Dr. Brooks says we're supposed to ignore our emotions and follow scientific procedure." Addie took the pitcher from her and placed it on the folding table.

"That doesn't answer the question," Tess said, opening a Tupperware container of cookies. "Earlier, you told me it didn't matter what he'd done. Something about neural whatever . . ."

"Pathways. This morning it didn't, but . . ." She aimlessly picked a cookie from the bowl and bit. "I don't know what to think."

Not even hours of immersing herself in the latest bulletin from the Caltech Neurophysiology Department and flipping through images of coronal brain sections had been able to stem her whirring thoughts of Kris and Kara and the awful things they'd done to her.

Tess called at five to remind Addie about dinner, even if she wasn't the least bit hungry (another disturbing after-effect of the adrenaline rush), and that she was supposed to help out with the evening games as Assistant PC.

"I can't," Addie said, scrolling to a particularly fascinating axial section of the interpeduncular cistern. "I'm working."

"I don't care. You need to meet the girls and get out of that dark, windowless cave. Anyway, you promised Foy you'd help. You begged to be made my assistant."

So Addie packed up her computer, grabbed a tasteless turkey sandwich from the vending machine, and ate it as she hiked up to the quad, dreading the prospect of having to be social.

When she arrived, she found Tess on the green, wrestling with a folding table, practically near tears.

Addie dropped her backpack and grabbed the other end. "Let me help you. Geesh, Tess, it's not worth crying over." She pulled out the four legs and rolled it to standing. "Voilà!"

But Tess was in a full sob. "Ed was supposed to help me. He completely blew me off."

"No, he didn't. It's my fault, I . . ."

Tess snapped up. "Your fault? Oh, come on, Addie." She wiped her nose with the back of her hand. "Don't do that."

"Do what?" Addie moved the table under a tree, for shade.

"Cover for him."

"I'm not . . ."

"If Ed thinks of me as just a little high schooler because he's off to college next month, then screw him."

"I don't think . . ."

Tess threw open the lid of a red cooler and removed a bottle of limeade. "Do you know what he said to me last night? I asked him when he was planning on coming to visit next fall. He said he didn't know if he could because he got only one break for three days in October and that wasn't long enough to fly all the way from Chicago to Boston, and Thanksgiving he'd have to be with his family." She blinked. "I mean, what a jerk!"

Addie bit her lip so she wouldn't accidentally blurt out something she shouldn't. "You might be blowing this out of proportion."

"Blowing this out of proportion?"

Addie winced.

"Unless he flies to Paris for Christmas, I won't see him until next summer!" Tess yelled. "That is, if he can work me into his schedule."

"You better get yourself together. Here they come."

Addie pointed to a pair of impossibly blond, skinny girls laconically strolling across the grass in absurd six-inch sandals. She feared for the integrity of their ankles.

Tess whipped out a mirror and dabbed a tissue at her smeared mascara. "Bree and Tay. The taller is Tay. She's the leader. Bree is the Igor to her Dr. Frankenstein. They're best friends back home in LA and they're super-pissed that they've been separated and put with different roommates."

There was a recipe for mean girl disaster, Addie thought. "Who are their roommates?"

Tess gestured briefly to a slightly chunky girl with a pretty face and brown hair streaked with purple. "That's Emma, Bree's roomie. Friendly. Midwestern. Type you can't help but like. How do I look?"

"Fine. Do you have Visine?"

"Do the Kardashians have plastic surgeons on speed dial? Of course." She rummaged in her bag and squeezed in a few drops.

"Who's the smiley girl sitting next to Emma?" Addie asked.

"That's Tay's roommate, Shreya Khan. She's from India, so she wins the farthest-from-home award—besides the exchange students, of course. Her dad's a massively famous Bollywood actor," Tess said. "Worth gazillions, with homes all over the world. Tay has no idea how cool she is. If she did, she probably wouldn't treat her like crap."

Several others arrived. Zuri, who was from Baltimore and took classes at Johns Hopkins; Rachel, an apparent piano prodigy from Manhattan; and Fiona and Mindy, the exchange students from China.

They made up Tess's "core peer group," which meant that she was completely responsible for handling all their concerns, including roommate conflicts and other problems.

"Tay and Bree keep threatening to run away, they hate it here so much," Tess said while they sat apart from the group on their own blanket. "I told them security wouldn't let them drive off campus but they said that didn't matter. They'd walk. Like, in those shoes?"

Shreya had her hand up. "Are we doing the Battle of the Sexes tonight?"

"That's the plan," Tess chirped, pouring juice into the cups. "Would you mind passing these around, assistant?"

It took a second for Addie to realize Tess meant her. "Oh, sure. Right." She carefully lifted the red cups and handed them to Bree and Tay, who curled their lips in disgust.

"Ew. What is this gross green stuff?" Tay took a sniff.

"It smells like toilet bowl cleaner."

"High fructose corn syrup, filtered water, lime pulp, and green dye number six. You want me to draw the carbon chain?" Addie answered.

The girls glanced at Tess.

"This is Addie," she said. "She's my assistant."

Addie said, "What's a Battle of the Sexes?"

"A chance for butt kicking," Emma declared with a fist pump, the rest of them applauding in confirmation.

Interesting. Physical combat did not pop up in Addie's research as an appropriate summer school field game. "Will there be artillery?" she inquired. "Any mortally wounded?"

"If I have anything to say about it," Shreya answered, setting off a round of giggling.

"We have a few minutes before the boys get here, so why don't you tell them a little bit about yourself," Tess suggested. "The normal bits."

She wiped her hands on her skirt and proceeded. "Like Tess said, I'm Addie, your Assistant PC, and a rising senior at the Academy who's here for the summer to manipulate sensory perceptions of the opposite sex . . ."

Tess murmured, "Be normal. Like we've practiced."

Zuri, the one sitting closest, said, "Normalcy is overrated. Let her speak."

"Yeah, I want to hear about manipulating the opposite

sex," Rachel said, smiling at Emma.

Addie lifted her chin and continued. "Thank you for that vote of confidence. Actually, I'm conducting an experiment measuring the male/female reactions to various stimuli at a chemical level. I can't really discuss it further."

Shreya said, *"Ooookay."*

"However, you should know that as your official Assistant PC, I will help you work through whatever relationship problems you are experiencing. So don't hesitate to come to me with any relationship issue. Straight. Gay. Bi. Transgender. I have extensively researched these concerns."

She gave Tess the thumbs-up, but Tess missed this, due to the fact that her face was in her hands. Clearly, she was so overcome by the sensitive insight of Addie's speech that she'd started to weep.

Addie said, "Now you know why the headmaster made me your assistant. To help."

"Yes," Tess said wearily, as a gaggle of male summer students rounded the corner, Ed in the lead, tossing a white volleyball.

If he had any clue that Tess was pissed, he didn't show it, even when she turned her back to him and folded her arms.

"The field is really muddy thanks to the rain," he said.

"Afraid of getting dirty?" she grumbled.

"Not us. We're game if you are."

She snorted. "Yeah, right. You want us to call it off. Like we would."

The girls cheered.

"We're so totally going to win this," said one of the boys, snatching the ball out of Ed's hands and jogging down the hill to the field, everyone following.

Tess got up and started collecting cups. "You go without me. I'll be right there."

"Ed and I will clean up," Addie said. "You go with the kids, Tess." She slid her eyes to Ed. "He and I need to talk, anyway."

Tess looked from her to Ed and back to Addie again. "Okay. Thanks."

They watched Tess stroll off, her sundress fluttering in the summer breeze, exposing the bright pink bikini she wore underneath.

"She's so amazing," Ed said with a sigh of longing.

"She's super-mad at you." Addie recapped the limeade and replaced it in the cooler. "Did you know that?"

Ed cocked his head, surprised. "No. Why?"

"Because you said you weren't going to see her again."

"I didn't say that."

"You said you wouldn't be able to get away this fall to visit. Can you help me with this table?"

"I'll do the whole thing. Stand back." He flipped it over and folded in the legs. "I was only being honest. I have no idea how hard school's going to be or whether I'll be able to get away. I might have to study constantly. It is the University of Chicago. You know, where fun goes to die."

"Sounds like my kind of place," Addie said.

Ed laughed.

"I'm serious."

"I don't doubt it." He carried the table to the gazebo and came back, frowning thoughtfully. "Okay. I'll talk to her and explain what I meant and I'll try to get away over break if I can. But she has to understand that everything is up in the air for me, too. Give me the cooler. I'll put it with the table."

She handed him the cooler. "She's afraid you're going to leave her behind when you get to college and that you've already begun thinking of her as a little high schooler. Her words, not mine."

"Tess? A little high schooler? There is nothing little about Tess."

"She might not take that the right way."

"Fair enough." They headed down the hill to the field. "How you holding up?" Ed asked.

"Okay. Still trying to process the fact that Kris is Kara Wilkes's boyfriend. I don't know how I missed that. Even with that long conversation on the flight, I never put two and two together. Must have been the turbulence that addled my otherwise perceptive faculties."

Ed grinned. "If you say so."

"You won't tell Tess about my call, will you?"

He slid a finger over his lips. "It's in the vault."

"What vault?"

"It's an expression. Means I won't tell anyone."

"That's a relief. Because she would not understand."

"She will, eventually. By the way, I ran into Kris at dinner and asked if he wanted to join us tonight. I hope you're cool with that."

That was a surprise. Ed had been so cold to him in the car. "*Suuuure*. He's in my experiment tomorrow so it's not like I can avoid him."

"Not if I have anything to do with it." Ed punched her lightly on the shoulder. "Hang in there, you rodent slayer."

For a second, she was shocked, until she realized he was making a joke and laughed.

"See? Humor's the best medicine," he said.

That wasn't true. The best medicine was the one that had been genetically targeted to treat a particular illness. But Addie supposed that was too awkward to embroider on a pillow.

A couple of students were resetting the spikes to hold

up the volleyball net at the far end of the athletic fields near the woods. Ed hadn't been exaggerating when he called it muddy.

Since it was straight-up boys versus girls, there would be none of that choosing sides for volleyball awkwardness, though Tess insisted on taking Addie aside and offering her pointers such as not to duck with her hands over her head when the ball came to her.

"Hit it back. You can do that, right?" Tess paused. "I mean over the net."

"Right. Absolutely," Addie lied. Anything to get the game going so it could end and she could go back to the lab.

"She can do it," a voice said from the other side.

Kris was in black running shorts and a tight gray T-shirt constructed from some sort of magical material that clung to his muscles and triggered a gush of epinephrine while her amygdala attempted to reconcile two conflicting signals from her prefrontal cortex: attraction and revenge.

"All right, everyone, play clean," Ed shouted, tossing the ball to Shreya. "Girls go first."

Addie and Kris faced each other.

"I know what you did, Kris Condos," she said. "You and Kara."

Shreya served the ball. It hit the net. Tess tossed it back

to her for another chance. "Warming up!"

Kris said. "I'm sorry. I didn't . . ."

"You did. That's why you . . ."

"Addie!" someone screamed just in time for her to look up and see the business end of the volleyball plummeting downward.

"I got it!" Tay cried, saving it with a pass to Emma, who spiked it over the net, where it fell between Dex and another boy.

"That was yours," Dex said.

The other boy squinted and chucked the ball back to Shreya. "What? It was right on top of you, man."

"Look, I can explain," Kris said. "It's complicated."

Addie rolled her eyes. "Please, don't even." It was a phrase Tess occasionally used, much to Addie's annoyance, since it lacked both a transitive verb and a subject.

Kris punched the ball to the girls' side. Zuri was on it, easily hitting it to the far line, where Ed and one of his PCs nearly smashed into each other to get it.

It landed next to Addie with a thud. "My bad," she said.

Tess picked it up and gave it to Kris. "Next time, look *up*, not *at*."

Addie assumed that meant she wasn't supposed to talk to Kris. Tess became so competitive when it came to sports. It was annoying.

The next time the ball headed toward her, Addie yelled, "Tay. Get it!" Which Tay did. Problem solved.

Until it was her turn to serve.

"You can do this," Tess said, positioning the ball in Addie's left hand. "Just make it mathematical. You know, calculate the arc of the curve or whatever it is you do."

"Calculate the arc would suffice," Addie said. "You don't have to add . . ."

"Freakin' serve already!" Dex shouted.

She pretended the ball was his head and lobbed it over. Kris spiked it back to Emma, who passed it to Shreya, who let it drop.

The boys were winning twenty-three to twenty, which, as far as Addie was concerned, meant it was merely a matter of minutes before she was back at the lab to set up for tomorrow's experiment.

Then she found herself opposite Kris again.

"Hi there," he said. "Miss me?"

"You do know you made my life hell, you and your girlfriend, don't you?"

He threw up his hands. "I know. I'm sorry. I'm sorry. I'm sorry. I thought you understood. After our talk on the plane . . ."

"I did. Now I don't. I'm . . ." What was she? "Unresolved. I need closure. An apology or something."

"I've apologized a million times. I don't know what

else I can say. I was messed up then. A different person. I got in with the wrong people. I was still getting over what I saw in Nepal. Hey, you were the one who told me about the neural pathways."

The ball was back in the boys' court.

"You can't use my research against me," Addie said, flinching as the ball, thankfully, sailed past her to Emma, who lobbed it back. "And you don't go trashing a lab, destroying expensive equipment, just because you don't feel like you fit in with society."

"That wasn't it. And I never wanted to trash the lab. We went there because you guys were torturing mice . . ."

"Gerbils!"

"Okay, *gerbils* . . ."

"We weren't. Where did you get that idea? Who told you that?"

"I don't know." Kris volleyed the ball across the net. "Kara, I guess. She said you guys killed frogs and had bags of dead cats and we needed to send a message."

Well, they did kill frogs, that much was true. "She's right about the frogs."

"*See!*"

"We stun them first, though." Addie stepped aside as Tay dove in front of her, saving the ball and grumbling: was she going to talk or was she going to play? "They don't feel anything when we kill them."

"So, you admit you're an animal killer."

She gaped. Did he just say that? Did he actually . . .

"Go for it, Addie!" Tay yelled.

She glanced up. There was the ball plummeting at a fierce velocity, triggering a burst of adrenaline. And there was Kris, the words still on his lips.

Her fingers rolled into a fist. She threw her arm back and made contact, executing a follow-through to ensure that the sucker landed—*smack!*—square in the face.

"Whoa!" Ed yelled as Kris went backward, hands over his nose, from which streamed a line of bright-red blood.

"Awesome!" Tay slapped her on the back. "You knocked him out cold. We won!"

Addie lifted the net and went over to where Kris was sitting in the mud, blood on his shirt. "Is that enough closure for you?" he asked, wiping blood off his chin.

She breathed heavily, trying to think what she thought, and was delighted to realize that, actually, it *had* helped to knock the stuffing out of him.

"Yeah. That'll work. See you tomorrow, at noon." She turned and marched off. "I'm going back to the lab."

EIGHT

That'll work.

She'd actually said that. She'd spiked the ball directly into his face with the force of an NFL linebacker and didn't even blink.

He touched his swollen, tender nose. *Who even was she?*

On the plane, she'd seemed so sweet, with her nerdy ponytail and big gray eyes and her awkwardness in dealing with the crying kid across the aisle.

Okay, so it was mind-blowing to learn later that she was Addie Emerson. That only made the guilt worse, because now he'd met her in person, but, all right. He could deal.

Except yesterday in Dr. Brooks's office when Dex whispered that he was Kara's boyfriend—Kris had the impression that he'd been forgiven. He definitely sensed a warming of the relations. Then, four hours later, she hammered a volleyball into his skull. Man, did that hurt. She might even have broken some cartilage.

"Age?" Addie stood over him, pen poised, eyebrow arched.

"Seventeen. Eighteen in October," he answered, resisting the urge to touch his nose again.

She made an efficient tick on her clipboard. "Location of origin?"

"What does that mean?"

"Be easy on him," Lauren said, her lips twitching in amusement. "Looks like he messed with one angry guy last night."

He and Addie exchanged guilty glances.

"I just want you to know," he told Lauren, "that the guy was three hundred and fifty pounds, a black belt, ugliest person you ever saw, and I landed him in traction."

"Yeah?" Lauren arched an eyebrow.

"No," Addie added. "Not even close."

Still, he noted, no apology.

It was their first day of the experiment and he was in the Whit along with Lauren Lowes (who apparently was going to be his partner) and Dexter (who definitely had a pickle up his ass). The poster boy for Vineyard Vines was all pursed lips and rolling eyeballs as they filled out their introductory questionnaires.

"By location of origin, Addie means hometown." Dexter did yet another eye roll.

"Farmington, Connecticut," Kris answered.

"I bet you're a middle child," Dexter said.

Kris said, "As a matter of fact, yes."

"Interesting." And Addie jotted a note. "How many siblings?"

"Two. Sisters."

Grace and Elena. Grace had been the one to suggest that he drop out of Andover and try Academy 355, where the students were less stuck up, more worldly. She broke it to their parents that he wouldn't be going back and defended him when his mother had a freaking screaming fit at Christmas. For that, he would forever be in her debt—even if she did hog the car during school vacations.

For the longest time, it was just the two of them against the world, since Grace was two years older than he was and their parents were never around. Work. Travel. There was always an excuse. Sometimes he thought his mom and dad had made a mistake. Why did they even have kids if they made an appearance for only half the year?

On the flip side, he and Grace, who'd convinced him to be a vegetarian, had completely perfected the ultimate grilled-cheese-and-dill-pickle sandwich—their go-to dinner in a pinch.

Then Elena came along and rocked their world. She was born with a funky heart valve that required multiple surgeries, and for a while there, doctors weren't sure she was going to make it. That's when his mother went part time and his father found a job that didn't involve business trips.

They sold the mansion in Greenwich and downsized to a bungalow in Farmington to make ends meet. His parents were still insistent that Grace start Smith and that Kris take expensive trips like helping earthquake victims in China, since broadening one's horizons was at the top of the Condos family agenda. But compared with the wealth before Elena's birth, they were broke.

Elena went to first grade at the public elementary school in town and drew him notes that she wrote in crayon on construction paper with I MISS U BIG BROTHER and stick-figure drawings of the two of them holding hands. She'd never be sent away like Grace and he had been. She was lucky.

"Oh my god. Can we get on with this?" Lauren jiggled her leg impatiently. "Twenty minutes until my afternoon class and we still haven't had lunch."

"On its way," Dex said, attempting a flirtatious smile.

Lauren ignored him.

She reminded Kris of a former classmate of his from Andover, Alyssa Reynolds, a pole-vaulter with liquid legs who sailed over the bar in a physically impossible arc. Every guy on the track team had a crush on her. Even him. Once.

Not that he had that much experience with girls. Too introverted, perhaps. Too bookish. That was Grace's analysis, though he preferred the theory that, so far, no girls had flipped his switch enough to make him want to commit.

Kara didn't count. Yes, he'd been into her—in the same way a kidnapping victim becomes attached to his abductor. Mack was the one who came up with that brilliant line.

"You've got Stockholm syndrome, dude," he said one night when Kris returned to their dorm room so late from Kara's, he had to crawl through their window to avoid setting off the alarms. "She says jump, you say how high."

Kara had that effect on people. If she didn't want you to leave, she'd pout and cry to the point where you'd do anything to make her stop. But if she wanted you to go, she'd claim a sudden illness and demand to be left alone. Kris found himself neglecting his own homework to help finish hers, so his grades suffered and Mack declared him an idiot.

Within two months, after Mack started hanging out

with them, Kara would have him eating out of her hand, too.

She was pretty, that helped. Gorgeous, actually. Long, shiny black hair down past her shoulders. High cheekbones. Flashing midnight-blue, almost purple, eyes. And a personality so powerful that even when Kris tried to break off their relationship—which he'd attempted numerous times—she'd sink her hooks into him and drag him back.

Like Mack said—Stockholm syndrome.

Addie handed Kris a piece of paper, *X* marked next to the signature line. "This is your waiver. Please read, sign, and return."

"Am I signing over my soul?" Kris asked, marveling at all the fine print.

"Out of the question considering there is no such thing as a soul," Addie replied. "Therefore, it would be impossible to release through a written contract."

Oooookay. "Guess Goethe didn't get the memo."

"Just do it," Lauren said, texting on her phone. "You know those things never hold up in court anyway."

He scrawled on the line. Addie scanned the waiver with her phone and slipped it into a file. Then she placed a digital recorder on their table and handed each a small bottle of eye drops.

Dex gave them two sheets of lined paper and pencils.

"To start, we need you to write down your first impressions of each other in five words. They do not have to form a sentence. Neither of you will see the other's answers, so you can be completely honest."

Lauren picked up the pencil and paused. "But I don't even know him."

"Exactly." Dex set the timer. "You have thirty seconds. Proceed."

Kris rapidly scribbled five words that randomly popped into his mind.

Pretty.

Athletic.

Pole.

Flexible.

Nice.

Those were descriptions of Alyssa Reynolds, not of Lauren, he realized.

"Thank you!" Addie pinched the page from his grasp.

"I'm not sure those are right," he said. "Can I try again?"

"You'll have many chances to try again. You'll do this at the beginning and end of each experiment."

Lauren said, "I thought that *was* the experiment."

"No, this is the experiment." Addie set tiny bottles of eye drops in front of both of them. "You may find these helpful. Now, for the next five minutes, I want both of you to look in each other's eyes."

"But he's totally bruised up," Lauren said.

"Irrelevant," Addie said. "And while you're looking in your partner's eyes, try to remember what emotions you're feeling about her or him or about yourself. When the time is up, you'll return to your previous words and omit, edit, or keep them the same."

"This is like one of my sister's party games," Kris said. "I feel like we should be wearing electrodes or something." He fingered his scalp, pulling his hair to make it stand on end.

Lauren laughed.

"If only," Addie said with a sigh.

"The school drew the line at implanting electronic devices in our subjects' craniums," Dexter said. "It's a sore spot with us."

Lauren squirted in the drops and batted her eyelids rapidly, tilting her head back so as not to ruin her mascara. A drop rolled down her cheek and, without even thinking, Kris leaned over and thumbed it away.

"You're sweet," she said, smiling. "But you should learn to duck."

"Now!" Addie set the timer.

Kris focused his eyes on Lauren's, then blurred them, to see if that would make a difference in staying power. Lauren gazed at him with the stillness of steel, like they were in a competition. And who knows? Maybe they were. Maybe Addie was testing whether girls could stare longer than boys. But how would that connect to the brain?

Gold and brown. That's what Lauren's eyes were. Also, a bit of green. Did you call that hazel? No, hazel was blue/green/brown, right?

Addie's eyes were gray. Or were they blue? He looked away from Lauren to check. They were gray-blue, like the bands of limestone he'd seen in the Himalayans. Mesmerizing.

"Gotcha!" Lauren pumped her fist. "You broke the stare. I win!"

"Time's up, anyway," Addie said, flashing a smile.

There it was again. That sweetness. Next, she'd probably slap him down with a cutting remark. Or just a slap.

Dex plunked down two plates holding peanut butter and banana sandwiches, Granny Smith apple slices, and baby carrots. "Lunch."

Lauren lifted the top slice of bread to inspect the contents. "What are we, in kindergarten?"

"Peanut butter is an excellent source of protein, B vitamins, and zinc, especially when combined with whole-wheat bread," Addie said. "We've replaced the jelly with a banana to reduce the sugar intake. And the fat content in peanut butter is excellent fuel for the cerebellum."

"Are you saying I'm dumb?" Lauren bristled. "Or that I have a fat head."

Addie shook her head. "Neither."

"Thank you," Kris interjected before this turned ugly. "I was definitely getting hungry." He took a big bite of the sandwich, trying not to mind that Dexter was scrutinizing each chew with creepy interest.

Lauren pushed her plate aside. "No, thanks. Lost my appetite. Are we done?"

"One last thing." Dex returned the list of five qualities they'd written at the start of the day's experiment. "This is your chance to revise."

Lauren barely glanced at hers. "I'm cool."

"Me, too," Kris said, though that wasn't true.

There was something about the way Lauren had complained about the sandwich that he found off-putting. Okay, so peanut butter wasn't his favorite, either, but that didn't give you a license to be rude.

Or maybe something else was going on with him and it had nothing to do with Lauren or this pointless experiment and everything to do with these strange new feelings he had for, of all people, Adelaide Emerson.

"You have to work for her?" Kara shrieked through the phone.

Kris took a swig of water and leaned against the rough

trunk of a large oak, grateful for the shaded respite from the ninety-two-degree heat and summer humidity. For two days he'd been ignoring Kara's texts, until she threatened to come up to the school and find him.

Thought it might be a good idea if that was avoided.

"It's not bad." He inhaled the sweet scent of freshmown grass and gave himself an imaginary pat on the back for a job well done.

"It can't be good. They're rubbing your nose in it by forcing you to be in the lab, Condor."

"N.B.D." He dragged an arm across his forehead to dab off the sweat. "And I'm not working *for* her. More like, I'm helping her with an experiment."

"Sure," Kara said skeptically. "Except they've got you cleaning out the gerbil cages, so every day you have to see those poor, trapped, helpless little animals." She groaned. "It's like they're making a mockery of an issue you believe in passionately. Don't tell me that's not twisted."

So far, he hadn't felt sorry for the gerbils or the crabs. And he hadn't seen any frogs. "The gerbils are happy."

"How did you know? Did you ask them?"

He laughed.

"It's not funny. You should quit out of protest. So you don't finish Foy's boot camp. What's the worst that can happen?"

"Um, military school?" he reminded her. "Three a.m.

reveille. Uniforms. All guys? You know how I am with authority. I suck."

"And that's why I love you."

The words hung in the ether, begging for a response. Kris took another swig of water and let them dangle. Sooner or later she was bound to get the hint when he didn't respond to her fishing.

"The thing is," Kara continued, "there are tons of alternatives to the Academy and to military school. Look at me. I'm doing an independent study next semester to finish my credits and then going to Florence in the spring!"

"Nice to be rich." He checked the phone. Two more minutes until the end of his break.

"You should come with me!" she said.

"Where?" As if he didn't know.

"Florence, you moron. Just think. The two of us at twilight by the Arno, our days in museums studying the world's greatest paintings, our nights spent making our own art."

He scoffed. "Right now, I've got fifty bucks in my bank account."

"That's okay. I have enough money for both of us."

His cheeks went hot as the rectangular figure of a man in Academy green overalls and steel-toed boots got out of a school golf cart. Buster, the number-two guy in Buildings and Grounds and Kris's self-appointed immediate supervisor, was coming to check if he was slacking.

Which he was.

"Gotta go," he said, getting up.

"You have serious commitment issues, Condor."

He pictured her lounging by the pool on the roof of her parents' penthouse overlooking Boston, sipping something cool and fruity, stunning as always in a bikini the width of dental floss. "And you've never had a job."

"Never will, if I have anything to say about it. Employment is for girls who aren't smart enough to play the system."

Buster was motioning for him to end the call, but Kris saw an opening and wasn't about to let it pass.

"I don't ever plan on being rich, Kara. In fact, as soon as I'm done with school, I'm going back to Nepal, where there's no running water and your bed is a mat on a dirt floor. So . . ."

"Relax! I'm not interested in getting married," she said, with a tickling laugh. "I just want to have fun. With you."

"And I'm saying you'd be better off with someone else."

There was a long, angry pause. "Don't ever say that again, not even joking. Got that, Condor?"

He closed his eyes, wishing Buster would give him just five more minutes. "I was only being honest."

"You're not being honest; you're being a jerk," she shot back, her voice choked as if she was on the verge of tears. "Sometimes, I think you just really enjoy twisting the knife."

He swallowed anxiously. "Don't say that."

"Why not? What do you care?" she sniffed.

Buster was rolling his meaty arm, signaling for him to wrap it up.

"Okay, Kara. I gotta go back to work."

"Will you call me tonight?"

It was the last thing he wanted to do. But if he didn't, there was no telling how Kara might react. She might spend the night crying alone in her parents' apartment or take a wildly expensive taxi to see him or go to a party or . . . he didn't know . . .

"Okay," he said.

"You better," she said sullenly. "You owe me."

For what, he was never sure.

NINE

B.A.D.A.S.S. Experiment Part Two

Day One

Addie's Notes

Participant #1

Lauren Lowes

Age: 17

Siblings: 0

Location of origin: Dallas, TX

Year at Academy: Rising 4th

Interests: Field hockey. Violin. Potential college major: Graphic design.

Participant #2

Kris Condos

Age: 17

Siblings: 2 sisters (middle child)

Location of Origin: Farmington, CT

Year at Academy: Rising 4th

Interests: XC running. Nepal. China. Potential college major: Undecided.

NOTES:

Participants signed waivers. Lauren and Kris met first, at noon. Both acknowledged having no prior relationship.

A) Lauren's impressions of Kris were as follows:

Cocky

Cute

Mysterious

Strange

Trouble

(Observation: Lauren's impressions of Kris were in line with expectations. Excellent baseline values.)

B) Kris's impressions of Lauren were as follows:

Pretty

Athletic

Pole

Flexible

Nice

(Observation: Kris's impressions of Lauren were incongruous with her appearance. Perhaps did not understand assignment?)

Participants engaged in eye contact for the prescribed time. They then consumed peanut butter and banana sandwiches and exited. Neither changed his or her impressions.

(Observation: Though participants have engaged in just one session, no increase or decrease in attraction due to prolonged eye contact was detected either in observations or written responses.)

B.A.D.A.S.S. Experiment Part Two

Day One

Dexter's Notes

Participant #1

Lauren Lowes

Age: 17

Siblings: 0

Location of origin: Dallas, TX

Year at Academy: Rising 4th

Interests: Field hockey. Violin. Potential college major: Graphic design.

Participant #2

Alex Tavarez

Age: 17

Siblings: 1 brother

Location of Origin: Sacramento, CA

Year at Academy: N/A. Summer PC.

Interests: LAX. Potential college major: LAX.

NOTES:

Participants signed waivers. Lauren met Alex at 8 p.m. Both acknowledged having no prior relationship since Alex attends school full-time in California. Lauren's body language was closed—arms folded, legs crossed. Alex was confident: posture reclined, knees spread.

A) Lauren's impressions of Alex were as follows:

Bro

Jock

LAX fiend

Smiley

Meh

B) Alex's impressions of Lauren were as follows:

She

Is

So

Freaking

Hot

(Observation: Clearly Participant #2 did not understand that he was not supposed to write in a complete sentence. Error? NOTE: Next time, write out detailed instructions so there is no room for misunderstanding on the part of participant.)

Participants engaged in eye contact for the prescribed time. They then consumed coconut water and trail mix. Small talk ensued. There were several attempts at humor on the part of Participant #2. Afterward, Participant #1 changed her final impression—"meh"—to "funny," while Participant #2 kept his the same except for adding an exclamation point after the word "hot!" (Observation: The upgrades on each participant's list support the thesis that intense eye contact alone may be enough to stimulate the production of PEA. Coconut water a factor? Next time will offer H_2O. More research needed.)

"Hmmm." Addie chewed on her lower lip as she absorbed the results of Dex's experiment with Lauren and Alex. "This wasn't the outcome I had predicted."

Dex lifted the scrubber from his tank of crabs. "Tell me about it."

"Well, the outcome I had predicted was that neither would show much interest with mere . . ."

"No, that's just an expression, Addie. It means I had already reached that conclusion. Ditto. Exactly. Or, in your patois, obvi." He sighed with impatience. "To be quite frank, I am beginning to have my doubts about this experiment. There are too many variables and not enough controls."

"Such as Alex not being able to control his instant attraction to Lauren?"

Dex's cheeks turned red as he shoved his scrubber back in the tank and began scraping furiously. "That only validates my concerns. If Alex and Lauren, um . . ."

"Commingle."

"Not that a girl of that caliber would have anything to do with that . . . *jock*."

"That jock is very visually appealing." Addie peered for a closer look at the crabs hidden amid the brown gravel and two tiny caves he had constructed, unaware that Dex had moved them to another tank.

"Sometimes you are so clueless." He tossed the scrubber into a sink and rinsed his hands.

"Because the crabs aren't here."

"That, too." Snatching a paper towel, he dried off each finger one by one. "I'm making great progress with the crabs and have accumulated more than enough documentation for an award submission."

Addie straightened and regarded him squarely, the clues now clearer. "You're saying we should terminate B.A.D.A.S.S. prematurely due to undesirable results."

"The crabs' reactions, at least, are quantifiable."

"But the crabs are *your* project. Not mine. I haven't even helped."

He tossed the paper towel into the garbage. "You had the chance to participate when I started working with them last fall. I can't help it that you're so love-starved that . . ."

She slapped a hand over his mouth. "Don't. Say. It."

"Please." He peeled her fingers away. "Never apply your hand to my mouth. It's highly unsanitary. You know as well as I that there are one hundred and fifty unique germs on the surface of a human palm."

Addie wiped her hand on a paper towel. "I just want to set the record straight. I am not now, nor have I ever been, *love-starved*. I am practical. You know my philosophy: no romantic entanglement until my doctoral thesis is complete."

"You say that, but I've seen the way you look at Kris, all puppy-eyed."

She suppressed a groundswell of irritation. "Never! I feel nothing for him other than a determination to treat him with professional courtesy, which, admittedly, is somewhat of a challenge."

"Because you think he's cute?"

A blast of heat shot up her neck. "Because it's a challenge not to resent him for destroying the lab."

"You seem to have given him a pass on that. I saw the way you two were chatting last night."

"You mean before I spiked the ball into his head?" Addie exhaled. That had been nothing to be proud of. She was ashamed she'd let her emotions spin so out of control.

Speaking of which, she needed to get on top of hers ASAP before she did something else she regretted. "Look. You're upset because you like Lauren and she likes Alex and not you."

"Get out!" He plunged his hand into the tank to rearrange the caves. "Unlike you, I've never been susceptible to my emotions."

"That's because you don't have any, you, you . . . cyborg!"

Perhaps this was the wrong thing to say, as his face immediately crumpled. Though that might have been due to the crab chomping down on his pinkie. Hard to tell.

"Oww!" A small brown crab dangled from his hand. Dex shook it back into the water.

Addie tore off more paper towels and dabbed his wound. "Breathe deeply to offset the pain. Does it hurt very much?"

He examined the raw red spot. "Not too much."

"Good. Keep pressure on the bite. That will interrupt the nervous system."

"Thank you. See how I'm being brave?"

She felt a rush of motherly sympathy. Dex could be rather sweet when he was vulnerable. "I'm sorry I got so angry at you. I guess, deep down, I'm mad at myself for letting Kris get to me. I never should have spiked that ball into his head. I can't believe how much damage I did." *To that perfect nose,* she didn't add out loud.

Dex went, "Hmph." Then, reluctantly, he added a stingy, "I'm sorry, too." Though that might have been less of an apology and more an expression of his regret that she couldn't control her emotions.

"I have a suggestion," Addie said, wrapping his pinkie tightly in the towel. "Let's just stick to the plan. We told Dr. Brooks that if Lauren didn't choose Kris at the dance, then we'd go back to the drawing board. Why not see what happens on Saturday? If it doesn't work, then we can make your crabs Plan B."

Dex stroked his injured digit. "I'm not going to the dance. You know my aversion to random socialization."

"Everyone has to be there. Headmaster's orders."

"Yes, but . . ." A fine sheen of sweat glistened on his forehead. "There is the possibility that I will be required to, you know, do . . ." He shook a leg and twirled, barely missing the table. "*That.*"

She studied his spastic twisting. "Didn't your mother send you to a professional dance school?"

"When I was twelve, in order to be invited to the Antediluvian Debutante Ball. And they taught me only how to do the box step and hokey-pokey."

Oh dear. She was pretty sure the hokey-pokey would not meet Tess's approval, and Tess was the arbiter of all matters socially acceptable. "Then don't dance. You can bring your laptop and take notes."

"That's true."

"Anyway," she said. "It's eleven fifty-five. Lauren and Kris will be here any minute. We've got to set up."

Setup included the day's lunch, which Dr. Brooks had arranged to be specially prepared by the school cafeteria. Granted, the staff had initially balked at the menu, until Headmaster Foy stepped in and explained the purpose of the bizarre dish. Then, according to Dr. Brooks, even the head chef herself "got into it." (Though Dr. Brooks had to reassure Addie that, no, the chef had not literally "gotten into" the food.)

Lauren and Kris arrived together, the flapping of Lauren's flip-flops echoing down the lab's concrete hallway as they approached. At the sound of Kris's easy laughter, the muscles in Addie's chest clenched and she went up on her toes in anticipation.

"Your guinea pigs have arrived," he announced. The bruises on his face had faded to brown, giving him a particularly rugged appearance, especially after a morning of landscaping.

A V of sweat ran down the front of his dark green Academy Buildings and Grounds T-shirt, right between his pectorals. Interesting how his shirt hung off his shoulders, broad and hard, unlike Dexter's, which were soft and round. Then again, Dexter was in baby pink with a popped collar, a completely different style, and he'd been in an underground, air-conditioned laboratory playing with crustaceans.

It was not right to compare.

And it was hard not to be curious. She wondered—purely theoretically—what it would feel like to have those strong arms around her. To be pulled to that chest. To feel Kris's long fingers running through her hair.

"Might want to check those emotions again," Dexter murmured.

Chastened, she squared her own shoulders and gestured for them to sit.

Lauren plunked herself down on the wooden chair and immediately went to her phone. "I can't spend a lot of time today. I need to finish some homework for my one-thirty class."

"You should complete your assignment the night before," Addie said, giving each their lists from the prior experiment. "That way, your subconscious can process the new knowledge while you sleep so that you'll be fully prepared the next day in class."

Kris said, "So that really works, huh, the subconscious thing? I thought it was just something you saw on TV."

"I wouldn't know. I don't own a television," Addie said. "However, from my *reading*, I know the subconscious is a far too unutilized tool. It is wasted on dreams."

"Maybe *your* dreams." Kris grinned. "Not mine."

Lauren thumbed to Addie and Dex. "God knows what these two dream about. Bunsen burners and petri dishes."

"I, for one, don't dream," Dex said.

Kris said, "And why am I not surprised?"

"Can we start?" Lauren asked. "I have, literally, no time."

Addie handed them each a pencil. "Please write down your impressions of each other, limiting your responses to five words."

Lauren made a face. "Again? I did this yesterday with

Kris and then with Alex. What's the point?"

Jotting down the last of his words, Kris said, "Who's Alex?"

Dex and Addie glanced at each other, alarmed. He wasn't supposed to know that there was a parallel control experiment. "Never mind," she said. "We need to hurry. Lauren's on a tight schedule."

But suddenly Lauren didn't seem all that much in a hurry. "You don't have another girl for Kris like I have another guy for me?" she asked.

"Not integral," Dex said, though what that even meant was a mystery.

Lauren went back to writing. "How come I get two guys?"

"Not just two," Dex whispered.

"Pardon?" Lauren stopped writing.

"Nothing." Dex took her paper.

When the lists were finished, Addie entered their responses in the spreadsheet while Dex brought out two plates. "Lunch."

"I hope it's not PB & banana again," Lauren said, examining the tortilla, guacamole, and . . . "Ew. What *is* this?" She held up an inch-long French fry that was strangely ridged and black at the end.

"Taste it," Addie said.

"She doesn't have to," Dex said. "Those things are

loaded with unnecessary fat, salt, and calories."

"Those *things*?" Lauren arched a brow. "Wait. They're not French fries?"

Kris dipped his in the sauce and bit into it. "I thought so. Delicious!" He wiped his fingers on a napkin. "Fried agave worms. Am I right?"

Addie lifted her finger up, pleased he was so smart. "Correct! Though the Mexicans call them *chilocuiles*. *Aegiale hesperiaris* is their scientific name. Your basic moth larvae."

"Oh god." Lauren clutched her gut. "I think I'm going to be sick."

Dexter began writing madly.

"Aren't you at least going to try one?" Addie asked.

"No. Way."

"That's part of the experiment," she singsonged.

"Then you do it." Lauren flicked a worm across her plate. It landed on the table, right by the sauce.

"All righty." Addie pinched it between her fingers and took a deep breath.

Dex gestured to the worm with the eraser side of his pencil. "It's unorthodox for researchers to participate in experiments with their subjects."

"It's also unorthodox to force people into eating putrid moth larvae," Lauren said.

"This helps." Kris held out the sauce. "It's not bad.

I used to eat stuff like this all the time when I was in China—silkworms. Same thing. They're considered a delicacy."

Lauren hugged her knees. "I don't eat anything that's considered a delicacy in a foreign country."

Turning to Addie, Kris said, "Go for it."

His brown eyes brimmed with amusement. It was as if he was saying, *I know what kind of person you are. You take chances. You're open-minded. You don't mind being different. In fact, you wouldn't have it any other way, would you?*

She liked that.

Addie dunked the worm and then popped the whole thing in her mouth, crunching down with one bite, whereupon it exploded in a burst of salty, spicy goo. Swallowing, she snatched up Kris's napkin and patted her mouth.

Lauren insisted on inspecting the napkin. It was empty. "She did it."

"Of course." Addie rubbed her stomach (or, the location on the abdomen commonly referred to as such). "Not bad."

"There you go! Have another." Kris held out his plate.

"I will if you will."

"Game on." He took a worm and, bypassing the sauce, bit it in half.

"Back atcha." Addie did the same, and then they toasted with their worm halves, dipped them ceremonially, and consumed.

"Um. I have to go, like, immediately before I barf." Lauren was already half out of her chair.

"Wait!" Dex said, waving the notebook papers. "You need to do your list."

Hastily, Lauren scribbled down five words, then grabbed her bag and, without so much as a good-bye, dashed out the door.

"I hope she's going to be okay," Kris said, completing his own list. "She did look kind of green."

Which was silly, Addie thought, reading over Lauren's latest five impressions, considering the worms were really nothing more than . . .

"Fried cheese?" Tess exploded in laughter.

"Shhh." Addie scanned the cafeteria to check if anyone overheard. "Quiet. Kris must never know."

"Oh, right. Sorry."

"I can't wait to report this to the Athenian Committee." Addie took a sip of her iced tea. "You are coming to my presentation, aren't you?"

Tess dipped a spoon into her pineapple Greek yogurt. "You know I wouldn't miss an opportunity to listen to you detail the peptides and riptides of love."

"There are no riptides. Riptides are currents. Peptides are amino-acid chains." Kind of embarrassing that she didn't know that, Addie thought.

"Whatever," Tess said, not the least bit embarrassed. "Let's get back to what we were talking about. Weren't you worried Kris would figure out that your worms were fake?"

Addie put her finger to her lips. Seriously. Years of being coached to project to the back of the room had ruined Tess's ability to keep her voice down.

"I was," she whispered. "Especially since he'd eaten silkworm larvae in China. I hadn't accounted for that. But the chef did a superb job. Cut them perfectly and made them look like the photos on Wikipedia."

"I bet Dex was apoplectic that Lauren wimped out, right?" Tess shouted.

Addie smacked her forehead. She would have to quit conversing about this in a public place if Tess insisted on being a human bullhorn. These updates were supposed to be confidential, not broadcast to the greater Academy 355 community. Dex would have a hissy fit if he found out she'd been blabbing about the experiment to her best friend, particularly since he and Tess didn't get along to begin with.

Dex dismissed Tess as a vapid drama queen, and Tess thought he was a psychopathic robot with an Oedipus complex. And now he was a psychopathic robot who maybe had a crush on Lauren. After the agave worm experiment, he kept sulking about her being "ganged up on," as if somehow her unwillingness to try a strange food had been Addie's fault.

"That was too much for her," Dex had railed, slamming his clipboard so hard against the soapstone lab tables that it produced a hairline fissure.

"If she had been more adventurous, Kris would have had a more flattering impression of her than"—she read off his last list—"nice, pretty, timid, uptight, boring."

"Her impressions of him aren't much better. He was downgraded from cocky to egotistical and from mysterious to whacked." Dex thumbed the crack he'd made, pulled a Sharpie out of his pocket, and drew over the line, to hide it. "I see she still kept strange and trouble."

"Also cute."

So there they were. Two days into the experiment and already Addie's thesis was being blown to smithereens and she and her lab partner were squabbling yet again.

"Sounds like the project isn't going as you'd planned," Tess said, finishing her yogurt.

"We'll see at the dance." Addie bit into her turkey sandwich, chewing thoughtfully.

"What's happening at the dance?"

Addie couldn't answer. She was only at eighteen.

"Oh, you're not doing that counting thing, are you?"

Tess rolled her eyes. "It is so weird."

She swallowed. "It's not weird. Thorough chewing aids digestion and ensures full nutritional value out of every meal."

"Before you take another bite, tell me what's so important about this stupid dance."

Addie put down her sandwich. "That's when we'll see if Lauren puts the moves on Alex or Kris. It will be our one chance to observe our subjects out of the lab and in their natural habitat."

"We need to buy you a new dress."

"I don't care what I wear." She lifted her sandwich to take another bite and was blocked by Tess.

"Also, we should do something with your hair. Get it out of that ponytail. Have you considered eyeliner? You need something to bring out your eyes."

"The dance is not about me. Besides, Kris and Lauren might not even be able to attend." She wiggled her brow. "That's okay because their next experiment is even more dangerous than consuming fake insects."

"Uh-oh. I hope you're not going too far, Addie, like when you got your hands on some cyanide to turn those iron nails blue and . . ."

"Please, that was eighth grade. And it was sodium ferrocyanide, which is barely toxic."

"You accidentally released enough poisonous gas to

send the entire class to the hospital!"

Addie dismissed this with a wave. "Middle schoolers craving attention. Everyone was perfectly healthy."

"Sure. After twenty-four hours in the ICU with round-the-clock supervision."

"Like I said. Everyone was fine." Addie took another bite of her sandwich and counted back from twenty.

"Exactly what kind of so-called trauma are you going to inflict on these poor people?" Tess groaned and waited for her to finish, counting out loud until she was done. "Five, four, three, two, one."

Addie patted her lips. "Nothing too strenuous. Just enough danger to really get the amygdala pumping out those survival chemicals. It's the only way my thesis can be proven."

"You're hella sick."

"We'll see. If they fall madly in love, you might think I'm hella genius."

"Hey, I wonder if that's what happened to Ed and me," Tess said, her green eyes wide open in fresh revelation. "We were stuck on a mountain in super-high winds with lightning all around. Could have easily died. Maybe that's why I fell for him . . . because, otherwise, he's so not my type. Did you ever think about that, *genius*?"

Addie thought, If you only knew. "How are you two

doing, by the way? Did you have a talk?"

"Yeah. Thanks for giving him a push. He said he's going to try to visit in October." She twirled her spoon. "I just love him *sooooo* much."

"I know." Addie gave her arm a pat.

"You do?"

"Actually, I . . ."

A shadow darkened their table and there was Kris, showered and clean, hands in his jeans pockets. Addie's pulse quickened.

"Got a minute?" he asked.

"I better go set up for evening games," Tess said, sliding out of her chair. "See you in about five minutes, Addie?"

Addie put down her half-eaten sandwich and shook her head. "Can't. I've got some more work to do at the lab. There's a paper that's just been published on . . ."

"Um, you are my Assistant PC," Tess chided. "The girls are going to be all over campus tonight and I can't be three places at once."

Shoot. That paper was vital to her Athenian thesis, a really fascinating breakthrough in the role of cells in regulating emotions.

"What are you guys doing that you're going to be in three places at once?" Kris asked, taking a seat across from Addie.

Tess picked up her tray. "It's Choose Your Own Adventure. The rock-climbing wall, ropes course, or kayaking."

"Which adventure are you doing?"

The question was directed at Addie. She met his gaze under that brooding brow and swallowed the bite she'd just taken. "I don't know. Kayaking, maybe. I could read in the boat."

"Five minutes." Tess tapped her watch. "We're starting off with circle, where we talk about the latest crises, and I don't want you to miss it. Your adolescent brain research could come in handy."

Addie gave her a tiny salute. "Yes, boss."

When she was gone, Kris leaned across the table and smirked.

"What are you up to?" she asked.

"Fried cheese."

Her heart skipped a beat, though it was hard to tell if that was because he'd figured out the scam or because he was so close the tip of his nose almost touched hers. "Affirmative," she said, sitting back a bit and twisting off the top of her water bottle. "When did you deduce the secret ingredient?"

"When you put it in front of me and I smelled mozzarella. Do you know how many pizzas I've eaten in my life? I'm something of an expert."

She took a swig and recapped it. "Why didn't you tell Lauren?"

"And ruin your fun? Nah."

"That's humorous," she stated.

"Humorous?" He made a face. "I've never actually heard someone say that. Usually people just laugh."

"Ha."

"You're messing with me, right?"

"Ha. Ha. Ha."

"Getting there. Let's try a joke. A duck, a pig, and an aardvark walk into a bar . . ."

"This sounds bad."

"It only gets worse." He frowned. "Shoot. I forgot the middle. Anyway, the punch line is, And the pig said, 'I don't have any balloons!'" Kris slapped the table, howling with laughter.

Addie remained straight-faced.

"Don't you think that's hi-lar-i-ous?" Kris asked.

"How could I? You totally messed up the middle."

"Okay, but the punch line. You have to admit, that's pretty good."

"I admit nothing." Addie held up her hand and ticked off her fingers. "For starters, your story didn't make sense. A pig, a duck, and an aardvark wouldn't walk into a bar. That would violate local health ordinances. For another, animals do not speak. Their brains have not evolved to the point where . . ."

Kris smacked his head. "Forget it. Do you have to pick everything apart?"

"An unexamined life is not worth living."

"Now she's quoting Socrates."

Addie crumpled her paper napkin and tossed it onto the tray. "I'm right here. You don't have to refer to me in the third person."

"Now she's giving me a grammar lesson." He looked up. "By the way, word is that right before the volleyball game Ed teased you about being an animal killer"—Kris covered his nose protectively—"and you didn't give him a concussion for it."

Poor Kris. The space under his eyes was still ringed with purple from the burst capillaries. She'd really done a number on him. "Ed was joking."

"So was I. It was an attempt to break the ice. You know, to clear the elephant from the room, so to speak."

"What elephant? And we weren't in a room. We were outside."

Kris ruffled his hair so it stood on end. "Man. Tough crowd."

Now that made her laugh. She giggled so hard, she coughed. "It's the hair. It's so wild. Do you ever get it cut?"

"Really? That's where we're going?" But he was smiling, and she couldn't help but smile back.

This phenomenon was fascinating, but also disturbing.

Her growing feelings for Kris were becoming a problem, not only because he had a girlfriend who just happened to be her arch enemy, but also because falling for a volunteer in your experiment definitely did not comport with scientific protocol. She would have to force herself to keep a professional distance, otherwise the entire B.A.D.A.S.S. project could be in jeopardy.

Her phone dinged and a text from Tess screamed, *WE'VE STARTED. WHERE ARE YOU?????*

"Gotta go," she said, getting up. "See you tomorrow. Don't forget, we're meeting at the gym, not the lab."

Then she dumped her tray and left without another word.

The girls were sitting on the grass in a circle when Addie arrived way late because she'd had to stop off at the dorm to pick up a notebook.

"Yay, it's Spike!" Emma said. The other girls broke out in applause since, thanks to her, they'd beaten the boys at volleyball the day before.

Being hailed as a hero, especially for athletic prowess, was an entirely foreign experience—and strangely gratifying. Academic achievement was a solitary endeavor. Getting all As on your report card didn't earn you high fives from your fellow students. Even when she and Dex won praise for their lab reports, it still felt lonely, since he inevitably took all the credit.

But yesterday she'd been part of a team, and now the team rallied around her. It was warm and welcoming.

She took a seat next to Mindy, who asked, "Is it allowed to hit a ball into someone's head? At home, that would be illegal."

"That's only if you reach across the net," Fiona said. "And she didn't do that."

The truth was, Addie couldn't remember if she'd reached across the net when she jumped up to hit the ball. All she could recall was being overcome with rage when she heard the words in Kris's mouth.

"We were talking about the dance on Saturday," Tess said from the opposite side of the circle, where she was sitting between a glum Tay and Bree. "The theme is A Midsummer Night's Dream, and Shreya asked if it was a costume party. It's not. You can dress up, dress down. It's all good."

Mindy raised her hand. "But isn't the dance on the day we're going to Harvard?"

Tess shifted uncomfortably. "We'll be back from our field trip by then. You'll have plenty of time to get ready."

"I was thinking of staying over." Mindy pointed to Fiona. "I mean, both of us. We're leaving for Chicago the next morning. We'll be closer to the airport."

Tess shot Addie a knowing look. "Maybe we should

talk about that later. The administration hasn't said anything to me about this."

"Really?" Zuri asked with a giggle. "That's a surprise."

Tess craned her neck. "Do you know something I don't?"

"It's okay," Mindy piped up. "Skip it."

Fiona said, "You should just tell them. Everyone knows, anyway."

"This is about the guy, isn't it," Tess said. "David or whatever."

Mindy ducked her head and plucked a few blades of grass. "We were going out last year. Then my parents said I couldn't see him because a relationship would hurt my studies. His parents agreed."

"That's a valid argument," Addie said. "I follow the same philosophy myself."

"You probably don't have a boyfriend," Tay said snarkily. "It would be different if you did."

Addie thought about this. "Noooo," she said slowly. "I don't have a boyfriend because I've sworn off boys until after I finish my doctoral thesis. See how that works? Chicken. Egg."

"But if you *did* have a boyfriend . . . ," Bree said with a half shrug. "I'm just saying."

"You do realize what you're 'just saying' is totally

illogical, right?" Addie said. "I have made a conscious decision to . . ."

A piercing whistle shut them up. Tess took two fingers out of her mouth and said, "Excuse me, ladies. We were talking about Mindy. She's the one with the problem. Let's turn our attention to her. Go on."

Mindy let out a sigh. "We knew our parents would get suspicious if we went on the same exchange program. So he went to Harvard's summer school and I did this. Our week here is the only chance we'll have to see each other until we graduate."

"Oh, no," Tess moaned, massaging her forehead. "This is so not what I wanted to happen."

But no one else seemed to notice her distress.

"What about at school?" Rachel asked.

"We go to different schools. His is all boys; mine is all girls."

"That blows," said Emma. "You two should rendez-vous after class."

Fiona and Mindy stared at each other, puzzled.

"Arrange to meet," Emma explained. "That's what rendezvous means in French."

"We know what rendezvous means," Fiona said. "We don't have time after class. Or before. We start school at eight and finish at five. That's how long our day is. We take one hour for dinner and then study until eleven.

Everyone does at least two hours of work before school."

"Are you serious?" Tay asked incredulously. "I would tell my parents no way. I have a life, thank you very much."

"You're lucky," Mindy said. "You can go to any college you want. We can't go unless we get high marks on the *gaokao* senior year. Three days of testing. Armed guards outside. Even drones overhead to make sure there are no radio signals helping students cheat."

The group hummed in uniform outrage.

"From what I've read," Addie offered, "the SATs are nothing in comparison. Girls go on the pill so they don't get their periods. They have ambulances in case students faint."

Zuri dropped her jaw. "That's a lot of pressure. How do you handle it?"

Mindy shrugged. "No boyfriend."

The circle erupted in laughter. Addie took advantage of the momentary distraction to send a text. When the reply was a thumbs-up, she said, "We better get to Choose Your Own Adventure before it's too late."

"Oh, you're right," Tess said, checking her own watch. "Okay, so who wants to go kayaking?"

Mindy and Fiona raised their hands.

"Ropes course?" Tess asked.

No takers.

"Rock wall?"

"Meh," said Rachel. "It's too hard."

"I choose the adventure of going to Thwing, getting an iced coffee, and watching bad TV in lovely air conditioning," Tay said, turning to Bree. "How about you?"

"Extreme slacking? I'm there."

They got up and brushed off their shorts. Emma, Shreya, Rachel, and Zuri followed.

Tess threw up her hands. "So much for team building."

"Look at it this way. They chose their own adventure. It just happened to be on reality TV." Addie stood and brushed off loose bits of grass. "At least some of them are kayaking. By the way, what are you going to do about the Mindy situation?"

"I have no idea. Hope she comes to her senses? Hope she's too busy to go to Harvard. . . . This?" Tess crossed her fingers.

Addie made a face. "Ah, yes, when all else fails, rely on the power of superstition. While you do that, I'll head back to the lab. That paper on spindle neurons isn't going to read itself."

TEN

How Kris happened to be down at the boat launch that evening was tough to explain.

Later, he would claim that he went to check out the sunset across the bay to the mainland, an obvious lie to anyone who knew that in the beginning of July, the sun set around eight thirty, not seven, which was when he was strolling the beach, skipping stones into the water, watching birds and generally hoping that at any minute Addie Emerson would arrive to go kayaking.

At the sound of footsteps thrumming on the wooden stairs, he spun around a bit too eagerly, only to be disappointed by the appearance of two summer students.

"The kayaks are over here," said the shorter girl, whose

name, he vaguely recalled from the volleyball game, was Shreya.

"Do we have to sign them out or anything?" asked Emma, the taller of the two, a heck of an athlete.

Shreya emerged from the boathouse holding two life jackets, tossing one to Emma. "There's a sheet inside. I wrote down our names."

"Okay." Emma snapped into her jacket and went over to the rack of kayaks, debating the virtues of each.

"Need a hand?" Kris asked, loping across the beach to help.

"I'm trying to figure out if there's a difference. They look the same except for the color."

"I think they are. Which one do you want?" Kris gravitated toward a yellow boat. "The brighter it is, the better for speedboats to see you."

"Makes sense. Okay. Thanks." Emma went inside the boathouse to get paddles while Kris fetched a red one for Shreya.

"They're fairly light," Kris said, setting hers half on the beach and half in the water. "Just awkward to carry."

Emma snapped her paddle together and then did the same for Shreya. "We were in the student lounge watching TV and it got really boring. Bree insisted on a reality show about buying a wedding dress with a bunch of screaming brides, so we left. We ran into Tess's boyfriend, who said it was a perfect time to kayak with the sun setting on the water."

"You know, I don't think those women say yes to anything," Shreya said.

"Except a diamond ring," Emma added, stepping into the boat. "I pity the guys who have to marry them."

"They're probably just as bad." Shreya got into hers. "Anyway, there was nothing wrong with the first dress. The one she picked out made her look like an exploded marshmallow."

Kris offered to give them each a push. Which they accepted. It wasn't until they started paddling off that he had a disturbing thought.

"Hey, you guys do know what you're doing, right?" He was particularly worried about Shreya, who didn't seem to have a clue and was spinning in circles, splashing the water frantically.

"I do," Emma said. "My parents have a house on Lake Michigan. We go kayaking all the time. I'll show Shreya how."

"Good!" Shreya said with a laugh. "Because I've never even seen one of these things before."

He stood on the beach and watched them round the point to the causeway. Then he lay down and closed his eyes in the warm evening light, inhaling the timeless scent of the sea and listening to the purr of motorboats chugging through the channel, the gentle lapping of the bay water on the shoreline, and the call of seagulls. It was so peaceful here that he didn't realize he'd fallen asleep until someone kicked sand in his face.

"What the . . . ?" He bolted up and shook his head.

Addie loomed over him, hands on hips. "Did you see two girls come by to go kayaking?" she asked, panicked.

"Yeah," he said, getting up and feeling a twinge of remorse. Dammit. He knew he shouldn't have let them go by themselves.

"How long ago did they leave?"

"Not sure. I think I might have fallen asleep."

Addie smacked her forehead. "Tess is going to kill me!" She hurried to the boathouse and grabbed two pieces of a paddle and a life jacket. "I didn't think anyone was going to be here. That's why I was at the lab. Then Ed texted me and asked why I wasn't at the beach because he'd . . ."

"Suggested they go kayaking." Kris already had his own life jacket on and was grabbing a paddle for himself and a kayak for Addie. "It's okay. I'm sure they didn't go far. Here." He slid hers into the water.

Addie stepped into it. "It doesn't matter how far they went. Shreya's used to swimming pools, not oceans."

"A fairly significant ocean borders India." He dumped a green boat on the beach. "They call it the, um, *Indian Ocean*."

"Ha. Ha."

Was that a real laugh? Or was she mocking him?

He pushed his boat out, stepped in, and fell right over. He hadn't done that since he was a kid. Total humiliation.

"Not much of a Boy Scout, were you?" Addie asked, swinging around.

"Must be last year's model. I'm used to the newer ones," he joked.

"You should read *How to Kayak like a Pro* by Walter P. Jinger. He's a former Olympian, you know. That's what I did, and now look!" She speared the water with her paddle. "Knuckles up!"

He was tempted to let it be known he'd spent four summers, including two as a CIT, in an all-boys canoe camp in Canada and probably could paddle circles around Walter P. freaking Jinger or whatever, but they had bigger troubles. Like making sure Shreya hadn't capsized. He got back in his own boat and caught up to Addie with ease.

"We have to get around the point to see the beach on the mainland by the bridge," he said, taking the lead. "That's where they went."

They negotiated a rocky outcropping that scraped the bottom of their boats. He had to swing around and extract Addie from a hidden boulder barely underneath the water's surface.

"So, about this experiment I got roped into," he asked, trying to strike up a conversation, "what's it really about?"

"I told you. It's about how males and females react in certain situations," Addie answered, coming up next to him.

"Then why did you start off with a staring contest? That doesn't make much sense."

"I can't explain further." Her ponytail bounced with each stroke. She was splashing water everywhere, even on him. So much for Walter P. Jinger's expert advice. "A researcher must always be mindful not to cloud the results with her subconscious feelings."

"Like violent urges to pummel your guinea pig into the ground?"

She dipped the end of her paddle and flung so much water at him, for a second he was blinded.

"Thanks for that," he said, wiping his face. "More abuse."

"I told you I was sorry. Stop bringing it up."

"When did you tell me you were sorry?"

She thought about this. "In my head."

"Yeah, that's not how you apologize. You actually have to make the words come out of your mouth. Otherwise it doesn't count."

"Watch out!" Addie shouted as a sleek cigarette boat passed by, heading toward the underpass in the causeway. "I despise those things. They're noise pollutants and regular pollutants." She pinched her nose at the pungent gasoline scent that permeated the fresh ocean air.

Kris sensed his kayak going backward. Fast. "Whoa. That's one hell of a current. I hope the girls didn't get caught in this."

"We would have seen them if they had, going out to sea," Addie said. "Though I guess they could have slipped away while you were asleep."

He thrust his oar in the water, to counter the force. "Hey, at least I was here. You were across campus in the lab, Ms. PC."

"Assistant PC, and . . . Kris . . . you better stop that."

"I can't," he said, employing deep, efficient strokes to be clear of the current. "I'm almost free."

Addie, he noticed, was relaxing in her kayak, oars across her knees like they were out for fun instead of desperately searching for two novice boaters who were in way over their heads.

"I'm telling you," she said in a strange, eerily calm voice. "Get your hands away from the water. It's not safe."

"What?" He lifted his oar. "Why?"

She pointed to a large gray triangle cutting through the water between them. "It's circling."

Kris swallowed hard as its sleek body passed like an underwater ghost. The shark was easily as long as his kayak, maybe even longer. A man-eater.

Addie bent over for a closer look. "It's huge. I think it might be a great white. How absolutely fascinating!" Against her own advice, she bent over as if to reach out and touch the fin, her kayak leaning precipitously to one side.

"Are you crazy? That thing will take your arm off!"

"When else will I get a chance to be this close to a great white?"

"Hopefully never. What's it doing here, anyway? I thought they were way out in the ocean."

"They've been spotted in Cape Cod Bay, so it is technically possible that one would be in the inlet." She pulled her hand back reluctantly as the fin disappeared. "They're very intelligent, you know. The assumption is that because their brains are small compared with their body mass that they're stupid. It's merely that their brains have different structures than ours, especially the great white."

What had he read about sharks? That you had to hit them on the head, hard, to stun their nervous system. He may have loved animals, but there were exceptions, including poisonous snakes, big, ugly spiders, and these guys. On impulse, he smashed his oar into the water, making a terrific splash.

"Don't!" she protested. "You'll hurt her."

"Exactly. While I distract it, you paddle as fast as you can to shore." He slapped the water again and this time the shark swerved from Addie's kayak and undulated toward his.

"Be careful!" Addie cried. "She's just lost. She probably came into the bay looking for chum that the fishermen throw off the docks. As an animal rights activist, I'd have thought you'd be all over this."

But he had stopped listening because the shark had changed its swimming pattern, darting into his kayak and then out. It reminded Kris of how bats bounce radar off objects to find their way . . . and to find food.

Poor choice of words, that.

Perhaps if he hadn't been so intent on the shark's movements, he would have paid more attention to the roar of a boat engine as it left the channel, zooming across the inlet at full throttle, the girls in the back screaming for him to go faster.

It wasn't until he heard Addie's shouts that he looked up and saw Ed at the wheel of an official Academy Campion, which he realized was the same cigarette boat that had passed them earlier. And in the back, crisscrossing their arms excitedly, were none other than Emma and Shreya, having the time of their lives, their colorful kayaks dragging off the stern.

"They're safe!" Addie yelled.

"Wish I could say the same for us."

"Go away!" she shouted, waving Ed off. "Shoo!"

Wait. Not go away. Come here! "We need to get on his boat," Kris hollered over the roar of Ed's engine.

Addie cupped her ear. "Can't hear you."

Ed obviously took her cue to leave, because he banked hard right, circling back, and setting in motion a chain reaction that, had Addie been sitting, might have resulted in less of a catastrophe.

Waves.

Kayak wobbling.

Addie's shriek.

Capsize.

Splash.

It happened so fast, Kris didn't hesitate. With four fast strokes, he was by her side as she clung desperately to the hull of her own overturned boat.

"Get in," he said.

"What about you? It's a one-person kayak."

"Exactly." And with that he slid out of his boat, into the water. It was shockingly cold.

"What are you doing?"

"Don't argue. The longer I'm in the water, the faster I'll be dead meat. Get in."

After a moment's hesitation, she maneuvered from her boat to his as Kris kept both steady by madly treading water. He did not want to think what his dangling legs must look like to a hungry shark. He hoped not like chum.

Safely in his seat, she said, "I'll help you flip the boat." But as soon as she reached for it, the kayak slipped out of his hands and floated away.

"Crap!" he swore, swimming freestyle to catch it.

And there, in the corner of his eye, was the fin—headed in his direction.

"Hurry!" Addie screamed.

No, really? he thought, reaching the kayak at last and snagging it with one massive stroke. In order to right it, he would have to duck underneath and push up with all his strength. And he would have to do it fast with the shark on his tail.

He dove into the cold, dark water, reached up, and flipped the thing. Water sloshed in the hull as he hoisted himself up and in, just as the shark slipped by.

Panting, blood pumping, he lay on top of the kayak, never feeling more lucky or grateful in his life. With shaky hands, he released the plug to drain it before the entire thing sank.

"Oh, man," he mumbled, resting his head on his arms. "That was close." He envisioned the creature's blind eyes zeroing in on his warm body, sinking its massive teeth into his leg, ripping muscles and veins.

He took a few deep, much-needed breaths and rolled over. Addie was gripping her oars and wearing, to his total confusion, an ear-to-ear smile.

"That," she announced, barely able to contain herself, "was *very* invigorating!"

"Invigorating?" He coughed out a lungful of seawater and got back in the seat. "That was scary as hell! I nearly got my leg bitten off."

"But you didn't."

"I was seconds away."

"That's what made it so stimulating," she gushed. "I

could literally feel my zona fasciculata pumping out tons of cortisol." She giggled hysterically, a truly spontaneous laugh. "I'm still on a high."

Who was this girl? They'd been seconds away from becoming shark Cheetos and she was having a blast.

"We need to get out of here," he said, searching for his paddle and finding, much to his dismay, that it had disappeared. "The oar's gone!"

Addie pointed in the direction of the ocean. "It's over there. I'll get it." Paying no heed to the shark, wherever it might have been, she rowed spastically in the direction of the open ocean and snatched it.

As she returned, the setting sun reflecting off the water and onto her smiling face, Kris was suddenly gifted with almost supernatural clarity.

He could see every golden-brown strand of Addie's wet hair, which stuck to her head like a drenched mouse, the way her nose turned up just the slightest bit and how her front two teeth were parted by a teeny gap, how her knobby knees stuck out of the cockpit, and how when she sneezed seawater, she wiped her nose with the back of her hand.

Nice, he thought.

No. Really.

Nice.

ELEVEN

"It's amazing you weren't hurt." Tess cracked open a cold bottle of water and took a swig, before offering it to Addie. "Could have been very dangerous, capsizing like that."

"Not to worry," she said, wiping the bottle rim of errant germs. "My life jacket was a US Coast Guard–approved Type III flotation device. How are Emma and Shreya?"

"Oh, there's nothing wrong with them. Emma was bummed that Ed came to their rescue, though he said Shreya was relieved. She definitely did not have the strength or experience to handle the bay."

Addie finished the water and tossed the bottle back

into the recycling. "I'm sorry I wasn't at the boat launch. I assumed everyone was watching TV, so I figured what the heck and went to the lab."

"That's okay. Ed should never have suggested they go kayaking without first checking to make sure there was supervision."

"Let's just blame this whole incident on *Say Yes to the Dress*." Addie grabbed a towel she kept neatly folded on her shelf. "I need a shower. My skin is sticky with sodium residue."

She collected her anti-mold bamboo shower basket, along with a towel, and left—remembering halfway there that she'd forgotten to say good-bye to Tess.

That was okay. Tess was used to her abrupt exits and entrances, thankfully. Other people were so obsessed with the formalities of saying hello, and hey, and good-bye and see you and talk to you later. Must one always announce when one was coming or going like some town crier? It was so unnecessary.

She pushed open the door marked GIRLS, which struck her as redundant since, being a single-sex dorm, all the bathrooms were for girls. As if to reinforce the sexism, every feature from the tiles to the toilets was constructed of porcelain in what Addie thought of as fairy-vomit pink, a holdover from when Wren Hall was built in the 1950s.

Fortunately, the bathroom was empty, so Addie had her pick of showers. She chose the one in the corner. It had a small window through which streamed powerful ultraviolet light waves—sunshine to the layperson—which were well known to kill bacteria and viruses by scrambling their DNA. Fascinating. There was great comfort in knowing that she was cleansing herself at the site of mass germicide earlier in the day.

Methodically, she stripped out of her skirt, top, and underwear as the water warmed to a perfect 105 degrees and then stepped in, delighting in the dopamine rush as the spray washed off all the salt and freed her mind from its constant whirring.

She was slightly ashamed to find herself thinking back to Kris's braided quadriceps and back muscles visible through his wet T-shirt. For the sake of their experiment, she would have to force those images from her mind and quit comparing him to Dexter, who, although possessing a healthy BMI, found his backpack so heavy that his mother had purchased him the roller kind—with his monogrammed initials.

This was perfectly understandable, of course. Dexter was a genius whose domain was the library or lab, not the gym or athletic fields. No one of any substance would dare argue that brawn was more valuable than brains.

Had Dexter been in the other kayak, most likely he

would have reasoned that the most efficient way to assure their safety would be for him to paddle back to shore to seek assistance (while she clung to the boat for dear life).

Kris, in contrast, had acted first and thought later. Perhaps. She didn't really get a chance to speak with him once Ed deposited Emma and Shreya at the docks and then returned to fetch Addie and Kris in case they needed help. Which they definitely did.

The bathroom door slammed and Addie proceeded to busy herself by methodically working through her shampoo/conditioner/soap system.

"Where did he come from?" one of the girls asked, stretching out the question mark like it was a separate word. "Every guy here is a dud and then . . . bam! In walks heaven."

"He was at the volleyball game last night. Remember?"

"How could I forget?" *Giggles.*

Addie cocked her ear for a closer listen. Tay and Bree, if her auditory powers of deduction were correct.

"I am a total sucker for guys like him," chimed in Tay. "He's soooo mysterious."

"Ditto!" Bree said. "I think it's cause all the guys where we're from are blond."

"California blond."

"They're everywhere. Even the idiots who've never

been on a surfboard—especially the idiots who've never been on a surfboard—are like *duuuuuude*. It's so hypo-critical."

A hypocrite was someone who espoused a certain philosophy in public that he or she violated in private. But Addie wasn't about to rinse off and correct them, though there was that temptation.

"What I don't get is why he was kayaking *with her*?"

The soapy puff stopped halfway up Addie's arm.

"She's nice enough, but . . ." The other girl rinsed and spit. "Talk about awkward turtle."

"Ya think? She's like a cyborg in a ponytail. And what's with the skirts?"

"I bet she's never even been kissed."

Addie's cheeks burned. This was so not true.

But that wasn't the end of it. What they said next hurt the most.

"I heard that a bunch of PETA types last year spray-painted nasty stuff about her on the wall of the lab and got kicked out of school for vandalism."

"Really?" Another rinse and spit. "What did they write?"

"I don't know, but they destroyed all the lab walls. Can you believe it?" This resulted in two peals of laughter that echoed off the tiles.

Addie's stomach flip-flopped.

"That. Is. Harsh," Bree said.

"I know, right? But if I'd been her, I'd have left school."

"Seriously."

Addie hung her head, the water running over her body, dripping off her chin and shoulders along with a fresh set of hot, salty tears. The only reason she hadn't left the Academy was because she didn't want to go home. It was worse there, the way the kids stared when she constantly raised her hand in class. It was as if wanting to learn was gross.

When she got to the Academy, she felt like the ugly duckling meeting her fellow swans. Everyone raised their hands. The weird ones were the people who didn't participate. Class discussions were fast and furious and often heated, with teachers urging them to push the boundaries in how they thought about the most basic facts.

What makes prime numbers so special? If the universe is not infinite, then what's beyond it? Why is there "stuff" and where does stuff come from if energy can be neither created nor destroyed and there wasn't nearly as much "stuff" around one hundred years ago as there is now?

If she'd asked these questions back in her old school, she would have been laughed out of the classroom. So, yeah, going home was out of the question.

Tess often promised that things would get better. With the seniors from last year graduated, that was one less group who knew her. Also, memories faded and, ultimately, people were more preoccupied with themselves than others.

Lately, she was beginning to see what Tess meant. Since she'd returned to school a few days ago, no one had mentioned the graffiti or the vandalism, aside from Dexter, though that was to be expected with Kris popping up in their experiment. Everything was going just swimmingly, until . . . tonight.

The door slammed. Addie startled and tried to pull herself together. She could not let the summer students see her crying; she'd never live it down.

It helped if she could analyze her emotions from a purely biological perspective. Tears, for example, were such strange phenomena, with no evolutionary purpose aside from a temporary emotional release—unlike straight-up lacrimation, wherein the lacrimal gland between the eyeball and eyelid produced moisture. She pondered the three types of tears—basal, reflex, and psychic—until the production of acetylcholine subsided along with her heart rate.

More composed, she dried off, ran a comb through her wet hair, brushed her teeth, and regarded herself in the mirror. She wrapped herself tightly in a fluffy blue towel and padded down the hall to the safe seclusion of her single room. Except that when she opened the door, she found she wasn't alone.

"Hey. I hope this is okay."

Oh, god, it was *him*.

Kris was sitting on her bed holding two pints of Ben & Jerry's ice cream. Her PEA switch kicked into overdrive.

"What are you doing here?" she asked, pulling the towel snugger.

"Hazed & Confused?" He held up one pint. "Or Chunky Monkey? Both are ridiculously full of awesome deliciousness."

"Um." She inched toward the safe refuge of her closet.

"I checked, but they were fresh out of fried agave worm."

"Excuse me." With that, she shut the door of the closet and felt around in the dark for the nightshirt she kept on a hook. Throwing it over her head, she undid her towel, stepped into a pair of underwear, ran her fingers through her hair, and reappeared.

Kris's glance flicked to her nightshirt and then up just as fast. "I love Hello Kitty."

She examined her shirt. "You're mocking me, aren't you?"

"Absolutely not. I am a big fan of pink-themed cat logos."

"It was a gift last year from my mentee."

Placing the two pints on her desk, he said, "What did you mentor her in?"

Addie slipped a notebook under them so the water

wouldn't ruin the wood, and sat on the bed. "Organic chemistry. I don't know why she was having trouble. Those carbon molecules are so much fun to build. They're like toys."

"You might be onto something there." He pulled a scoop from his pocket and cracked open the Chunky Monkey. "K'Nex for the gifted child."

That *was* a good idea.

"Anyway," he continued, digging into the ice cream. "I'm sorry if you felt like I was razzing your shirt. You should see what I wear to bed. Ripped boxers."

The image made her slightly faint as she watched him produce two white bowls and thin metal spoons from inside his maroon Andover hoodie. "Did you steal those from the cafeteria?"

"Steal?" He opened the Hazed & Confused. "More like short-term borrowed without signed authorization."

She was doubtful that such a form existed. "That's a joke, right?"

He handed her a bowl with a scoop of each. "Right. You're catching on. We'll have a belly laugh in no time."

"It's better than your duck and aardvark one," she said, nudging a frozen walnut.

"And pig. Don't forget the pig because he has the balloons!" Kris recapped the pints, sat on the bed, and looked at her expectantly. "Usually at this stage of the game, most people would say thank you."

"Thank you for bringing me ice cream after breaking into my room."

"Touché!"

Actually, after her crying jag in the shower, it was nice to have him there. What had Bree called him? Oh, right: heaven.

He waved the spoon absently. "The thing is, I wouldn't have had to break into your room if the school hadn't turned into a prison. Since when did they close the dorms at ten?"

"Since the summer students required a curfew."

"Which I discovered when I buzzed the front door and Tess answered. She told me to go around back where your window was and try to get hold of you that way. It's not like I have your cell number, and . . . I was worried. That was pretty freaky out there, what happened to us. Wanted to make sure you're okay."

Addie was truly touched. "Thank you for your concern. I'm fine. How about you?"

"Good. Is there any reason why you're all the way over there?"

She scooched down from the head of the bed to where he was sitting, by the foot, and went rigid. Him being in her room in violation of curfew and eating Chunky Monkey was so risky! They could get caught at any moment and all hell would break loose.

The headmaster would summon her into his office and lecture her about being a lousy role model Assistant PC. Tess would be appalled that she was eating ice cream after eight p.m. when there was absolutely no chance of burning off the calories before sleep. And Dr. Brooks . . .

. . . better not to imagine how mad Dr. Brooks would be.

"Ice cream makes everything better, don't you think?" Kris said. "I figured maybe you could use some after capsizing tonight. That water was freezing."

"No, freezing is zero degrees centigrade. By my estimation, the bay was roughly 12.778 centigrade, which would have lowered our core body temperatures to—" She couldn't finish because Kris had shoved a spoonful of banana-chocolate yumminess into her mouth.

"Sometimes, Addie, it's nice to just sit together and eat ice cream. In silence."

She swallowed it in one lump and paid for it with the stabbing sensation of an instant ice-cream headache. "But I like to talk."

"I know you do." He smiled and took another spoonful. "What do you want to talk about?"

She massaged her forehead. "Your ambitions."

"My *ambitions*? I was thinking more along the lines of why the Red Sox suck so bad."

"Because they have no reliable hitting and their

bullpen has been decimated."

"Oookay. Guess we can put that to rest. So you want to know my ambitions, huh?" He stared at the ceiling, tapping the spoon on his knee. "Well, my short-term goal is pretty simple: get back on Foy's good side, do better than I did on the May SATs, up my GPA next semester, and go to school out west, like California. Major in Asian studies. Then, bam, back to Nepal!"

"Won't you miss your family?"

"Yeah, but . . ." He hesitated, as if about to say something. "Nah. I'll save it. What about you?"

"My family is of a non-nuclear structure." One more bite of ice cream. "Dorrie, also known as my mother, is a wildlife biologist who travels all over the world going from grant to grant. She's hardly ever home. My father remarried a younger woman and they have twin daughters who require as much time and attention as my stepmother's closet."

"So you're kind of out of the picture."

"No. I'm in the family pictures—in the back. I stand behind my stepsisters because I'm taller."

Kris closed his eyes. "What I mean is, you're pretty self-sufficient, so your parents can ignore you and not feel guilty."

Guilt. He was obsessed with it. "They never feel guilty." She crunched on a fairly large piece of dark chocolate. "They act like I don't exist." As soon as she said that out loud, she felt a little sorry for herself.

"Oh, Addie. That blows." He slid his bowl onto the desk and put his arm around her. She stiffened. Kris was warm and smelled of dried kelp from the bay.

"You know what I secretly loved the most about Nepal?" he said, still holding her. "Not the mountains or the people, though, don't get me wrong, they were awesome. It was the aloneness. No cell. No internet. It was like I'd slipped off the face of the Earth."

"Earth doesn't have a face," she began.

"It's an expression."

He laughed, turned to her, and they clicked. For what seemed like eons, she was lost in his deep-brown eyes. They were like tractor beams drawing her to him.

She wiggled free and concentrated on her nearly empty bowl, willing herself to get back in control. "You are going to the dance Saturday, right?"

He bent his head toward hers. "If I go, will you dance with me?"

"God, no!"

He flinched. "*No?*" The tone of his voice made it sound like she had hurt his feelings. Or maybe he was teasing. "Why not?"

"I can't, because . . ." Wait. She couldn't tell Kris that she needed to see him interact outside the lab with Lauren.

And yet, it was vital to her coursing emotions that they didn't. It was so confusing!

"Um, because PCs aren't allowed."

"What? That's stupid."

"I know. School rules. We have to be chaperones." She shrugged like it couldn't be helped. "Anyway, you have to go to the dance. The headmaster has made it mandatory."

He stood and stretched so high his fingertips grazed the ceiling. "I have to go to the dance because I'm on cleanup, so I'll probably only show up at the end."

This would never work with Lauren. He had to be there at the beginning. She watched him shove his two pints, bowls, and spoons under his hoodie. "You could come earlier," she said.

"Nope. No point if I can't dance with you."

"What if I found a way to sneak in one quick dance?"

He zipped up his bulging jacket. "Then maybe. Hey, I gotta go before I turn into a pumpkin." Then, without a thought, as if it was second nature, he leaned down and brushed his lips against her cheek before opening the window and disappearing into the night.

Addie fell back on her bed and listened to his footsteps crunch across the gravel, reminding herself that a personal relationship was a nonnegotiable, don't-even-go-there possibility.

She touched the spot where he'd kissed her, and sighed.

* * *

The next morning, much to her relief, Addie was back on schedule: A run on the beach at five a.m. Shower at 5:45. Blow-dry at 5:55, followed immediately by hair in ponytail, a slathering of SPF 50, and her hiking outfit, a white T-shirt and trail shorts. Technically they were gray, but also with enough of a denim-blue hue to quell her anxiety.

She was in the lab by 6:10 and had finished reading the paper on spindle neurons by 6:45 and writing up her own Athenian presentation five minutes later. There was one more experiment to run on Brad and Angelina—whether their behavior changed depending on their choline levels—and then it was off to breakfast.

At 8:15 a.m., she went to the café to meet Tess for iced coffee, oatmeal with almond milk, and one half of a sliced banana. It was the only breakfast she ate. Ever. Tess arrived right on Tess Time at 8:30. Fifteen minutes late, like clockwork. And, as usual, too flustered to consume anything but caffeine.

"Crisis alert!" Tess gave her latte a squirt of liquid death. "Tay and Bree's new weapon in their campaign to make their roommates' lives hell is to call each other at three a.m. and talk really, really loudly. It's totally unfair to Emma and Shreya."

"So watching TV at Thwing as one big happy family didn't work, huh?"

"Made it worse when they walked out." Tess tossed her stirrer in the trash. "I was up all night dealing with their complaints."

Addie took a sip of black coffee. "Unpalatable!" She reached for the half-and-half and dumped in a good-sized serving.

"Are you sure you want that much?" Tess inquired.

"Fat is excellent fuel for the brain. Why not put them together?"

"Brain and fat?"

"No. Bree with Tay and Shreya with Emma. That way everyone would get the necessary eight hours of sleep."

They left the café, Tess pushing open the door with her shoulder. "Giving in to their manipulation would defeat the purpose of a summer session. Tay and Bree are from the same town. They're supposed to branch out and meet new people."

She waved cheerfully at a group of her PCs lounging on the grass.

Addie followed behind, sipping her coffee. "Meeting new people is overrated."

"No, it's not. How can you say that?"

"The Broca's area in my cerebral cortex signals my lips to move."

Tess laughed and did the waving thing again as another group of summer students passed by.

This time, Addie attempted to join in with her own halfhearted hand flapping. In response, the students put their heads together and whispered conspiratorially. Maybe they'd heard about her, too.

Tess said, "Smile. No one likes a grump."

"They're talking about me, that I torture animals."

"Oh, stop."

"It's true." She walked deliberately, eyes averted. "I try not to let it get to me, but one cannot always control one's own synapses."

They stopped in front of the library, where Tess was scheduled to meet up with the exchange students. Today, finally, they were going to Harvard, complete with a tour of the campus, a special lunch with a representative from admissions, and shopping in Harvard Square. Mindy was going to be thrilled.

Tess pulled herself onto the brick wall to wait. "What's up with you this morning? Did something happen last night—I mean, besides the shark attack?"

"I got only five hours and twenty-three minutes of sleep."

"Ah. And . . . ?"

Addie opened the lid of her cup and downed a cube of ice that she then crunched. "Do you think I should give makeup another try?"

Again, Tess laughed. It was her "adorable" laugh, the

one she used with small children who were being cute and when Addie was being . . . Addie. "You swore off make-up when you got pinkeye, remember?"

"That's because you used violet eyeliner with carmine in it, and carmine is made from cochineal extract, which is made from the ground shells of the female *Dactylopius coccus* beetle, to which I am allergic."

"Ooookay. So we'll avoid the bug kinds. For Saturday night, I'm picturing you in a pale blue dress, so those colors would clash anyway."

Addie was flabbergasted. "How did you know I wanted to wear makeup for the dance?"

"Um, because you wouldn't wear it to a lab?"

This seemed to be more of a question than a statement, which Addie could parse for only a second, since the exchange students were approaching. "Do you think if I wore makeup, people would stop calling me weird?"

Tess cocked her head sympathetically. "Oh, honey. Something did happen last night, didn't it?"

"Not really." Addie didn't want to mention the incident in the bathroom—no telling how Tess might react. "Aside from Kris showing up in my room with ice cream."

Tess arched an eyebrow. "Really?"

"Don't act like you didn't know. You told him to go around back to my window where, in fact, he attempted anti-defenestration."

"Anti- defene . . . wha?"

"Defenestration." Addie finished the last of her ice. "To exit through a window, the Latin word for window being *fenestra*. Ergo, to enter through a window would be the opposite of that. Hence the anti."

"Whatever. Who cares? Kris brought you ice cream! How sweet is that?"

"Too sweet. Have you ever read the sugar content in Chunky Monkey?"

But she couldn't hide her smile. She'd been replaying last night over and over, how he teased her about the Hello Kitty nightshirt and complimented her on being brave. How he kissed her cheek.

And though it might come across as catty, she took secret delight in knowing that Tay and Bree would have killed for Kris Condos to climb through their windows. (Even if they were on the second floor.)

A shot of pain radiated through her shoulder as Tess hit her with a hard punch. "Look at you!"

Addie rubbed the spot on her arm. "What?"

"You are totally into him."

"I am not." She went toward a recycling bin to toss her coffee cup, but Tess slid off the wall and rounded on her, peering at Addie like she was trying to read her mind through her eyeballs.

"Oh, yeah. This is bad."

"We're just friends. And now that he's apologized for that thing he did last spring, I'm letting it go." Addie tossed the cup past Tess and, naturally, it missed the bin.

Tess picked it up. "Just the other day you almost killed him in volleyball for 'that thing he did' last spring." Tess tossed the cup. "And twenty-four hours later, you're blushing. I've never seen you like this with a guy before."

There she went with that hyperbole again.

"For the zillionth time, I am not interested in Kris *that way*. Besides." Addie waved to the exchange students, who didn't wave back, possibly because they were bent over their phones. "He has a girlfriend."

"So what? Ed supposedly had a girlfriend when we met."

"He did not!"

Tess tilted her head questioningly. "How would you know? Ed was just some guy in our art class before last fall . . . *right*?"

Addie clenched her teeth. She was this close to blowing the cover she had so carefully orchestrated. "Right. I mean, from what I know. Now. From what I know now." Her mouth went dry. "In light of . . . experiences with him. Hanging out. Et cetera."

It seemed as if Tess was debating whether or not to buy this bumbling answer. Fortunately, the exchange students were yelling about nearly missing the shuttle.

"We'll pick this up later," she said, backstepping toward them. "In the meantime, instead of planning everything, why don't you just relax around Kris and let nature take its course."

If nature took its course, Addie thought, the Netherlands would be under water and half of Earth's population would have been wiped out by smallpox. But as Tess had noted repeatedly, Addie should not correct others, so she kept this observation to herself.

And then she went to find Ed, before he ruined everything.

TWELVE

"So, what's this about you running into a shark?"

Except it sounded more like *shahk* coming from Boston native Buster, the six-foot, bald member of the Academy's Buildings and Grounds department.

Kris grabbed the top rung and tried not to look down, where he hoped Buster was anchoring the twenty-foot ladder securely with his size-thirteen boots. Inches away, under the eaves of the Chisolm Hall, hung a large, papery, gray wasp's nest. He searched for signs of life.

"See anything?" Buster asked.

"Not sure." Kris removed the crowbar from his belt and listened for buzzing.

The day before, two students had been stung while

chatting on the steps directly below, sending the administration into panic mode. It was too dangerous to spray the hornets when it was warm and they were active, so they had to do it at dawn while the bugs were clustered in their hive and cold.

And by "they," Buildings and Grounds meant Kris, or, as the regulars had nicknamed him, "The Kid," because he was at least six years younger than the youngest member of the grounds crew. Climbing to the roof and killing hornets was definitely a job for The Kid, they'd decided without bothering to ask his opinion.

"Consider it a rite of initiation," Buster had said, though Kris suspected the rest of them were too scared to deal with a swarm of angry, stinging hornets.

Now, several hours later, they were back to assess the death count.

Kris extended the crowbar to the nest and gave it a poke.

"I never heard of no great white in the bay," Buster said. "Could have been a basking shark. The things look scary but don't bite."

The hive shook slightly. Kris recoiled. "I don't know. The fin was white."

"Pure white? Or gray white?"

Why was he peppering him with questions at a time like this? The shark thing could wait. His neck could not.

"You'd better have this ladder steady, Buster, because I'm going to try and knock this thing down."

"Don't you worry your pretty little head about it."

The crew was always teasing him about his hair for being relatively long and wavy compared with their shiny, bald pates.

Kris gave the hive another knock. It wobbled. But no hornets.

"I'm just thinking that if it really was a great white, it would have been on the news," Buster said. "They have organizations that track those monsters, you know. Woods Hole or something."

Okay. This was it. Kris brought back the crowbar and gave the nest a whack.

"You sure the shark was real?"

Kris squinted. No wasps. Good sign. "I don't know. I guess." He dealt another smack.

"Could have been a fake."

"Get out of here. Who would have put a fake shark in the water?"

"Some sicko. To give you preppies a scare."

One more hit and it would be down, and then he could get off this freaking ladder. "Looked damn real to me."

"So did the one the drama department used when they put on *Jaws* last summer. Genuine Spielberg. One of the girls here, her parents are famous actors who know him.

Swear to god. They're buddy-buddy."

Kris raised the crowbar and stopped. "Are you telling me the school put on *Jaws*? How was that even possible?"

"They did it on the beach. Total pain in the butt for us, building that stage off the docks. But it was worth it. I brought my two kids and they loved it and they don't usually go for stuff that's not a video. Afterward, the actors showed them the mechanical shark so they wouldn't be afraid to swim and whatnot and that's why I'm asking— was your shark fake?"

The answer was obvious, and had Kris not been twenty feet above ground, he would have run to the drama department to see for himself.

Whack!

With that, the nest fell and shattered into thin, papery shreds.

The drama department was next to the gym in the basement of Albert Hall underneath the George C. Newbury Theater and box office. Kris took out his clippers and pretended to trim hedges before sneaking to the back entrance, an unmarked steel door that faced a currently vacant parking lot.

Unclogging gutters and toilets between knocking down hornets' nests and mowing lawns was definitely not his dream summer job, but working for Buildings and

Grounds did have its advantages: namely, a master key that he quickly swiped in the scanner.

The door opened onto a hallway of offices, dance studios, a random piano, and a bulletin board posted with programs, requests for rides to Boston, offers to babysit professors' kids, and a practice schedule.

The play this summer was *Little Shop of Horrors*, to be shown on August third, fourth, and fifth, the second-to-last day of the session. Next to it was a screamer of a note:

PEOPLE!!!!!!
ONLY 2 MORE WEEKS TO DRESS
REHEARSAL AND 1 WEEK AFTER THAT
FOR THE PLAY. THIS MEANS YOU CANNOT
MISS A SINGLE PRACTICE!!!
BE HERE ON TIME WITH YOUR LINES,
UNLESS YOU HAVE A WRITTEN EXCUSE
FROM THE INFIRMARY.
1 NO-SHOW = NO SHOWS FOR YOU!
SIGNED, YOUR MAESTRA
TESS

Maestra? Kris thought about this. Wasn't sure that was a word. Maestro, yes. Nevertheless, even though Tess was not at the top of his favorites list, he had to smile.

That posting was very her.

Fortunately, practice was in the afternoon before dinner and then after evening games. Guess it never occurred to the drama kids to get up early like the athletes.

His phone vibrated. Kara. Again.

She'd been after him to go to a party in Cambridge the next night, which just happened to conflict with the school dance—an easy excuse, especially since he had to work.

You better answer me. I know you're on break. I called Buildings and Grounds.

Holy . . . she didn't. Now that was really going too far. The guys would never let him live it down.

She answered his frantic call with a menacing giggle. "I knew that'd get your attention. You are such a sucker, Condor."

He exhaled in relief. "So you didn't call the office?"

"Of course not. I'm not that much of a stalker."

Though she was, in fact, stalkerish. "I'm working. What do you want?"

"Oh, have I interrupted your lunch? That's very working-class hero of you, to be so protective of your baloney and cheese time. Wait, you don't wear a tool belt, do you? Because I am there in a New York minute if you have a tool belt."

It was eleven forty-five. In fifteen minutes, he had to

be at the gym for the third part of the experiment. "Not to change this fascinating subject," he said, "but weren't you involved in drama for a while?"

"Don't remind me. *Annie.* I was orphan number three. The reviews were rave." She yawned. "Why? What are you up to?"

Above him, a door slammed, followed by footsteps. He had to hurry because he could not get caught, not with his ass already on the line with Foy. "Do you know where the prop room is?"

"Under the stage. Is that where you and I are meeting up?" Another shrill giggle that sent shivers up his spine.

"I'll tell you later. Thanks." He hung up and found the right door and unlocked it. His heart sank as he faced a maze of black walls, floors and ceilings zigzagging this way and that.

His phone buzzed. Kara. Seriously? Since ignoring her would only make matter worse, he answered with an irritated, "What now?"

"You didn't tell me what time you're picking me up for the party. We can meet in Harvard Square or"—she paused—"you could just come to the Back Bay. No parental supervision, remember?"

The prop room was marked, helpfully, PROPS. He flicked on the light and surveyed the racks of costumes and mess of odd scenery. These drama people were pigs!

Juliet's balcony was shoved in a corner, along with brightly painted plywood flowers that were either from the *Wizard of Oz* or Dr. Seuss. He had to climb over what appeared to be the remnants of a makeshift barn until he found it: a gigantic mechanical great white shark with no underside except for wires encased in Plexiglas.

He found the switch hidden in the "belly" and flicked it on. The motor had been insulated for total silence. Even when Kris depressed the forward button on the remote control, he could barely make out the gears churning.

"Score." Kris pumped his fist and used his phone to take a picture for proof. He couldn't wait to show this to Addie.

"You're not answering me!" Kara's voice came out small and far away as he took seven shots from various angles.

"Sorry," he said, getting back on. "What was that again?"

She sighed. "I'm talking about the party. What time are we meeting up?"

He shifted gears, turning off the light and shutting the door. "No can do. Seriously, I have to go to this school dance."

"*Have* to or *want* to?"

"Have to. Gotta work. Foy's orders." It was a half-truth. No point in further angering Kara in adding that he wanted to go because Addie would be there.

"You continue to be a disappointment to me, Condor, with all this obeying and industriousness. Good thing you're cute, otherwise I'd dump your sorry butt."

Wish you would, he thought, turning off the prop-room light and backing slowly out the door.

"That's it. You've left me no choice. I am coming over there to get you. What do you think about that?"

Kris did not take the bait. "I think I've got to get back to the job. Thanks for the help. Bye!" And clicked off.

Someday Kara would get the hint, right? She had to, because otherwise he would have to tell her, again, that they were over. History. Finito.

In the past, whenever he so much as mentioned maybe seeing other people, she'd burst into tears about how she was going through a lot and he wasn't helping, thank you very much.

"Go. Just go!" she'd order. "Leave me alone so I can do what I have to do."

And of course, he couldn't leave after *that*.

It'd been easier to stay put and tolerate her roller-coaster moods. Until now.

Until Addie.

Whenever he was in Addie's orbit, he instantly felt sharper and brighter, as if her genius was contagious. She made him want to match her point for point, fact for fact, with his intelligence.

The other night, motivated by a sudden burst of

academic curiosity, he actually went to the library to read. *For fun. Meditations* by Marcus Aurelius. Dude was alive 1,800 years ago and was still completely readable.

Ah, but he wasn't pure as all that. The other side of him also wanted to pull out that ponytail and kiss those sweet lips. He had an evil urge to coax out the passionate, fiery girl trapped in the perfect model of a straight-A student.

But none of that was possible with Kara in the picture. As long as she was texting him every hour and threatening him with surprise visits, he was trapped.

That had to change. Now.

THIRTEEN

What was the point of having a centrifuge, Addie wondered, if school rules prevented you from spinning down real, human blood? Because measuring her test subjects' hormone levels would have made this project so much easier.

She sighed and tapped her fingers on the black soapstone table in the Whit as she reviewed the evidence from the experiment so far. According to their before-and-after lists, Lauren showed no more interest in Kris than she did in Alex. Both were "nice." Alex even got an upgrade to "funny," whereas Kris was holding steady at "cute."

Granted, they'd participated in only two experiments—the baseline and the agave worms—but at this stage Addie had hoped for a flicker of admiration for Kris's daring, some sort of indication that Lauren's PEA levels were spiking in his presence.

It took Tess less than twenty-four hours to fall for Ed, though, to be fair, adrenaline was already coursing through her body from the sprained ankle and the storm.

If only Addie'd had the administration's permission to use a really daring activity like skydiving or extreme skiing. That would totally pump out the norepinephrine, with its love-like sweaty palms and beating heart. But there were those stupid school rules again. Also, money.

"Staring slack-jawed at the spreadsheets never won Crick and Watson a Nobel Prize," Dex said, flipping on the lab faucet with his elbow and washing his hands of salt water.

"True. Their brainstorming was done on paper napkins." Addie closed the laptop with its disappointing results. No doubt, Dex had already interpreted the data as more proof of defeat.

He flipped off the faucet and snatched a brown paper towel. "Don't look so glum. Nikolai Tesla was considered a failure for most of his career and he was brilliant." He tossed the towel in the trash. "Like you."

What was that supposed to mean? "I haven't failed. I just need more time to institute an instant attraction."

Dex smirked. "I love it when you contradict yourself

in one sentence. If you need more time to create an instant attraction, then you are definitely in trouble."

She fumed. Her cranium could have exploded, she was so frustrated with his constant negativity. He was such a Debbie Downer.

"Instead of bad-mouthing the project, why don't you be useful and give me some suggestions?"

"Okay, here's an idea. Let's call this project what it is—dead in the water—and use my crabs. There's still time to switch. I'm sure the Athenian Committee will understand when you explain that, when it came to the brain, unfortunately you got in over your head." He bent over, killing himself with laughter.

Addie hopped up so fast she almost knocked over the stool. "That's it, Dex. You are the Worst. Lab. Partner. Ever."

"Awww." He stuck out his lower lip. "Is someone having a bad day?"

She hated when he talked to her in a baby voice and came *thisclose* to actually slapping his smug pink face when her phone binged.

Ed.

All set up in the gym. Email + fax sent. Good thing I'm already in college 'cause this could get me kicked out, big time.

Right. She took two deep breaths to redirect the

oxygen. Priorities, Addie, she reminded herself silently. Concentrate on what's important.

Thank you soooo much!!!!! she texted back. And it was true. She couldn't have planned this without him.

You ready?

Yes! Thx. On my way.

Hope this works, Ed texted back. *I'm out of ideas.*

She nodded to the screen on her phone.

Me 2.

The Academy's legendary rock wall took up one whole side of the gym. At forty-six feet high and a hundred feet wide, with a twenty-foot overhang that required climbers to crawl upside down, to call it formidable would be an understatement. It had been designed by Günter Hammelsmith, a Swiss mountaineer and Academy alum who, unfortunately, plunged to an early death while attempting to paraglide off Mount Everest to the Indian Ocean.

It was rumored that Günter had been born genetically devoid of fear, which was obvious to anyone who had attempted to climb the wall. That's why the Academy students had nicknamed it The Beast.

And today it was Experiment #3.

Lauren and Kris were already strapped into their harnesses and tying on their shoes when Addie rushed into the gym, breathless. She'd made the mistake of swinging through the cafeteria to grab some lunch, only to realize she'd forgotten her ID in the lab, where she learned from Dr. Brooks that Dexter had already left for the gym. Which meant she was late *and* hungry.

"How nice of you to put in an appearance," Dex said, not looking up from his computer, where he was inputting baseline information.

She ignored him and went over to Lauren and Kris to offer a hand with the harnesses.

"These are the ugliest things ever," Lauren whined. "They're like leather diapers."

"You ever climb a rock wall before?" Kris asked, hopping up and down to test his shoes.

She gave her shoelace a particularly violent tug. "No. You?"

"Uh-huh. And I think you'll appreciate the support when your feet fly off the top rocks. Thirty-five feet is a long way down."

Lauren glanced toward the ceiling. "No freaking way. I'm agoraphobic."

"Agoraphobia is fear of open places," corrected Addie, who'd been quietly observing this exchange with intent interest. "Acrophobia is fear of heights."

"Whatever," Lauren answered. "I'm not going up there."

Carl Eldred, an impossibly fit teacher, bald with

muscles the size of cantaloupes, bounded from the gym office, clapping his hands. "All right, people. Let's go over the ground rules before we get started."

Addie took Lauren's and Kris's "before" lists, which they had dutifully completed without having been asked, and craned her neck to catch a better glimpse of Kris, who was handily maneuvering the ropes. His gastrocnemii were bulging today, undoubtedly due to the strenuous physical labor from being part of the grounds crew. That would also explain his firm triceps and enlarged deltoids.

Her heart did a little flutter. Which reminded her. "The cardiac monitors!"

"Another task of yours I completed. The straps are on their wrists and synched." Dex called up an app that showed Kris's heart beating at a calm 63 BPM and Lauren's at a relatively high 82.

"Why is hers so elevated?" Addie asked.

Dex smiled to himself, like a bird preening his own feathers. "Perhaps because she's in my presence?"

"You're not her type," Addie shot back, still smarting from the way he'd put her down back in the lab. "She's attracted to boys with way more testosterone."

His feathers folded. "Excuse me for dabbling in a little self-deprecating humor."

"Excuse accepted."

Carl was winding down his spiel. Addie went over to

stop him before they took another step. Literally.

"Thank you so much," she gushed, as if his instruction had already saved their lives. "I know you have another class after this and you probably want to grab some lunch, so we'll take it from here."

"What?" he asked. "Leave?"

"Yes. We're fine. You can go."

"Can't do." He crossed his arms and widened his stance. "I've got to be here when newbies are on the ropes. School orders from our insurance carrier."

She took out her phone, called up a group email that appeared to be from Dr. Brooks and Headmaster Foy, and showed it to him. He gaped at it for a second. "This is completely out of the ordinary. I could be sued!"

"There's a waiver in your office printer waiting for your signature," Addie said. "It frees you of all liability."

"I'll have to read it myself. Don't do anything until I give the okay." He held up a finger of warning and then marched off.

"Addie," Kris said softly.

She turned and their eyes met. They had a connection now. She could sense their growing bond in the deepest recesses of her ventromedial prefrontal cortex. The near plane crash, the shark, the late-night ice cream in her room, even the bogus agave worms, had trained their synapses to release neurochemicals on sight. This was a phenomenon she'd researched, of course, and observed from the sidelines as Ed and Tess's friend. But those situations couldn't compare to actual, thrilling experience.

"Addie," he said again.

She startled. "Yes?"

"I found out something about yesterday. We have to talk."

"We are talking."

He did that half grin thing of his.

"Alone."

"No." Lauren shook her head.

"What?" Kris asked, spinning around to look at her. "Why can't Addie and I have a moment alone?"

He said *a moment alone*. Addie felt her PEA surge!

"I just want her to understand that I am not climbing that." Lauren pointed to the wall. "It's too dangerous."

Addie said, "There are cushions." To prove it, she jumped on the mat. "You can drop like a rock and, at most, sprain something or break a pinkie."

"Exactly!" Lauren said. "I'm not going to risk being benched from track for this stupid experiment. Field hockey is my ticket to a full scholarship. I am not going to screw it up with a broken wrist this fall!"

Dexter sauntered over, playing the elder, more mature lab partner. "What have you done wrong now, Addie?"

"Addie hasn't done anything wrong," Kris said. "Lauren

doesn't want to climb the wall."

"Did you tell her that was the experiment today?" Dex asked Addie accusingly.

"I think the big giveaway might have been the harnesses and rock-climbing shoes, along with Carl giving them pointers," Addie said wryly. Dex was always so quick to judge.

"That's an idea. What if we brought Carl back?" Kris asked. "Would you feel better then?"

"I'd feel better watching someone else climb The Beast, like one of our Dr. Frankensteins." Lauren flicked her finger between Dex and Addie.

Dr. Frankenstein?

Dex's hand flew to his chest. "I wish I could. I do. But due to a childhood illness, I simply don't have the muscle strength. The doctors are amazed I'm as high-functioning as I am, considering my limited lung capacity."

"Scarlet fever?" Kris asked.

"Smothering mothering," Addie said under her breath as she went over to Lauren and unsnapped the harness. "Okay. I'll climb the wall, and once you see how safe it is, you can try."

Lauren slipped out of the harness and kicked it to Addie. "And if I don't?"

"Then I'm afraid you can't get the extra credit for AP Bio. Not that the Ivies care about GPAs or anything."

Addie stepped in, glad she'd decided to wear shorts today instead of her favorite skirt.

"This is so unfair," Lauren said, slipping out of her shoes. "It's like I'm being held hostage. Damned if I do; damned if I don't."

"You could always climb the wall with a lifeline, get the extra credit, and actually have something interesting to write about for a college essay," Kris said, helping cinch up Addie's straps.

Dex wiggled his finger. "A moment of your time, lab partner."

Addie shuffled a few measly steps. "Can't go any farther. Strapped in."

"What are you doing?"

"I'm demonstrating." She slipped on the climbing shoe Lauren had been wearing. A tad loose for her smaller feet.

"You're going to jeopardize the entire experiment. Bad enough that you ate the 'agave worms.'" He put *agave worms* in finger quotes. "Now you're actually interacting with the participants. And by participants, I mean Kris."

She tried tying the left shoe while standing, a bit of a challenge. "The timbre of your voice would indicate that you are growing angry. Either that or you have a cold. Which is it?"

He bent down and knotted the laces for her. "The

issue is that you're developing a thing for one of your guinea pigs."

"A thing?" She frowned as Dex moved to her other foot like she was a helpless toddler. "What kind of thing? That is a very nonspecific term."

He whipped back his blond bangs. "A crush."

"As in to compress by force? I do not wish to squish Kris." Admittedly, she was having fun with him now, playing on her reputation for overliteralism. No one expected her to joke around, and that made it even funnier—at least to her.

He stood and put his hands on his hips. "Your bias toward him is yet one more reason to terminate this experiment immediately."

"And what about your obsession with Lauren?"

Dex paled and then recovered. "So you don't deny your feelings for him."

"I neither confirm nor deny," she shot back, so tired of his constant riding. Just once it would be nice if he cut her a break. "But I am completely confident that the results of this experiment remain untainted by either me *or* you."

He scowled.

"Can we hurry?" Lauren said. "Did you say Carl has a group coming in? I need credit for this and Addie's going to take up all my time."

"I'm good to go," Kris said.

Dex uttered one last halfhearted protest as Addie returned to the mats and shuffled back to the wall. "The purpose of this experiment is to chart the difference between male and female reactions to certain physical challenges."

"Like falling on your face," Lauren said.

Addie picked up the rope tied to the other end of her harness and tossed it to Kris. "Would you mind belaying me?"

His lips twitched in amusement. "It would be my pleasure."

"I should do it. I'm her lab partner," Dex said.

Addie touched her palm. "Calluses, remember?"

He couldn't argue with that, as his mother had often warned her that Dexter suffered from particularly sensitive skin that made it impossible to shake hands, for instance, much less secure a rough rope.

"Here. Take this, I don't need it," Lauren said, tossing her the heart monitor.

Addie strapped it on and then pivoted to the wall, assessing the best route up. The rocks were different primary colors—yellow, red, blue, green—which must be portentous in some regard. Yellow, she deduced, were easier footing. Blue were safeties. Red were advanced. Green . . . no clue.

Gripping a red, she hoisted her right foot on a yellow

and proceeded in logical fashion. The process provided an interesting challenge vaguely reminiscent of chess. It wasn't just the next move you had to contemplate, but the move after that, and even one after that.

"All right!" Kris shouted as Addie reached the halfway point. He gave the harness a reassuring tug of the rope. Something felt off and she reached behind her to adjust the carabiner, tightening according to the rule of thumb her mother used to sing:

Righty tighty, lefty loosey.

Calling down to Lauren, she said, "See how easy this is?"

"You're, like, only six feet off the ground. As a kid, I slept on a top bunk that was higher."

Bunk bed, eh? Hmm. Setting her sights on where the wall bent to the overhang, Addie assessed the available rock outcroppings and proceeded accordingly, rising a good twenty feet. Her arm muscles—accustomed to holding books, not pulling up her entire weight—began to ache and her knees were slightly unsteady.

She dared not look down; already her palms were turning moist, thereby raising the possibility of slipping.

"Grab that green rock over there," Kris said, gesturing to her left. "That'll put you in the sweet spot for the final ascent."

Except the green rock was a bit of a stretch. In order to

reach it, she would have to extend her leg a good five feet, almost her entire body length.

"Be careful!" Lauren cried.

"You can come down now," Dex said. "Your heart rate is one forty. That's enough."

No, it wasn't. At her age, her pulse should be able to exceed two hundred and be fine. Anyway, if she relinquished at this stage, Lauren would refuse to go any higher during her turn and that would defeat the purpose of the experiment.

She had to give it a shot. Reach for the red, swing to the green, right foot on the yellow. Perfect. With a deep, oxygenating breath, she summoned all her courage and followed the plan. Anyway, if she fell, there was the harness and the rope. Backups.

"I'm going for it," she declared.

Gripping a rock with her right hand, she extended her left foot to the green rock. It was like doing a midair split. Her anterior thigh muscles balked in protest. Tentatively, she reached for the red rock with her left hand. Now she was splayed against the wall like a splattered spider.

"Halfway there," Kris said. "Hold on. You can do it. I'll keep a tight grip on you while you do."

She had no choice. Removing her right hand from the safety, she was about to bring her right foot over when she felt another tug and heard an ominous *snap!*

This was followed by an "Oh, crap!" as the carabiner she'd just adjusted released the clip, which flew up to the grommet on the ceiling where it remained, a good ten feet above her head.

Addie clung to the wall with all her might. She was thirty feet off the floor, higher than the top story of her house back home. Below her, Kris, Lauren, and Dex were the size of toys. Or so she imagined. She didn't have the guts to check.

"Help her!" Lauren screamed.

Dex read off her heart rate. "It's one sixty-three. And climbing."

"You're cool, Addie," Kris said calmly. "There's another rope right off your left shoulder. If you can reach it and hook it on, you'll be back in business."

She could barely turn her head, much less grab a rope. "I'm afraid that's a negative, captain."

Lauren said, "We should get Carl. He'll be able to . . ."

"No!" Addie surprised even herself by shouting. "That will only cause administrative problems. Kris is right. If I can get rehooked, I'll be fine. When I adjusted the carabiner, I must have accidentally loosened it instead of the opposite."

"No problem. I'm coming to get you," Kris said, throwing the other end of his rope to Lauren and taking to the wall.

"Here we go," Dex said. "Countdown to disaster. Don't worry, folks, I have 911 on speed dial!"

Addie watched as Kris climbed with sure footing. "You've done this before."

"Camp in Canada. We had a tradition of racing each other to the top of a cliff every night after dinner," he said. "None of us had these wimpy harnesses."

Which raised an interesting question. "What will you do when you get to me?"

"I'll attach my rope to your clip." He paused to contemplate the best route to get next to her.

"You can't. There'll be too much distance between us."

Kris was close enough now that they could talk without having to shout. "I agree," he said. "But not for long." Two more climbs and he was inches away. "See?"

Addie grinned. She was so relieved to have him next to her. "Thanks."

"No problem. You look really pretty today, by the way. I don't know what it is."

A stimulated ventromedial prefrontal cortex, she almost replied, choosing instead to respond with a simple shrug and a blush.

"One hundred ninety-five and rising!" Dex announced.

Kris reached behind his back, holding on to the wall

with one precarious hand, and undid the carabiner. Then, leaning far to his right, he attached it to her clip and twisted it tight. "There. Safe and secure."

"But you're . . . free!" Addie said.

He shrugged. "No biggie. Want me to help you down?"

Addie thought about this.

Her hands were sweating so profusely she had to wipe them off on her shorts before each grab. Her heart felt like it was about to crack through her ribs. Every inch of her was screaming to descend to safety, to get off this godforsaken wall with its tricky rocks and ridiculous purpose. Only sick adrenaline junkies would call this fun.

"That's okay," she said. "I can do it myself."

"But . . ." Kris went silent as Addie summoned all her courage and forced her left hand to reach for the red rock to the left.

"All the way to the top," she said shakily, "like I promised."

He broke into a wide grin. "Me, too. I'll go first so you'll know which rocks to use."

"I can't look." Lauren hid her face in her hands.

"You have to look," Kris called to her. "Because you're holding the other end of her rope."

"Oh, right." Lauren scrambled to get the end lying on the mat. Kris climbed all the way up without a safety!

They worked in unison, Addie following his trail. The trick was to keep looking up. If the brain did not know how far off the ground it was, it could not flip the switch into panic mode. Of course, descending would present its own problems, though Addie wasn't worried.

Kris was with her, and just having him around made everything all right.

"You go first," he said when they got to the top. "Step on that red rock and reach for the yellow."

She took his advice, and as she passed him, he touched her back to steady her. There was something so gracious about this simple movement that her heart wanted to break. Maybe other people thought she was weird, but Kris didn't. And realizing that, she was overcome with such a boost of confidence that with a burst of energy, she took the next, precarious step and slapped the ceiling.

"Done!"

"Booyah!" Kris said, giving her a fist bump. "And you did it all yourself. No support."

"Except the moral kind," Addie said. "From you."

"Oh my god. Two hundred and twenty!" Dexter shouted.

"That's my pulse?" Addie asked.

"No. That's Kris's. It's gone . . . off the charts."

But Kris wasn't even panting or out of breath. Hadn't broken a sweat, either. So that heartbeat made no sense,

Addie thought. Unless it had nothing to do with the wall climbing . . . ?

He winked. "Damn monitor."

Lauren let out a scream. That was how Addie realized that she must have let go of the wall, because suddenly she was dangling in midair, Lauren valiantly holding on to her end of the rope.

"Let her down slowly," a man's voice said. "Hand over hand."

Addie swung around to see Carl standing at the computer next to Dex and Dr. Brooks. No one seemed especially pleased—especially Dr. Brooks.

"In my office," she said once Addie's feet touched the mat. "Now!"

FOURTEEN

"I'll take that," Carl said, removing the rope from Lauren's hands. "You kids had better move along. My group is almost here."

Lauren watched incredulously as Dex and Addie gathered their laptop and notes and disappeared around the corner with Dr. Brooks. "Hey! What about my extra credit?" she hollered.

Too late. They were out of earshot. Either that or they were simply blowing her off. "Can you believe that?" she cried. "We agree to do their stupid experiment and they just walk away as if we're chump change. It's so disrespectful."

Kris sat on the floor, removing his climbing shoes,

only half paying attention to Lauren's bitching. Wow, total complainer.

"I would have climbed the wall. Really, I would have. I just wanted them to see what it was like first. Oh, hi, Alex!"

In a flash, her lips reformed from pout to a beaming grin as a poster boy for high-school jock entered the gym. Alex was about Lauren's height—which was, granted, tall—with black hair and deeply tanned skin. Judging from his cocky walk, he played either soccer or lacrosse. Kris put his money on lacrosse, since he was guessing this Alex was his counterpart in Lauren's other experiment.

"Whoa, hey!" Alex returned Lauren's dazzling smile. "What are you doing here?"

"Getting royally screwed." Whereupon she launched into a tirade about the stupid experiment and how Dex and Addie had "totally lied" about it being a measurement of male versus female reactions to certain situations because they were a couple of "psychos" who made them do things like eat fried Mexican worms. Seriously.

"So, wait, they were going to make you climb that?" Alex chucked his chin to The Beast. "No. Way. Without a spotter? You could have gotten seriously hurt."

"That's what I told them and they didn't care, even when I explained about making sure I didn't get injured before field hockey started up and the scholarship and all that."

"They never make us do stuff like that when it's you and me." Alex took this as an excuse to touch her, reaching out. "So what's up?"

"I know, right?" Lauren smoothed an errant strand of blond hair behind an ear. "We just stare into each other's eyes and write down our observations. I have no idea why they put me together with . . . oh, sorry, Kris, forgot you were still here."

Kris had forgotten he was there, too. He had rewound to minutes before, watching Addie biting her bottom lip in focused concentration, bravely forcing herself to finish the climb. He was more nervous for her than for himself, even though he was the one without the lifeline, and the world fell away as he guided her to the top, mentally willing her his strength.

And yet, today's crisis was but one of a series he and Addie had survived in less than a week. They started off with the gut-churning turbulence, then the "shark" attack, and now this. Through it all, Addie had been upbeat, positive, even giddy after the shark incident. Now he wondered if she'd be disappointed to learn that the "thrill" had come from a theater prop.

"Kris?" Lauren snapped her fingers in his face. "Get with it. This is Alex. Your counterpart."

He stood and greeted him with a quick nod. "Hey."

"Hey." Alex nodded back. "You go to school here?"

"That's kind of a loaded question at the moment," Kris said. "We'll see in a couple of weeks."

Lauren grabbed her backpack. "Gotta go. Class in twenty minutes. You headed out, Al?"

Alex was so not headed out. He'd just arrived with his gym bag and was obviously at the gym for a workout. But he didn't even hesitate.

"Yeah. Sure. You have lunch yet?" Alex thumbed to the exit.

"No, and I'm starved." Lauren let him open the door and passed through. "You?"

"Not really."

Which, in guy speak, meant that of course he'd eaten. Well, good for him. And good for her, Kris thought, tossing his climbing shoes in the bin. Glad some people were happy.

He picked up his phone from the corner, where it was mixed up in his groundskeeper uniform, and winced. Seven messages from Kara. He was in the process of deleting every one when the group Carl had mentioned tromped in, six summer students led by Ed.

Exactly the person he was looking for.

Ed was listening to Carl lay down the rules with the group when Kris strolled over casually, the pack holding his uniform and work boots slung over his shoulder, and clapped him on the shoulder. "Yo. What's up?"

He turned and nodded, his expression hard to read, though Kris went with wary. "All right, all right. How you doing, man?"

"Not bad." Kris motioned for them to step away so they wouldn't interrupt Carl's presentation. "Listen, I just want to thank you for what you did yesterday, coming back for Addie and me. That was really solid of you."

"No problem. Lucky I was in the area. Who'd have thunk there'd be a great white shark in the inlet? When I told Tess, she freaked."

Kris toed the edge of a mat. "Freaked, huh?"

"Oh, yeah. She lives in fear of those things. Beach girl." Ed rolled his eyes.

He was slightly shorter and stockier than Kris, light blond where Kris was dark, short hair where Kris's was long, and probably pound for pound packed more muscle. That said, Kris figured he could take him. If forced.

"Now that's surprising," Kris said, reaching into his pocket.

"Yeah? Why?"

"Because I found this in your boat when I was cleaning it out last night." He placed the black remote control in the palm of Ed's hand and took a step back for a complete view of his reaction.

Ed turned it this way and that, frowning. "What is this?"

"A remote control. But you know that."

"I do?" He did an excellent imitation of a confused person. Tess, the thespian, must have taught him well.

"Don't play dumb. I found the shark."

Ed squinted at Kris like he was insane. "What are you talking about?"

"The mechanical shark? The one Tess's parents got for her from Spielberg when she put on *Jaws* last summer? Seriously. Don't BS."

"I wasn't here last summer. Tess and I started going out in October."

A frisson of doubt surfaced in his mind. Kris dismissed this and plowed forward. "It was still wet, dude. It was in the water yesterday and you operated it with that. That's why you happened to be in the exact location where the shark was. It wasn't 'luck.' It was a prank."

The tips of Ed's ears turned red, and Kris expected steam to blow from them at any minute. "Look." He kept his voice low, out of eavesdropping range. "I don't know what the hell is wrong with you, but clearly, you have issues."

Kris took a step. "I don't have . . ."

Ed put up both his hands for him to back off. "Tess said I should give you a second chance for Addie's sake even though, you know, why would I do that when you were the one who wrote—"

"I didn't . . ."

"*Shut. Up.*" Clearly, Ed's temper had crossed an invisible line, and there was no reeling it in. "Let me finish. The only reason I'm not knocking you flat is because Tess would kill me if I did. But I'll tell you this. I did not put a shark in the water; I wouldn't have done that to Addie. Tess'd kill me if I had."

When Ed phrased it that way, it all made sense. Of course he wouldn't have teased her with the shark. He and Tess treated her like their kid sister, and they were her self-appointed bodyguards. Kris realized then that he'd made a terrible mistake, one from which there was probably no coming back.

One that could forever turn Addie against him. He needed to set the record straight, fast, before it was too late.

"Hold up," Kris said as Ed stormed off.

He spun around, fists still clenched.

"I just want you to know that it was Addie that I was worried about. I don't care about me getting pranked. Heck, after what I've done, I deserve it."

"Got that straight." Ed flexed his fingers.

"It's just that . . . I like Addie. A lot. And . . . if you were coming after me, whatever. But her . . ." God, what was he saying?

Ed just stood there, sizing him up. Kris braced for the inevitable punch in the gut, to be followed by Carl pulling them apart with a stern lecture and, finally, the meeting with Headmaster Foy, who would present him with a bus ticket back to Boston and a warning never to return.

All because he'd been worried about Addie.

"Look, man, I'm sorry." Ed uncurled his fists.

Kris shook his head. "Huh?"

"I can understand how you thought I might have done that thing with the shark, but I didn't. Swear I didn't."

"Okay. Good to know."

"The thing is, thanks to Tess, when it comes to Addie, I . . . I get kind of protective. It's like . . ." He scratched his military-short cut and winced. "I don't know. I can't explain. It's complicated."

Ooookay, Kris thought. "No big deal. We're cool."

"Look, I'll ask Tess if there's a sign-out sheet for props so she can track down whoever took the shark. But I never saw that remote control before in my life, so I don't know where that came from."

The prop room, Kris thought. Obviously.

Ed walked off, paused, and turned back to Kris. "You might want to give Addie a heads-up, though. I think my guys are planning to get her back for the spike that nearly took you out. They're still claiming that they should have won by default for that." Ed nodded to his group, which was suiting up for the climb. "Might be wise for her to sleep with one eye open for the next few nights. I'm just saying."

Kris felt bad. He didn't want Addie paying for his poor reflexes. "They shouldn't take it out on her. Wasn't her fault; I didn't get out of the way fast enough."

"Whatever." Ed shrugged. "Everyone likes a good prank. See ya."

Kris checked his phone. He had ten minutes to sneak the remote back to the prop room and then report for duty at the lab for a fun-filled afternoon of cleaning gerbil cages and fish tanks, the bathrooms, and mopping all the floors. Pure hell . . . if he didn't have a chance of running into Addie.

FIFTEEN

"Sit!" Dr. Brooks motioned to two seats in front of her desk. Dex and Addie did what they were told, as usual, while their advisor paced, her cheeks inflamed as brightly as her orange batik dress.

"Is something wrong?" Addie asked, hugging her laptop.

"We'll let the headmaster decide," Dr. Brooks snapped, folding her arms in disgust. "I called him and he said he's on his way."

Dex poked her in the ribs. "Nice work, Emerson."

Addie slapped her chest. "What did I do?"

"Why don't you ask your amygdala? It seems to be calling the shots these days."

She was getting so sick and tired of him blaming her for every tiny hiccup. "Shut up!"

Dr. Brooks quit pacing. "What's going on with you two?"

"Dexter just accused me of uncontrollable norepinephrine emissions in the presence of Kris," Addie said.

He stabbed a finger toward her. "Busted! I never said Kris."

"But you did say amygdala." She tapped her temple. "I know how your brain works."

"Please! You're acting like children. Let's just save our complaints until . . ."

There was a polite rap on the door, and in walked Headmaster Foy in his standard summer attire: dark green Academy 355 golf shirt and khaki shorts. He frowned slightly, as if annoyed to have been called from the sunshine to the dark office of the lab.

"Dr. Brooks." He bowed slightly. "Dexter and Adelaide. I assume there is a reasonable explanation for this."

It was then that Addie noticed he was clutching two pieces of white paper. She straightened her posture and set her lips in what she hoped would be interpreted as an expression of innocence.

"What's that?" Dexter asked.

Dr. Brooks sat on the corner of her desk. "Why don't you tell us?"

"I don't know. I can't see it from here."

Mr. Foy handed him the paper. Addie peered over his shoulder, admiring the official language and impressive replication of the Academy 355 letterhead. Well, not so much a replication as a cut and paste.

"It's a waiver excusing Carl from having to supervise the climb." Dex gave it to Addie, who pretended to study it intently. "So?"

"So who faxed it to the gym office?" Mr. Foy tapped the fax address at the top. Displaying the other paper, a printout, he added, "Along with the fraudulent email?"

"Not I," Dexter was quick to say. "Maybe Addie."

Seriously, Dex would sell his mother for medical experimentation if he thought it would save his reputation, she thought. "Why would you think I did it? What in my track record would even hint that I would be capable of committing such a transgression as manufacturing a waiver and then faxing it to the gym office?" She added a tiny gulp at the end of this speech, the way Tess did whenever she was trying to squeeze out sympathy.

"Oh, dear, of course we don't think you had anything to do with this," Dr. Brooks said soothingly.

"Why not? She was the one who told Carl to check his fax machine!" Dex said.

Dr. Brooks and the headmaster exchanged uncomfortable glances. Mr. Foy said, "If that's the case, then you need to explain, Adelaide."

"To restate," Addie said, "why would I violate my nature by committing fraud?"

Dexter threw up his hands. "Because you've got it bad for Kris Condos and, I don't know, you didn't want Carl around to stop you. Maybe because you knew all along that Lauren wouldn't climb the wall and so you did it just to trigger Kris's PEA levels."

The boy didn't receive a gold-engraved invitation to join Mensa for being stupid.

Dr. Brooks rounded on her. "Is this true, Adelaide? Have you developed feelings for one of your test subjects?"

"My PEA levels are under control, as are my amygdalae." Addie shot a glare at Dex. "Meanwhile, I regret to report that my lab partner possesses an ulterior motive. Namely, he wishes to have his project submitted for an Athenian Award instead of mine."

Now it was Dex's turn to be in the spotlight. "What do you say to this?" Mr. Foy asked.

Dex hesitated for a second and then blurted, "I deny the accusation but not the conclusion. Addie's experiment has been compromised twice, not only today at the rock wall, but yesterday when she ate the fake agave worms and Lauren didn't."

Mr. Foy said, "Agave worms?"

Dr. Brooks said, "I'll explain later. Anything else, Dexter?"

Addie curled her toes as her lab partner—*former* lab partner—proceeded to slice and dice her in front of the two most powerful people in the school.

"I regret to inform you that there is more. Specifically, it has come to my attention that Addie went kayaking with Kris yesterday evening."

And he snuck into my room through a window past curfew, she added silently, the memory of Kris on her bed with the ice cream tickling her with faint shivers. Fortunately, Dex didn't know about this bit of rebellion, or she'd really be in trouble.

"Addie's errors aside," he said, "my project is more substantive than proving that feelings of love can be created . . ."

"And destroyed," Addie added.

"My project shows that crustaceans can feel actual pain, which could have tremendous potential implications for transforming the shellfish harvesting industry, and I'm sorry, but I think that's a *leeeetle* more important than helping teenage girls get over being dumped."

Another glare from him.

Addie saw his glare and raised it with a pair of squinty eyes.

Foy brightened and smacked his hands together.

"Excellent. Nothing more true to school tradition than a dose of academic rivalry. This is how rockets are sent to the moon, how cancer is cured. Einstein didn't develop the theory of relativity without Gunnar Nordström nipping at his heels."

Addie doubted highly that Nordström would have debased himself by crawling on the ground and engaging in such puerile behavior with the most renowned physicist ever. But probably now was not the time to correct her headmaster, especially since, much to her relief, he had moved from the awkward fax issue to insisting that Dex demonstrate his crabs.

Dexter was only too happy to comply. The four of them tromped out of Dr. Brooks's office and down the hall to the main lab, where Kris just happened to be mopping the floor.

"Oh, sorry, I'll get out of your way," he said, picking up his bucket.

"Heartening to see you industriously at work," the headmaster said with a nod. "Keep it up."

"Yes, sir." Kris stole a sideways glance at Addie, who returned a shy smile, before heading down the hall to dump the bucket.

"Okay, so here's the main tank." Dex led them to a large brightly lit tank, about three feet long and only partially filled with water. The bottom was covered in sand,

and there was a small island where the crabs could get out of the water at one end. In the middle were two artificial caves.

"As you will note, both caves appear identical." Dex slipped on a pair of rubber gloves, removed the cover of another, darkened, tank, and scooped out a flailing blue crab, its claws snapping into the empty air with frustration.

Addie's fingers clenched. She hated this part.

Mr. Foy leaned forward. "Now what?"

"You'll see." Carefully, Dex lowered the crab into the lit tank, placing it in front of the one nearest to Dr. Brooks. Eager to shield himself from the light, the crab scrambled into the nearest opening.

And that was when Dex gave him the juice.

Zzzzzz!

Mr. Foy tottered backward as the crab went flying from the cave hole. Addie wanted to snatch it herself and deposit it in the ocean so it would never have to be tortured by Dexter again.

"You electrocuted him!" Mr. Foy said. "Doesn't that constitute abuse?"

Dex clearly couldn't be more pleased with this reaction. "Apparently not, because crabs, lobster, and all crustaceans are exempt from animal-cruelty laws on the premise that they don't feel pain."

"Dexter's right," Dr. Brooks said. "I have checked the laws myself. In light of, ahem, recent events on campus, I wanted to be sure the Whit fully enforces a policy of ethical treatment."

Mr. Foy gestured to the tank. "But you can't argue it doesn't feel pain. Look what just happened."

"The shell-fishing industry would counter that the crab's response was the result of reflexes, such as when you pick up the handle of a hot pot and automatically drop it," Dr. Brooks said. "When you throw a lobster in a pot of boiling water and you hear its claws scrambling, isn't that what people say? 'Oh, that's nothing. It's just reflexes.'"

Mr. Foy rocked on his heels. "Yes, that's true. Wait, that crab. You're putting it in the tank again? Don't. I think you've made your point, Dexter."

"Actually, no, I haven't." Dexter deposited the crab in the water and they all waited.

It sidled slowly to the entrance of the cave where it had been shocked. Then it paused, as if debating whether to risk another zap, and decided to try the other cave, where it snuggled in safely, digging itself into the deep sand.

"Impossible!" Mr. Foy exclaimed. "Crabs can't think."

There was a clatter as Kris returned with a metal folding ladder, his mouth set. He must have overheard or seen part of Dex's little presentation because he looked ready to kick in the tanks, which made sense, she concluded, seeing as how he was so passionate about animal rights. After all, he wouldn't be here doing janitorial work if he weren't.

Dexter cleared his throat and continued. "You're right, headmaster, in that the crab's white nerve clusters that serve for brains do not process much, except information transmitted by the eyes. Instead, ganglia in each segment of the crab, including the legs and flippers, help it to efficiently respond faster than they would if a central brain were in charge. However, I would posit that my experiment proves that on some level not only is their reaction to stimuli more than reflexes, but that crustaceans will seek alternatives to being, um . . ."

"Tortured?" Addie offered, checking with Kris, who nodded back appreciatively.

"Hurt," Dexter said. "Again."

"This is why Dexter's research is so groundbreaking," Dr. Brooks said. "Recently he's been able to repeat his findings, which is one of the criteria for the Athenian Award."

You didn't have to be a genius like Addie to see that she was losing Dr. Brooks's support. Mr. Foy, too, appeared to seriously contemplate submitting Dexter's crabs instead of her B.A.D.A.S.S. project. She held her breath while they decided.

Kris opened the ladder and climbed to replace a flickering light bulb in the ceiling.

"Why didn't you apply for the Athenian Award by the deadline?" Mr. Foy inquired.

"I hadn't designed the right experiment by then so, being Addie's lab partner, I conceded defeat and joined her team. But now I've worked out the flaws, and I'm sure you agree that my project is superior. We should scrap Addie's immediately, and submit mine instead."

Tess believed you could hex people by directing negative energy toward their spirits, and for once Addie wished she didn't know so much about science so she could believe her.

Dr. Brooks bent over to examine the caves. "Considering how Addie's project has already been breached, Dexter's suggestion might have merit."

Great. Even her own trusted advisor was jumping ship. Though of course not literally, as they were in a lab, not a boat.

"Hmmm." Mr. Foy looked up at Kris, frowning, clearly annoyed by his presence. "You may take a break, Mr. Condos. Return in ten minutes."

Kris climbed down the stool and tossed the old light bulb in the trash with a bit more force than necessary. "Don't go down without a fight," he whispered in her ear on the way out.

Her heart surged. "Excuse me," she piped up, after Kris closed the door behind him.

Three faces regarded her glumly, proving just how far she'd fallen from their favor. She lifted her chin in defiance.

"Dexter can submit his crabs, but please let me finish the B.A.D.A.S.S. project. We've come so far and it seems a waste not to follow through. There is only one more experiment to go—the island—and I've been tracking weather reports. I'm quite optimistic that we will gather fascinating results."

Mr. Foy, seeming completely out of the loop, had just opened his mouth to ask a question when Dr. Brooks interrupted. "If we were to green-light this," she said, shoving her hands in her white lab coat, "then you will have to make every effort to ensure against future compromises."

"In other words, no kayaking or hanging out with Kris," Dex said.

"I know what she means," Addie shot back. "Yes. Absolutely. From here on out, I will adhere strictly to the scientific method without deviation. No interfering in the experiments and no"—this was nearly impossible to utter out loud—"fraternizing with the test subjects."

Dr. Brooks and Mr. Foy conferred privately while Addie studiously avoided making eye contact with Dex.

All those late-night sessions in the library discussing their work and future plans and he undercut her at the first chance. Perhaps he was a psychopath with a malfunctioning frontal cortex. That could be the only explanation for his easy disloyalty.

Dr. Brooks and Mr. Foy returned from their corner. "The headmaster and I are in agreement," she said. "Dexter, you may continue to refine your thesis. You will need to work very hard, as you only have a few days to write your reports and submit them for peer review."

"So I won't have time to work on Addie's experiment, right?" He was barely able to contain his glee.

"Correct. Therefore, Adelaide, you will have to conduct the island experiment as well as write up your findings alone, without Dexter's assistance. Is that doable?"

"Of course," she said, though, if she were being honest, she was far from certain. "But we can't submit both of our projects. Athenian Committee rules state that each school is permitted to submit only one."

Mr. Foy beamed. "Of that I am fully aware."

Nothing more was said; he'd said it all.

It was either her. Or Dex. And she could not afford to lose.

SIXTEEN

First and foremost, the intent of the Academy's discipline system is to educate students and treat them justly when rules are violated. Please note that the Academy is a private school and therefore not obligated to adhere to the same rules as public schools; our discipline system is not a "trial," as one might encounter in a court system; nor do the rules of evidence apply . . .

MAJOR OFFENSES

A student may be expelled from the Academy at any time for committing or attempting to commit any of the following offenses, including when it is a first offense:
1. Hazing other students. Hazing is defined as

*harassing, intimidating, bullying, or coercing another
student with the purpose or result of embarrassment,
disturbance, or humiliation.*

*2. Dishonest acts of any kind, including academic
dishonesty. Academic dishonesty may include plagiarism,
cheating, and theft and/or sabotage of another student's
work product with the intent of harming said student
and/or improving one's academic standing. Such acts
are cause for immediate dismissal without delay.*

*—from the Academy 355 Handbook of Student
Academic Policies and Standards*

Kris closed out of the student handbook and let out
a big breath. So that made two offenses, ironically one
committed *against* and the other committed *for* the same
girl.

"You're an idiot, Condos!" He pounded his desk once.
Stupid, stupid, stupid.

It was like he was hardwired to self-destruct. Case
in point, Nepal and China last summer. Spent six weeks
volunteering to do backbreaking labor removing rubble,
rebuilding a school, and digging wells in a country where
he knew no one, got sick, slept on a stranger's mattress,
and took a shower twice, only to come home, raise funds
for the organization, and drop out of Andover because he
couldn't handle the phonies.

You know, you just could have sucked it up. If he had, he'd be starting his senior year now instead of second semester junior year. And why was he behind? Because after begging and pleading his way into the Academy, he again flipped the destroy switch and exploded the week before finals.

And now, the day Foy praised him for working hard and making amends for past transgressions, he decided that the wise thing to do would be commit another "major offense."

Self-destructive. Absolutely. Maybe he should get help.

He got up and turned out the light, anything to make his closet of a room cooler. When he got to the Academy, he found his regular room in Jay Hall had been taken over by two summer students, so he had a choice: a janitor's room in the basement next to the boiler, or a former maid's room in the attic. He chose the attic to avoid spiders. Big mistake. He should have known that a ten-by-ten space under the eaves of a fifty-year-old clapboard building would be a virtual sauna. Except most people didn't sleep in a sauna unless they had a death wish.

The grounds crew had taken pity on him and brought in a plastic fan to fit in the small window. This was definitely progress, as they'd shunned him those first days on the job because he was a prep boy. Or, rumor had it, a spoiled, rich prep boy who'd defaced the wall of a lab to get back at some girl.

Thankfully, Don, a security guard who shared cigarettes with Buster, set them straight during the lunch break yesterday.

"Nah, he wasn't the one who wrote the graffiti; he was the one trying to cover it up," Don had said, gesturing at Kris with his lighter. "I caught him red-handed with the black spray paint, going over the words. Tried to get him to stop, but he insisted on finishing, said he didn't want anyone to see what they wrote. Still, I had to do my job, so . . ."

Having decided that Kris had been manipulated by a girl (a partial truth), the crew gradually came around, even offering him a smoke—which he declined. And then they surprised him with the fan. It was sweet.

Maybe it would have been sweeter if the fan actually cooled the air instead of pushing more hot air into the room, but beggars couldn't be choosers.

"I'll tell you what, Condos," his supervisor, Robert (never Bob), said to him just this afternoon while he was signing out, "you keep up the hard work and I'll personally write you a recommendation to the trustees. That hornet business alone earned you a gold star."

A recommendation that would be tarnished as soon as his latest crime was discovered, which, considering

Dexter's elevated IQ and vengeful mind, would be simply a matter of hours. Whereupon Kris predicted he'd be booted off campus and sent directly to the all-boys military academy in Colorado without passing *go* or collecting two hundred dollars.

Tentatively, he opened the email that had been forwarded from his mother with the subject line: Please Read, Important!

> Your father and I agree that this is the best school for you
> at this stage in your life. While we admire your resolve
> to pay for your mistakes back at the Academy, there is
> no substitute for a fresh start and good old-fashioned
> discipline!
> Love, Mom
> P.S. Wish you were on the Cape. The weather is perfect!

This was followed by several photos of his sisters lying on the beach, riding the waves, and eating lobster, sunburned and smiling, at a picnic table overlooking the ocean.

Thanks for the morale boost, Mom.

Kris wiped sweat from his forehead and continued to the message she'd forwarded. It was from his would-be advisor at the military academy, reminding him that course registration would begin in two weeks and that, in preparation for his anticipated matriculation, it would behoove him to read up on school policies. Handbook attached.

Why even bother? He'd just violate that, too.

Unable to sleep, he went down one floor to the bathroom and took as cold a shower as he could handle before his muscles cramped. On the way back to his attic prison cell, he ran into Ed in his underwear coming down the stairs.

"Tess needs to talk to you." Ed handed him his phone. "It's an emergency."

Immediately, he thought, Addie.

"Sorry to wake you, Kris, but can you get over here?" Tess said, sounding panicked. "I need your help, *desperately.*"

Kris took the stairs two at a time, Ed on his heels. "I just need to get dressed and I'll be over. What's wrong?"

"I'll tell you when you get here. Come to the front door of Wren. It's right by my room. Hurry!"

He turned off the phone and threw it to Ed, slipping his key card in the door. "You have any idea what the problem is?" He stepped into a pair of shorts and grabbed a T-shirt from a pile on the floor.

Ed stood in the door, half awake. "I dunno. She should have apologized to me, though. I was the one she woke."

Aside from the lights illuminating the walkways, the campus was pitch-black and dead quiet. The ocean roared beyond the breakers with a steady rhythm of crashing and sighing that was both haunting and eternal. Perhaps because there were no other distractions, the smell of salty sea air was particularly strong, and by the time he reached Wren, his face was damp from the fog.

He buzzed the door and was instantly greeted by a short girl in pink PJs who looked not much older than a child. "In there." She gestured to a door on the left that was half open.

The dorm room was twice as large as his and fully decorated with wall hangings, a funky multicolored standing light, a pink shag rug, enough pillows for a sheikh's harem, and gauzy curtains that matched the gauzy bedspread, on which sat a cross-legged Tess, Mindy and Fiona, and . . . Addie.

Addie smiled at him briefly and then dropped her gaze to the cup of tea in her hands.

"Thanks, Shreya," Tess said, motioning for her to close the door before the girl's curious inspection was complete. "Kris, you might want to grab that chair. This could be awhile."

Kris sat backward on the chair facing the girls.

Tess said, "I'm so sorry to get you out of bed . . ."

"It's okay. I wasn't sleeping." He snuck a glance at Addie, who seemed fixated on that cup of tea. "Crazy hot in my room."

"Oh, that's good. Well, we have a kind of crisis and

we need your translation skills." Tess took Mindy's hand. "We went to Harvard today on a field trip and Mindy saw her boyfriend from back home. . . ."

A big tear rolled down Mindy's cheek.

"And, um, it didn't go well. She's devastated."

"After all she did for him!" Fiona blurted.

In Mandarin, he asked Mindy what happened. She answered too fast, and he had to take her hand and gently request she slow down so he'd get the gist.

She pushed strands of hair off her face, revealing eyes swollen from crying. "He told me that he wished I hadn't followed him from China, that when we got home, he didn't want to see me ever again." This was punctuated by an almost silent sob. "He said I was an embarrassment."

Kris translated this for the group.

Tess threw herself back on one of the cushions. "That's disgusting. He cooked up the plan to come here and for them to meet up, you know," she said, as if for some miraculous reason Kris would.

"Mindy's and David's parents have forbidden them from seeing each other back home," Addie said, finally making eye contact.

Kris might have been mistaken, but Mindy hadn't been the only one crying. Addie had been, too, judging from the red rims around her puffy eyes. Dexter, that jerk. He was the one who'd made her miserable by deep-sixing her

Athenian Award. Man, what he would give for ten minutes alone with him. It made his blood boil.

"They signed up for separate student exchange programs in America just so they'd have a chance to hang out," Tess said. "Their programs overlapped this week one time—when Mindy came to Boston—and their plan was to meet up. But that can't happen because that would be a total violation of summer school rules and could get both of us in major trouble. Mindy might even be sent straight back to China."

Kris said, "It's also hella romantic."

"Not that hella romantic," Addie said, "if he called her an embarrassment."

Kris bit his cheek to keep from smiling. "You guys seem to be on top of it, so what am I doing here?"

"I called you because Addie was trying to explain to Mindy about the brain during breakups and how neurohormones work and blah, blah, blah. It wasn't getting through, so we thought you could translate and now you're bored and want to go," Tess said, punctuating this with a pout.

"I'm not bored. But explaining neurohormones is a little beyond my abilities in English," Kris joked. "In Mandarin? Forget it."

"Seriously," Tess agreed. "I don't know which would be harder. Interpreting Mandarin or Addie-speak? I think I'd choose Mandarin."

Addie frowned. "My speech is perfectly normal. It's not my fault that you aren't familiar with the common terms of neurology."

"We're complimenting you, Addie," Kris said, "in a teasing way. Not all teasing is meant to be mean."

She arched a brow, doubtful.

"Mindy needs help," Fiona said, rightly bringing them back to the reason they were there. "She needs . . ."

"Reassurance," Tess offered.

Addie said, "What I've been trying to tell her is that love is the rush *in* of pleasurable brain chemicals, and breakups are the rush *out* of those same chemicals, like a tide. That's about as simple as I can make it."

Kris used his phone to Google the Mandarin words not in his vocabulary. *Dànǎo* for brain; *Huàxué zhìpǐn* for chemicals. Of course, there were a zillion different types of chemicals, and for all he knew, he was telling this poor girl that her brain was recovering from a loss of nail polish remover.

When he was finished, Mindy turned to Fiona and rattled off a string of sentences with such speed that Kris could barely make out the basics. He heard *meaningless, what's she taking about?*, and *not helping.*

"Mindy needs more explanation," Fiona said. "She is too heartbroken to understand."

Tess got up to refill everyone's tea from the electric—and illegal—pot on her desk. "Maybe it would help if you told her about your dating disasters, Addie. You know, to relate."

Kris said, "Yeah. I'd like to hear that, too." He grinned, but Addie only blushed.

"I'm not sure that'd help. I haven't been with that many guys."

His heart melted a little and he understood, maybe, what Ed had been trying to say earlier about the urge to protect Addie and her innocence.

Piping up, she said, "What about you, Tess? You're the one in a rocky relationship."

Now it was Tess's turn to redden from embarrassment. "Um, discretion?"

"You were the one who is all about being relatable," Addie retorted. "It was fine to talk about my dating disasters, but not how you're worried that Ed is losing interest in you because he's going to college next month?"

Tess slapped her forehead. "Can we not?"

"Now that I think of it, Mindy," Addie said, "you and Tess have a lot in common. You both feel like your boyfriends are pushing you away, and Tess's mothers would die if they found out their daughter was head over heels for a pro-military, conservative . . ."

"That's enough!" Tess declared, jumping off the bed.

"Who cares what my mothers or Ed's super-strict parents think? All that matters for Mindy and for me is that we can't help ourselves. We're in love!"

Addie groaned. "Oh, please. For the zillionth time. There is no such thing as love!"

Kris gave her a questioning look. "You really believe that, don't you?"

"I don't *believe* anything. I *know*. Love doesn't exist. Just chemicals." She returned his gaze steadily, her pale gray eyes intelligent and also hopeful. "Society would be better off if it abandoned amorphous notions of love and recognized the science: the survival of the species hinges on reproduction, and to further that effort, upon entering maturity, our brains enter a phase of increased neurohormone production, otherwise referred to as adolescence.

"If we were back in the jungle, we would be procreating now. Since we're not, we're sitting on Tess's bed trying to explain to a girl in the thick of dopamine cravings why she can't have more of the 'drug' to which her brain has become addicted."

Addie may not know it herself, he thought, but she wants love, too.

"You guys," Tess said softly. "You don't really think Ed will break up with me when he goes to college, do you?"

Tess didn't want to know his answer to that, Kris thought, though he suspected Fiona and Mindy had reached the same conclusion, seeing as how they were also keeping silent.

Finally, Addie said confidently, "Are you kidding? You and Ed are like this!" And she intertwined her index and middle fingers.

"Really?" Tess asked. "Then how come he's been disappearing lately and being really vague when I ask him what he's been up to?"

Because guys are scum, Kris wanted to say. Half of them are constantly looking for the next best thing.

"You're making a big deal out of nothing," Addie said. "Give him his space. And if he is breaking up with you"— she shrugged—"so what? You'll be over him in eleven weeks, two days, and three hours. Studies have shown that's how long it takes for your neurohormone levels to return to normal."

"Provided," Tess added, "that you don't go back to your ex. Because what happens if you do that, Addie?"

She sighed. "The clock resets and you have to start counting to eleven weeks, two days, and three hours all over again."

Mindy gasped. "But eleven weeks is almost three whole months!"

"No, three whole months is twelve weeks," Addie corrected.

"I think what Mindy's trying to say," Kris interjected, "is that if this is it with David, then it'll be a long time until she feels like herself."

"Actually, she'll never be herself," Addie said. "MRIs have shown that love alters pathways in the brain permanently, so that even when the eleven weeks are over, one's thought process is completely and irretrievably changed."

"What we in therapy call *personal baggage*," Tess added.

Kris ran his fingers through his hair, recalling the girlfriends in his past. There was Lissa, his first kiss in eighth grade, who taught him to love peanut butter and pickle sandwiches. Couldn't open a jar of Skippy without thinking of her. Sophie—who went even further than a kiss, for whom he would be forever grateful—and Kara.

What Tess said about baggage? Yeah. That was Kara.

Fiona checked her phone. "It's late. One thirty a.m. We leave tomorrow."

"I thought that was Sunday?" Tess said.

"It's Saturday." Fiona pointed to her screen. "Mindy won't see David until school starts in September."

"Five weeks after that. Then I'll be okay, right?" Mindy looked terribly sad, but somewhat improved, Kris thought. Not so out of control and weepy. More like resigned.

"Well, the trip wasn't a total waste," Fiona said hopefully. "We got to tour Harvard."

"And all I got was a lousy T-shirt." Mindy smiled.

"There you go!" Tess said. "You're getting better already. Only eleven weeks, two days, and two and a half hours to go."

"Do you have a girlfriend?" Fiona asked flirtatiously as he escorted them to the door.

Kris grinned. "*Wǒ xīwàng*," he said with a wave goodnight. He shut the door and said, "You think she'll be okay? She seemed wicked upset."

"She'll be fine," Addie said. "I'm the one who's going to be a mess. I can't operate on five hours of sleep."

Tess yawned. "Yes, you can. I do it all the time. Be thankful you're not going to toss and turn worrying that you're about to be dumped by the love of your life."

"Don't borrow trouble, Tess," Addie said. "Take the advice you're always giving me. Relax and go with the flow."

"Ugh. As if I could." They hugged each other briefly before Tess closed the door and Addie and Kris found themselves alone in the hall.

He noticed then that Addie was in her Hello Kitty nightshirt looking fresh-scrubbed and pink. It was all he could do to stop himself from unleashing that ponytail.

"You better get out of here before one of the summer students sees a boy here way after curfew," she said, pushing open the front door.

"Can't you go with me?" he asked, following her out.

Her eyebrows flew up in shock. "Go with you? *Where?*"

"To my room. No one will see. Or care. It's a guy's dorm. We can, um, talk." *Lame!* "Sorry. I mean, I would like to talk. Honestly. But also . . ." Gag. He should just shut up before he lost his last shred of dignity.

She took his hand and led him behind a tree. It was so dark here, he could barely make out her expression aside from her slight smile and eager eyes.

"What's wrong?" he whispered. "Why are we here?"

There was a pause, and then Addie said, "Kris, I regret to inform you that we must terminate all further contact."

At first he thought she was joking, but then, seeing her frown, realized she might not be.

"You're serious?"

"I am. Yes."

He was stung. He hadn't even made a move and already he was being rejected. "Don't tell me you're still mad about last spring."

"No. Well, yes, but that's not it. This has nothing to do with you, really. It's more about me."

He chuckled cynically. "Please, just be honest. What's the truth? Because if you're worried about me and Kara, forget it. We're through. We were done a long time ago."

There was a pause, as if she was absorbing this news flash. He wished he could see her face so he could read her expression. It was killing him, not knowing what she was really feeling.

"It's the dictates of the scientific method, I'm afraid," she said at last. "Don't blame me. It's all thanks to Roger Bacon."

"Roger Bacon? Who the hell is he?"

"The father of scientific procedure. One of his core tenets would be that I, as a researcher, cannot have any sort of relationship with my researchee, for lack of a better word."

Kris was swept in a wave of relief. She really hadn't been lying when she said this was about her. "Scientific procedure, huh?"

"Yes. It's vitally important to preserving the outcome of an experiment. Without following it to a T, the whole project is up for scrutiny."

"Oh, okay." He was glad she couldn't see how wide he was smiling, because knowing Addie, she'd probably take offense. "Whew. For a minute there you had me worried that I'd forgotten to put on deodorant or something."

"No. You actually smell quite nice. Like you just took a shower."

"I did."

She swatted a mosquito. "Anyway, already I've violated Bacon's rules by kayaking with you and that night in my room and now this, with Mindy. If the Athenian Committee finds out . . ."

"They won't. I could drop out!"

"Oh, please don't," she said, reaching for his arm.

"That will ruin everything. If this experiment fails, then Dr. Brooks will submit Dexter's project instead of mine and my scholarship chances will decline by twenty-two point six percent."

"Twenty-two point six percent, huh?"

"Don't be patronizing. I've analyzed the statistics and done the math."

"Okay. Sorry. Yeah, I could see how that would suck."

"It would more than suck. It would be ruinous. Unlike Dexter, I have no college fund with hundreds of thousands of dollars. My father spent it all on his new wife's shoes."

"Shoes?"

"They were very expensive shoes. From Paris and Milan. Also, she insists on driving Land Rovers, those hideous gas-guzzlers. The result is, I can't afford to take chances and lose."

"But you have taken risks. And that's good," he said, wishing she would unwind herself for once. Let go and give in to her passions instead of constantly fixating on awards and grades. "Life is too short to play it safe."

"It's even shorter if you don't."

He pulled her closer. "Yeah, but it'll also be more boring." He swallowed the urge to just get it over with and kiss her to drive the point home.

"What are you doing?"

"I was thinking of kissing you."

Another pause. "I would not object." She lifted her face.

Okay, that was odd, but he wasn't about to get into another argument. He bent down and placed his lips on hers, softly, gently. For a girl not used to boys, he had to be careful not to . . .

What?

Before he could come up for air, Addie Emerson brought him to her and kissed him hard and long.

It was nothing like what they did on the plane.

"Wow, um . . . Where did that come from?" he asked, his head swimming.

"I told you. I read extensively." She wiped her mouth with the back of her arm. "*Cosmopolitan* magazine is very helpful in this regard, but the models on the cover are disproportionate to reality."

"That came from you, not a magazine." He played with her ponytail. "Addie, can I just say that was amazing and that you're unlike anyone I've ever met. You're so . . ."

"Weird?" she asked. "That's usually the word people use when it comes to me."

"Weird isn't right. How about unique? Smart. *Cool.*"

"Cool is a new one." She laughed and so did he.

"Good. I'm glad I was the first to call it."

She wiggled out from his arms and stepped back abruptly. "Look, I do have to leave before we're caught.

Just please do as I ask and don't ruin anything. If Dexter finds out about . . . *this*, there would be huge consequences."

"Screw Dexter. What can he do to us?"

"You'd be surprised. Scans on his brain have shown seriously diminished gray matter in parts of his cortex." She clucked her tongue. "Textbook sociopath."

Kris fought a sudden impulse to confess his latest crime even though, obviously, telling her was out of the question. It would reopen old wounds that hadn't fully healed, especially after he swore he had turned over a new leaf. What little trust he'd managed to gain with her would be instantly shot.

"I'll do whatever you want," he said. "You want me to act like I'm nothing but your guinea pig, you got it. But once this project is over and you win that award, I want us to go out, okay?"

"We *are* out."

"No . . ." God. This relationship, if it ever happened, was definitely going to have its challenges. "I mean, hang out. Be together. What do you think?"

Addie reached up, kissed him softly, and whispered, *"Wǒ xīwàng."*

The words went straight to his heart.

I wish.

SEVENTEEN

"Yes! He kissed you. I knew he would!" Tess pumped her fist and danced around Addie's room. "I want to call Mindy and Fiona and personally thank them for making him come to my room last night. I totally won that."

Addie propped herself up on her elbows and checked the time. "It's not even eight o'clock, and I've had only five hours and thirty-six minutes of sleep, far short of the requisite for optimal health and cognition."

Tess flopped on the bed. "I couldn't wait. I heard you two last night through my window and have been dying to get the lowdown ever since. So how was it? Please tell me he wasn't one of those slobbery kissers. That is the *worst*. No, the worst is a pushy tongue, like they're trying to imitate some awful movie."

Addie had no intention of divulging any details. Besides, Tess had her own problems to keep her tossing and turning instead of how Kris kissed or if Ed would drop her after the UChicago freshman mixer. For example, what kind of college she had a chance of getting into. If the girl spent as much effort on biology as she did on gossip, she'd be acing the AP exam with a 5 instead of a 2.

"Come on, Addie," Tess whined. "A clue. A hint. I'll take anything at this moment."

"Let's just say that in scientific terms, the sensory stimulation was highly satisfactory." She hopped out of bed and proceeded through a set of early-morning yoga poses to shake off the sleepiness. Warrior. Downward dog. Headstand, or whatever you called it in yoga-ese. It had to have a name.

"Ugh. You're killing me!" Tess cried, rolling over onto her back. "How can you be so calm when there's so much to do?"

That reminded her. The weather report!

Addie ran over to her laptop, where the National Weather Service outpost for New England was bookmarked. Forecast for the next twenty-four hours was brilliant sunshine. She clicked on the radar and scrolled down. This was it; her one remaining chance to snag the Athenian rested on a moving low-pressure area swirling off the coast of Delaware.

"You have to leave," she told Tess bluntly, gathering her shampoo and towel for a fast shower. "I need to prepare."

"I'll say. Hair. Nails. And what about a dress? You didn't bring one, did you?"

Addie paused at the door. "Why would I need a dress for Owl Island?"

"Owl Island? Forget that. I'm talking about the dance tonight. Kris is going to be there and you need to deliver the one-two punch. Impulsive kiss, knockout dress. Leave him flat on the floor."

It would be impossible to flatten Kris, as he was at least 185.42 centimeters high and 67.13 kilograms in weight and, therefore, able to withstand any blunt trauma she might be capable of delivering. But never mind. She couldn't stand around quibbling with Tess about her wild hyperboles. There were reports to be written.

"I don't care what I wear," she said, hoping Tess would just drop this makeover business. "And I don't have time to shop, not with my Athenian Award on the line."

"All right. All right. I'll go to Boston and find something for you," Tess conceded reluctantly, as if that hadn't been her plan all along.

It didn't surprise her that Dexter was already hard at work when Addie breezed into the lab singing a nonsensical tune about the periodic table of elements, a snappy ditty her mother taught her as a child. Her heart was light, and outside, the morning fog was burning off to reveal a warm summer day with a few fluffy white clouds drifting over the calm turquoise sea.

"No humming." Dexter pointed to the handwritten sign to that effect that he had tacked up next to the posters about the importance of safety goggles and what to do in case of a chemical spill.

If there were anything out of the ordinary, it was that instead of being at his usual post with an eye to a microscope or staring at the screen of his laptop, Dexter was on his hands and knees crawling around underneath a lab table.

"Are you okay?" Addie placed her own laptop on the table and knelt to his level. Perhaps he was suffering from food poisoning or appendicitis. Dexter lived in fear of dirt.

"Of course I'm not okay," he snapped, inspecting a junction of black wires at the base of the wall. Tentatively, he probed one with a plastic spoon.

"What are you doing?"

"I am following this UA wiring from tank number two to identify why, exactly, my caves are no longer electrified." He fiddled with a plug. "Incredible. I don't know how he did it."

"Who?"

"You know who."

"No, I don't."

Dexter was making no sense. Maybe he didn't get the recommended minimum 7.5 hours of sleep, either.

"You are being extremely vague," Addie said. "I might be able to assist if you were more forthcoming with specific information."

He yanked the plug and tossed it aside. "Trust me, Addie, the last person I want to assist me is you."

That hurt. Dex was being so nasty to her lately, bad-mouthing their experiment, tattling on her to Dr. Brooks and Headmaster Foy. It was becoming difficult to remember when they used to be partners, even friends!

Forget it, she thought, booting up her laptop. "There's no reason for you to lash out at me just because you're experiencing lower serotonin levels. Get your meds adjusted."

He rose and brushed off his knees. "Guess what? Not every action, mood, and/or emotion has to do with brain chemicals." He slammed her laptop shut and glowered, though if his intent was to be threatening, then the spouting whale monogram on his peach-colored golf shirt was working against him.

"I happen to have a perfectly legitimate reason for being furious," he said. "Do you remember yesterday when I showed Mr. Foy my crabs?"

"How could I not?"

He waved an accusatory finger, which, Addie thought, had been getting quite a lot of action lately with all his nagging. "*That* is why you did what you did."

"What did I do?"

"You know."

"Again, I don't." Honestly, this was beginning to resemble a seventeenth-century witch inquisition. "Would you just tell me?"

Dexter's chest heaved, prompting a spasm of coughing. "Look at my tank."

She peered into the tank. Same sand and rocks and a little island. Same two caves. "So?"

"Do you see any crabs?"

"No. But you keep them in the other tank, the darkened one."

He flicked on the light above the other tank. "See anything here?"

It, too, showed no signs of life. "No."

"Exactly." He switched off the light. "That's because you took them!"

"I didn't!"

"You did. You stole them because you were jealous! You'd do anything to prevent my project from being submitted to the awards committee. Admit it!"

"I'll admit no such thing. What's wrong with you?

We've been lab partners since ninth grade. You know I wouldn't sabotage your work." Though that wasn't to say freeing the crabs hadn't also crossed her mind. "It's unethical!"

He chewed on his lower lip, thinking. "An alternative theory: under the influence of Kris Condos, you've had a sudden awakening to the plight of test animals, so you snuck in here last night, put the crabs in a bucket, and carried them to the ocean. Then, to give me a dose of my own medicine, you rewired the caves."

"Dexter, the electricity must have damaged more than your dendritic nerve endings. When I tell you I had no part in this crab-napping, you know it's true—it's physically impossible for me to lie. As for influenced by Kris? Don't forget, I was the one who bore the brunt of his attack last spring. So it's highly unlikely I would come around a full one-eighty to his way of thinking."

"Yeah . . ." More lip chewing. "Therefore, the only other person who would have had the means—a universal key card—and the motive—his proven fanatical obsession with saving lab animals—along with a history of reprobate behavior is . . . Kris Condos."

As soon as he said it, Addie knew he was right. Not that she was about to let on. "Get over it. Kris doesn't care about your crabs. He's learned his lesson." Though she wished she sounded more confident.

"Really? Then when I reached into the supply tank this morning, why did I get a"—tears welled in his eyes as he displayed his right hand—"shock!"

"Oh, Dexter! Let me see." Addie clasped his hand in hers. It was a normal temperature and coloring, aside from having a tad more color than its usual fish-belly white. "Is it painful?"

"Stings slightly. More like . . . a tingle." He sniffed.

"Do you want me to take you to the infirmary?"

"No, I'll tough it out, thank you." He removed his hand and held it, limp-wristed. "That's why I was examining the wiring. I can't detect his method. If it hadn't been for the circuit breaker switching, I could be . . . dead!"

That was unlikely, since the voltage to the cave was much lower than the average dog fence. But she was intrigued.

Stooping down, she inspected the wire for damage and found it intact. Dexter was correct in that the power couldn't have been altered at the source. A resistor must have been added, and a fairly significant one at that, considering water's conductive properties.

"And you're positive the saboteur was Kris."

"He was in the lab yesterday when I was demonstrating my method, and I don't know if you noticed, but he wasn't exactly happy."

She'd noticed.

"Next day, crabs gone." He shook his head as if gravely disappointed. "I had hoped he'd reformed, and it seemed like he was making amends working for Buildings and Grounds and, as you know, agreeing to the experiment." He sighed deeply. "I hate to do what I have to do."

Her stomach seized. "What are you going to do?"

"Tell Dr. Brooks and Headmaster Foy, of course." He cocked his head in false sympathy. "I'm sorry, Addie, but this is a safety issue and your Kris is beyond repair. He's a danger to society and maybe even . . ." Dex touched her lightly. "You."

No, no, no. This was the worst possible turn of events! She squeezed her temples with both hands, trying to block out the inevitable. Foy would receive Dexter's report and expel Kris without question. He'd be sent off to military school, where he'd be lost to her forever.

And last night had been so magical, too. So much promise.

There was no other option except pleading for mercy. "Can't you not tell Foy? You know Kris is already on academic probation. He'll be gone by tomorrow."

He responded with a smirk of superior self-satisfaction. "Hate to say I told you so, but . . . I told you so. Didn't I warn you about letting yourself get involved? This is what happens."

Ergh. Dexter was an insufferable, relentless, giant douche, she thought, fists forming. How she had ever admired him for being brilliant was a mystery.

Her phone pinged. Ed again.

Got your message. Want to meet at the docks?

She replied. *Now? I'm kind of in the middle of something.*

T just left for Boston. Better do this before she gets back.

There was valid logic to that statement. *Okay, thanks. After this, we'll be even?*

Yes.

Good. Because with this last one, I'm def skating on thin ice.

It was absurd of Ed to say he was on thin ice when temps were climbing into the low nineties, even on the open water. The only ice was in the red cooler at the back of the boat, which, in Addie's opinion, he drove way too fast, cranking the engine to maximum speed and bouncing on the waves so hard she had to hold on to a railing to keep from being catapulted into the water.

She shielded her eyes from the blazing sun to make out Owl Island, a barren outcropping of rock, sand, and scrub oak on the horizon.

"Awesome day. Not a cloud in the sky," Ed shouted above the engine's roar.

Addie clutched her hat—an absolute necessity in thinning ozone. "One consistency of weather is that it changes!"

They approached the first buoy marking shallower waters, and Ed cut the engine to a chug. Once upon a time, probably not that long ago in evolutionary terms, Owl Island had been connected to the Academy's peninsula. Then the glaciers melted, and water rushed in and separated the two land masses.

But they were still connected in the minds of the Academy trustees, who retained ownership of the island despite its uselessness—aside from on the occasional field trips or bird-watching outings, as the island boasted several species of nesting terns—and not a single owl.

Addie supposed that the island got its name because it was shaped like a pair of owl eyes with deep craters at each end now filled with fresh water. More glacial scarring.

They bobbed slowly as they got closer to shore. Out here, away from other traffic, the sea smelled salty fresh. Gentle waves lapped on the beach, where clusters of small white terns scurried in flocks, their black stick legs moving in the same coordinated unison as schools of tuna.

It was almost enough to take her mind off Dexter and what he was doing right now—most likely sitting in Foy's office signing Kris's death warrant.

"I'm dropping anchor here. The tide's going out and I

don't want to get stranded." Ed killed the engine, went to the rear of the boat, and depressed the automatic winch. The anchor landed in the soft sand with an audible thud.

There was electronic equipment to remove, including a camera and wires that were especially vulnerable to the corrosive impact of salt water. Ed told her not to worry, he was one step ahead of her, which was an underestimation, as he was already waist high in the water and carrying the equipment in a dry bag.

She jumped in and followed behind, dragging the floating cooler of bottled fresh water. Tiny translucent jellyfish undulated around her waist. She made a mental note to bring vinegar to treat their stings.

"Where do you want this stuff?" Ed stood on the beach, searching for a place to stick the dry bag.

Addie pointed to a silver weather-beaten cabin tucked in the woods. Actually, it wasn't so much a cabin as a rough shelter with four wooden walls and a roof not much bigger than the average garden shed. The Academy had built it to store equipment so school visitors wouldn't have to lug kayaks and fishing rods out to the island. Then the shelter was burglarized and that was the end of that. The school didn't even bother locking it now.

Ed kicked open the door and looked around the dank interior. It smelled musty and was desperately in need of a thorough sweeping, but it would do. "Spider city."

Addie pulled the cooler inside. "If it weren't for spiders, humans would have been killed off by mosquito-borne diseases eons ago."

Ed dumped the dry bag on the floor. "But still, you know, spiders."

They spent the next hour quickly setting up the camera. Ed taught her how to zoom in for a shot and switch to record. The Athenian Committee insisted that each project be accompanied by a video, a task Dexter had eagerly offered to undertake before all hell broke loose and he quit. Now she was scrambling to get something, *anything*, to show at her presentation.

When they were done, Addie and Ed trudged back to the beach, grabbed a bottle of water each, and lay on the sand, staring up at the clear blue sky.

"You think it will work?" Ed asked.

"If they don't chicken out."

She considered that expression. It was another quirky euphemism that traced its etymological roots to the era when Roman armies kept sacred chickens, according to her Latin teacher. If the sacred chickens ate the grain that had been blessed by the gods, then the Romans took that as a sign to commence fighting. If the birds didn't, then they withdrew from battle. Hence, "chicken out."

Addie couldn't conceive of a situation in which chickens wouldn't peck at free grain. Maybe if it was poisoned.

Or moldy. Anyway, Ed was talking so she had to pay attention. He was reminiscing, and people did not take it kindly when you ignored them during moments of sentimentality.

". . . I remember when you stopped me after class and said you noticed I had glanced over at Tess thirty-four times that day." He laced his fingers behind his head. "I was like, Who is this person? What does she care?"

"It was a scientific observation." Addie took a swig of water. "I was searching for a prospective boyfriend who was attracted to Tess and whom Tess had theretofore ignored. I apologize if I made you feel uncomfortable."

"Uncomfortable wasn't the word for it."

Then what was the word? "Uneasy?"

"Awkward. Totally awkward, especially when you showed up after practice and said you had a proposition: participate in a brain experiment and end up with Tess. I was like, whoa. Freaky."

That wasn't exactly how Addie remembered the conversation. From her recollection, Ed would have done anything to be with Tess, even camp out on a mountainside and wait in a pelting rain for them to reach the appointed destination. (In Tess's ridiculous designer sneakers, it took 2.5 times longer than planned.)

Ed had had his doubts. When Addie explained, in short, that she could make anyone fall in love with anyone else by putting them in dangerous situations, he'd burst out laughing.

"Oh, yeah? Then how come they let men and women serve in the Marines?"

"Gender is separate from sexuality," she said dismissively. "Besides, people in the military do fall in love sometimes, and who's to say that's not because of their surging brain chemicals."

So Ed was pleasantly surprised to learn that, in fact, B.A.D.A.S.S. did work after all. Tess found a boyfriend who catered to her every whim, Ed won his dream girl, and Addie proved that her theory could be applied in the field.

"Has Kris been asking you more questions about the shark?" Addie reached out to a seagull that was flatfooting up the sand to inspect the intruders.

"Nah. I shut that down. I think he suspects Tess, though, what with the prop room and all."

The seagull pecked tentatively at her bare toe. She kicked it off and it flapped its wings, insulted. "That's okay. Tess won't talk." Addie finished her water. "Thanks for jury-rigging the harness, by the way. I was worried Carl would fix the catch."

"Me, too." Ed propped himself up on his elbows and surveyed the sea. "I never did learn how you got the idea to pull this stunt."

She sat up, too, and lifted her face to the cooling ocean breeze. "Promise not to tell?"

"Sure. It can be our little secret. One of many."

"Came to me in a dream."

Ed turned to her, stunned. *"A dream?* That doesn't sound like you."

"I don't know why not. The subconscious is a powerful tool. Give it a problem and it works behind the scenes to find a solution, and when it does, sends it to your conscious brain."

"Wow. Hey, I almost forgot." Ed removed a folded Post-it Note from the pocket of his T-shirt. "Kris gave this to me."

Keep taking risks.

Addie crumpled the paper into a ball and tossed it into the ocean, where she watched it disintegrate into the waves and disappear.

EIGHTEEN

"Dude, you messed with my crabs."

"What?" Kris dumped the gerbils' soiled cedar shavings into a bucket for the compost. "You should see someone for that."

Dexter snapped up from his laptop, where he had been typing furiously for the past hour. "That's not funny."

"Sorry."

"You're not. You have no idea what those crabs mean to me. They're not just crabs."

"They're *your* crabs," Kris said, scattering fresh shavings into the tank and pushing them around.

"Exactly. With my highly sensitized specimens, I stood a chance of securing the most prestigious award any student neuroscientist could receive. Not only that, but I would have become famous by proving crabs can feel pain."

"By making them feel pain over and over again. That's sick, man. Not cool."

Dex bristled. "I'm not sick, I'm thorough."

"So thorough that you went too far and fatally electrocuted a few?" Kris had no proof this was true, but Dexter didn't refute his bluff.

"Science isn't always pretty, my friend. That's what you and your girlfriend need to understand. The only reason you haven't died from polio is because the vaccine was tested on rhesus monkeys. That's what Jonas Salk did. No one dares mention his monkey killing because he's practically a saint, but it's true. Monkeys, dude. *Monkeys.*"

Kris wished Dex would quit saying "dude." It was as if he'd read somewhere that this was the way guys their age spoke.

Superficially, Dexter's argument about animal testing could have passed muster, *perhaps*. Except if the goal was to not inflict pain on living creatures because you knew for certain it hurt them, then why would you do it repeatedly?

That's where the cruelty came in, and from what little Kris had seen of Dex, including his derisive treatment of

Addie, it was possible he got a thrill every time one of those crabs flailed in misery. You could tell he enjoyed zapping them from the way he pumped his fist whenever they flinched.

Not thorough—sick.

Kris took the shavings outside. When he returned with food for the gerbils, he found Dexter with his arms folded, looking particularly smug.

"Now what's up?"

"A proposition. Tell me what you did with the crabs and we can keep this incident between ourselves. You need a report to Foy like you need a hole in the head. He hears about this, it'll be automatic expulsion. No questions asked."

"I didn't do anything with the crabs. I told you." A gerbil snatched a peanut from Kris's hand and ate it greedily. Cute little guy, he thought, scratching the top of its head, none too eager to get his finger anywhere near those yellow incisors.

Dex opened his laptop. On the screen was the letter he'd composed to the administration outlining allegations that Kris had intentionally stolen and freed the crabs. Worse, he had rewired the caves so as to produce a mild, though potentially dangerous, shock. All unproven. Didn't matter. One rumor and Dex was right—he'd be history.

Kris gave the screen a cursory glance, tamped down a bolt of panic, and went back to feeding the gerbil, reminding himself to be cool.

"Tell me once more that you had no part in my crabs' disappearance and this letter is going straight to Mr. Foy."

Kris placed the mesh top on the tank and wiped up some shavings that had fallen on the table. "*Dude*, what crabs?"

Dex pressed send.

NINETEEN

"It's green!"

Tess held up the adorable dress with the barely there straps she'd bought that morning at a couture shop on Newbury Street in Boston. She supposedly got it on deep, deep discount for twenty bucks, though Addie suspected she'd conveniently left off a zero.

"It's not green," she insisted. "It's turquoise—to bring out your eyes."

"Turquoise is a shade of green and my eyes are gray." Addie fingered the hem doubtfully. "It's very short and the material is almost transparent."

"I know, right? You're going to drive Kris wild." Tess tossed the dress onto her bed and wheeled Addie to the mirror on her desk, which was littered with baskets of makeup, clips, combs, and pink cans.

Addie picked up one and read the label. "This might be an aerosol. That's bad for the already damaged ozone layer."

"The ozone can survive a couple of spritzes. Now let's talk about your hair." Tess ripped out the omnipresent ponytail holder.

"Ack! What are you doing?" Addie's hand flew to her head in protest.

Tess batted it away. "Relax. We need to get you cleaned up—and I'll give you a blowout."

That sounded painful. But, after enduring the process, which required hot air and big round brushes, Addie decided a blowout was simply annoying and a huge waste of energy. Her scalp was super-sensitive and she cringed with each tug. When the ordeal was over and Tess had finished applying teal eyeliner, mascara, light foundation, a few quick swipes of blush, and lip gloss, Addie decided she resembled her aunt Jo's spoiled Pekingese.

Woof.

"You. Are. Gorgeous." Tess stood back and appraised her work.

Addie examined her bare feet. "I don't have shoes to go with this."

"You're right. You can't wear sneakers or those hideous sandals. . . ."

"My sandals aren't hideous. They're very practical—in or out of water."

"Exactly. Let me try one of the girls since my feet are twice the size of yours."

A half hour later, Addie had on a borrowed pair of silver strappy spikes that were, in her private opinion, ergonomic disasters. Unable to stand, she sat on the bed reading the latest issue of *Neuroscience Today* while Tess vacillated between peach- and orange-colored dresses for herself.

Addie checked her watch. "We'll be late. The dance starts at eight."

"So what?" Tess was at her desk, carefully applying yet another coat of mascara. "No one arrives on time."

"I do. And so does Dexter. Promptness is a courtesy we extend to others, he says."

"Why are we even talking about him?" Tess recapped the mascara. "After the way he treated you, he should be invisible."

Addie stood to go, only to sit back down again when Tess started rifling through her lip gloss. Finally, at nine p.m., the ritual of their hair and makeup was complete, and Addie was close to apoplectic that they had so deviated from the schedule. She tripped behind Tess, who broke the laws of physics by striding on her own tiny spikes with ease.

"How pretty!" Tess stopped so suddenly at the

entrance to the dance that Addie, who'd been concentrating on kilograms per square centimeter, bumped into her and nearly fell.

From the rafters inside the white tent hung dozens of multicolored paper lights, thereby creating the effect of red, blue, green, purple, and yellow bubbles.

"Chinese lanterns," Addie said, hesitating. The tent was packed with strangers swaying to the pounding music. It was so loud she had to clap her hands over her ears.

"Now, now," Tess said, gently lowering Addie's hands. "We'll have none of that."

"Maybe I should go back to my room. I feel slightly sick."

"No, you don't. You're excited, not scared." Tess took her by the elbow.

"I just don't do well in crowds. You know that. I'm not good with strangers."

"I also know that you have an experiment to run, right? I thought you were here to watch how Lauren interacted with Alex and Kris."

Just the mention of his name sent her stomach tumbling, though Tess's reminder about the experiment was helpful. Yes. If she simply focused on the assignment, the residual fears of inadequacy and having to engage in small talk—much less actually dance in public—would vanish.

Tess escorted her safely to where Dex was standing

by a potted fern, clipboard in hand.

"You're late." He checked his watch. "By seventy-two minutes."

"Whatever," Addie said, slipping behind the plant, where she could observe without being seen. "What's with the clipboard?"

"Documentation," he replied, tapping his pen. "When Lauren and Kris get together, I want to note the time when I was proven right about your thesis being flawed."

How sweet of him to sacrifice his Saturday night to prove me wrong, Addie thought sourly.

"Adorable bow tie." Tess flicked a finger at Dexter's pink plaid one. "Did mother pick that out for you, too? Or was it nanny?"

He touched it defensively. "Mother, of course. She has impeccable taste. But aren't you supposed to be with Ed? Though, this is a *high school* dance, so it might be a little young for him."

Tess brushed a thread off her arm, playing the part of the ever-confident girlfriend. "Ed can do what he wants. I'm not his keeper. Doesn't Addie look nice?"

Dex turned to Addie and scrutinized her from head to toe. "What did you do to your hair?"

"Tess applied friction and heat," Addie said.

He set his lips together disapprovingly. "Well, it looks different and not at all efficient."

"You really know how to flatter a girl," Tess said, twirling away. "Now don't go all crazy on the dance floor, Dexter. I know how you get with a couple of Cokes in you."

They watched her saunter off, laughing as she threaded through the crowd.

Addie didn't wait a beat. "Did you go to Foy?"

"I sent him an email. He has not responded."

Good. Maybe he wouldn't check it until the morning.

"For the record, I did give your crush an out. I told him that if he admitted to taking the crabs, that I wouldn't tell a soul."

Addie's heart leaped. "And?"

"And he denied it three times. So I sent the email."

Dammit. Why didn't Kris confess? Then again, knowing Dexter and his evil leanings, it was highly unlikely that an admission of guilt would have gotten Kris off the hook. Probably, Dex would have used it as blackmail or forced him to do his bidding all next year.

"Uh-oh. Too bad for you." Dex pointed with his pencil to the snack table, where Lauren appeared to be in deep discussion with Alex, who was wearing a bright-green button-down shirt with dark-green shorts.

"Clash," Addie observed.

"I agree. She is a beautiful blond goddess and he's a cretin."

"I was referring to his choice of attire. The greens conflict."

Still, Dexter's point was not lost on her. Alex and Lauren were together socially. Bummer.

"Don't fret. You gave it your best shot." Dex patted her back awkwardly. "As with all failed experiments, it is incumbent on scientists to analyze the underlying fault in their theories and procedures."

"Stop it with the failure talk. It's annoying." She shifted to the left so his hand fell.

"Hmm. Looks as though he hasn't been expelled yet," Dex said, gesturing to Kris, who was standing on a ladder in the corner fixing one of the lanterns. He was in jeans and a dark green Academy 355 T-shirt that allowed for an unobstructed view of his biceps. She couldn't help but smile.

Kris climbed down, tossed a spent light bulb to another member of the grounds crew (Addie deduced this because he, too, was in a dark green Academy 355 T-shirt), folded up the ladder, and carried it to the door. Along the way, he passed Alex and Lauren, who abruptly left the conversation to turn her full attention on Kris.

Lauren threw an arm around Kris's neck and whispered in his ear. Addie experienced a surge of PEA, aka jealousy, and categorized it as such, refocusing her attention on the importance of this interaction.

She tapped Dex on the shoulder. "Don't start documenting just yet. Look at Lauren now."

Dex blinked. "Inconsequential. They're just talking."

"Then why is she throwing her head back and laughing? And why is *he* enjoying physical contact with another girl?" Addie nodded to Alex, who was dirty dancing with the girls' field hockey captain. "Look. Their hips are touching. He didn't do *that* with Lauren."

Dex was speechless, especially when Kris had to literally push Lauren away and head for the exit. Lauren tottered after him, flipping her hair and employing the many methods to gain attraction that Addie had noted in her research.

"Fascinating," she said, taking Dexter's clipboard to record the series of interactions, complete with the coup de grâce of a lip-lock between Alex and the girls' field hockey captain.

Dex murmured, "Inconclusive."

She returned his clipboard. "There's your documentation of my success. You're welcome."

The music stopped along with the dancing. The lights went up and Mr. Foy went to the microphone, where he made a brief speech about how enriching it was to have the exchange students on campus. Before he invited them on stage to discuss their experiences, he wanted to remind everyone to sign up for a student exchange program so they might have a chance to visit other countries, too.

"*Addie!*" a voice hissed. "Add . . . *ieeeeee!*"

Tess was on the other side of the plant with Fiona. "What?"

"Have you seen Mindy?"

Odd question. Why would she have seen Mindy? "No. Why?"

"Because she's missing and Fiona thinks she went to Harvard to see David."

Addie slapped her forehead. "She can't see him in order to return her neurohormone levels to normal."

"Yes, yes." Tess rolled her hand. "The least of our problems. Foy's about to call them to the podium and everyone will be there except for her. He's going to go ballistic."

"And we have to be at the airport by five a.m.," Fiona added. "Early-bird flight."

Tess said, "You have to go down to Harvard and find her. I'll get Ed to drive."

"Why me?" Addie asked. "Why not you?"

"Because I'm going to be on stage with them! And hey, you're my Assistant Peer Counselor, remember?"

Fiona said, "You should bring Kris to translate since I can't be there."

Addie considered the logistics. It was close to ten. If she could persuade Kris to leave the party, a fifteen-minute endeavor in itself, it would take forty minutes to get to Harvard (a half hour if Ed could circle and not have to park), fifteen minutes to find David's dorm room (if Fiona knew where it was), another half hour to convince Mindy that the best course of action would be to leave him behind, and then forty minutes, give or take, to return to campus.

Which meant, depending on the parking situation, they wouldn't return to school until one a.m. That was if all went as planned. If not, then they had a four-hour window before Mindy had to be at Logan.

The scheduling alone was a nightmare.

"Okay. I'll do it on one condition. Real shoes." She lifted her spikes. "I'll never survive if I have to cross Harvard's campus on shiny silver toothpicks."

"All right, all right," Tess said, "but hurry. If you don't bring her back in time, there's no telling how this will blow up. Mindy's the daughter of a diplomat—if she's lost in Boston, we could find ourselves in an international crisis."

And for once, Addie decided, Tess was not resorting to hyperbole.

TWENTY

It took twenty minutes to convince Buster to let Kris leave work early.

"We are potentially facing a diplomatic crisis," Addie said, repeating Tess's admonition.

Buster was not impressed. China could declare war on the United States for all he cared. In the Buildings and Grounds community, a work schedule was a work schedule. "Your shift ends at midnight, kid. You have to help me break down the tent."

"That can wait," Kris said. "It's not like there's anything happening on the quad tomorrow. It's a Sunday."

He was standing really close to her and she felt a surge of excitement as a little tingle ran up her arm when the backs of their hands brushed—which he might have been doing intentionally.

Finally, after Kris promised to do most of the work on Sunday, Buster relented. He probably didn't want to stay late, either. "Okay. Just this once I'll give you a pass. If Mr. Foy asks, I'll tell him that you had to leave campus on an emergency to find one of the exchange students."

"Um," Addie said, "could you not? Diplomatic crises require utmost tact."

"Tact, huh?" Buster winked at Kris. "Sure. Mum's the word."

Actually, the word was *late*. They were now five minutes over their schedule, with no room for bickering about semantics.

She slipped off the idiotic sandals and ran to her dorm to get her practical ones while Kris went to get a shirt that didn't identify him as a member of the Academy 355 workforce. That added another five minutes until they rendezvoused at the prearranged meeting spot under the oak by the causeway.

"Hey," Kris said when she arrived breathless, her ugly sandals slapping the pavement as she approached. She could barely make out his white shirt in the dark.

"I didn't get a chance to tell you how beautiful you look tonight."

He took a step closer, triggering a rush of epinephrine

that made her swoon. He was so cute and tall and just super-nice.

"Thanks. Tess chose the dress and applied intense heat and friction to my hair."

"I like it out of the ponytail." He slipped his hand along her jaw. "Can I?"

She was touched that he asked before he kissed her. It indicated that he understood her quirks and didn't mind.

"Yes. But we have to be careful. No one must be able to catch us."

"No one will find us." He bent down and softly brushed his lips against hers. This time, Addie didn't take charge as she had the night before, but let him be in control.

She gave in to his embrace, and allowed him to kiss her deeper, stroking her hair and pressing his chest against hers. It occurred to her that letting go was a matter of trust. And that she should never fall for someone like Dexter because he was 100 percent untrustworthy.

Beeeep!

They sprang apart. Addie adjusted her dress. Kris grinned.

Ed was leaning out his driver's side window. "Enough with the PDA. Get in."

A musty old tarp covered the backseat, the kind Addie had seen on the school's boat when Ed rescued them after the shark attack. Ed told them to get under it so he could pass security without an interrogation.

"I'll tell them I'm picking up a couple of summer students from the bus stop since the shuttle stopped running an hour ago."

It was a plausible excuse. As a college-level PC, Ed was free to come and go as he pleased and often ran similar errands. Too bad the tarp smelled like rotting fish. It was suffocating.

Ed put on a huge show for the guard, complaining about how his Saturday night had been ruined because some idiot kids had stayed in Boston too long and missed the last bus. The guard commiserated and sent him off with a pat on the hood and a grammatically incorrect "Drive careful."

Kris and Addie threw off the tarp and gasped for air. "That thing was nasty, man," Kris said, kicking it to the floor.

"It was all I could think of. You two are going to have to hide under it again when we come back with Mindy. What's the story there, anyway?"

Addie briefed them with the little information Fiona had provided. David was in the Harvard summer program staying in Room 308 in Hollis Hall and Mindy went to plead with him not to end their relationship. That is, if she hadn't left yet. Fiona was afraid that he would close the door in her face and Mindy would have to make her way back to the Academy alone, all the way from Harvard . . . which would be a real problem.

The bus from the T stop in Wonderland to Marblehead had already stopped running and wouldn't resume until the next morning at six a.m., an hour after Mindy was supposed to be at Logan. A cab ride cost over fifty dollars and she didn't have cash or a credit card. She would be a scared girl trapped in a strange city in a foreign country and she would miss her flight to Chicago. Oh, and her father was some bigwig in the Chinese government.

See above: diplomatic crisis.

"Don't worry. We'll find her." Kris took Addie's hand and gave it a squeeze, releasing a burst of norepinephrine that made her want to break out in song.

Boston was lit up like a fairyland, and the lights along Memorial Drive reflected off the slowly moving Charles River. Ed crossed the salt-and-pepper bridge onto the section of Massachusetts Avenue that was home to MIT, with its modern brick buildings and ghost campus. Not a soul in sight.

From there they crept bumper-to-bumper through honking traffic. Addie tried to temper her anxiety. This trip was taking too long. Already they were off schedule by ten minutes, and if . . .

She closed her eyes. No. She was not going to slip into old habits. They would get there when they got there.

But they *were* late. *Really* late.

Although it was after eleven, Harvard Square was still packed with college students. They emerged in clusters from the red-tiled T station and gathered around amateur guitarists strumming behind the newsstand. Addie leaned out the window to inhale the smells of garlic and fresh coffee emanating from nearby restaurants mixed with the grit and grime of the city.

"Down that alley is a place with really good pizza," Kris said, pointing to a neon sign. "When I was at Andover, my friends and I would come here on Friday nights and hang."

It had slipped her mind that he used to attend a different school. There was so much about him she didn't know and yet she felt so close to him. Then again, one of the by-products of dopamine was a false sense of intimacy.

She made a mental note to mention that in her paper for the Athenian Committee.

Ed parked in front of the iron gates to Harvard Yard and activated his flashers, immediately setting off a chorus of angry beeping from fellow frustrated motorists. Addie opened the door and Kris followed.

"Addie will call you when we're ready to be picked up," Kris said, leaning in the window. "Thanks, man."

"I'll meet you on Summer Street." Ed thumbed over his shoulder, the blare of horns so cacophonous it was embarrassing. "Chill!" he yelled into the rearview, pulling back into traffic.

Kris and Addie took in the historic entrance to one of the most famous college quads in America. "Harvard," Addie whispered. "I am really here."

"You can get that on a T-shirt, you know. Buy it online for twenty bucks and save four years and two hundred and fifty thousand dollars in tuition."

"Yes, but it's the degree that matters, not the T-shirt."

"I dunno. The T-shirt might just do it for me."

They entered the quiet yard dotted with small white tables where students sat, chatting earnestly. Kris navigated the paths zigzagging through the worn grass with ease. "I had a friend who went here," he explained. "We used to visit a lot."

"After the pizza?"

He laughed. "Sometimes before the pizza. We were that reckless."

Though that wasn't really very reckless, so he had to be joking.

Addie said, "Hah! Good one."

That only made Kris chuckle again. They passed a large bronze illuminated statue that was decorated haphazardly with ribbons and flowers.

"What a fraud," Kris said. "I'm surprised they don't take it down."

Addie read the inscription on the base:

JOHN HARVARD

FOUNDER

1638

Kris ran his sneaker against the base. "The Statue of Three Lies, they call this monstrosity."

"Why?" Addie asked, staring up at the noble visage. "He's the founder of Harvard. It makes sense to have a memorial to him."

"First of all, it's the likeness of a nineteenth-century Harvard student, not of the seventeenth-century clergyman named John Harvard," Kris explained. "Also, John Harvard was neither the first president nor founder of this esteemed institution but merely some guy who chipped in seven hundred and eighty pounds, barely enough to buy a couple of PS4s. Finally, the date? Fail! The school was founded two years earlier."

"Why are you doing that?"

Kris lifted his foot, which he'd been running along the base of the statue. "For good luck. That's the tradition."

"I don't believe in luck."

"You should. John Harvard was a nobody and he ended up with a famous statue and the most prestigious school in the world named after him. How lucky is that?"

"Fortunate, perhaps. Not lucky. But we're wasting valuable time. Where's Hollis?"

Hollis turned out to be right around the corner. Now the question was how to get inside, since they didn't have a key card.

"It's after eleven," Kris said. "There might be a curfew for summer students like at the Academy. If we wait, someone is bound to come out and we can go in."

Sure enough, a girl opened the door, took one look at Addie in her expensive, brand-new Newbury Street dress, and opened it wider.

"Thanks," Addie said. "We're here for a party and didn't know how to get in. We buzzed but I guess they didn't hear us."

"I figured," the girl said, smiling. "There are parties all over campus tonight."

"So much for security," Kris said, taking the stairs two at a time.

Addie froze at the bottom step, covering her mouth. Kris turned. "What's wrong?"

"I did it," she said, simultaneously shocked and delighted. "I lied! And it was the easiest thing in the world!"

Kris gave her a thumbs-up. "Next you'll be laughing at my jokes. Come on."

They reached the third floor, their footsteps creaking

down the ancient hall's wooden floors until they found 308. Kris placed his ear against the door. "Voices. Male and female."

"Talking, or . . . ?" Addie asked.

He shrugged. "Only one way to find out." He rapped quietly three times.

"Who is it?" someone asked in a distinct accent.

Kris answered him in Mandarin, and after a moment's hesitation, the door opened a crack to reveal a boy in a multi-striped shirt and glasses.

"Yes?"

"We're friends of Mindy's," Kris said first in English and then in Mandarin.

The boy pushed up his glasses. "Who?"

"Mindy's not her real name, remember?" Addie tried to peer inside the room, which was pitch black aside from a glowing computer.

"I don't know a Mindy," the boy reiterated.

Kris tried a different approach. "She's in a student exchange program, staying at Academy 355. They're worried about her because she left without telling anyone where she was going."

The boy seemed like he was about to again deny any knowledge of such a person when a small voice peeped from the back of the room. "I'm here. It's okay. I know them."

David said something to her in Mandarin.

Kris put his mouth to Addie's ear. "He told her to stay back. That he would take care of it. Looks like she's not going without a fight."

"Then he wants her to stay?" Hmm. This was a new and perhaps troublesome twist in their relationship.

"Can we just talk to her?" Kris asked David in Mandarin. They spoke further, until David relented and let them in.

He switched on the light and closed the door. There was Mindy sitting with her hands folded at the end of his bed, her facial expression unreadable.

"I'm okay," Mindy said. "David and I talked and I'm fine."

"So, you're not breaking up?" Addie asked.

David said, "You told them about us?"

"Fiona did."

This wasn't exactly true, but Addie wasn't going to call her on it.

David plopped down next to Mindy, taking her hands in his and speaking in soothing tones. As a neuroscientist, Addie was confused. He seemed to regret causing her distress. He showed remorse and affection by holding her hands. These were not the standard behavioral patterns displayed by a person who wasn't in love.

Kris said gently, "You have to go back with us, Mindy.

Your plane leaves tomorrow morning. Everyone is wicked worried."

She nodded, tears welling in her eyes, and leaned against David, who patted her silky dark hair and in English said, "This is what I didn't want to happen. I broke it off with Mindy . . . because I knew that when we got back home, things would only be worse for her."

"Why?" Kris and Addie asked in unison.

"It's not just Mindy's parents who don't want us to be in a relationship. Mine, too. My father had girlfriends in school and didn't thrive academically. My mother thinks I'll be the same."

Mindy smiled ruefully. "He studies harder than anyone. From six in the morning until eleven at night."

"They found out from my little brother that Mindy and I were planning to see each other here and they called me—they were . . . angry," David continued. "They had spoken to her parents and . . ." He brought his lips to Mindy's hair. "I broke it off so she wouldn't get in trouble. If I hadn't, things would have been bad when she got home."

"Oh!" Addie smacked her chest, deeply moved. "That is the most touching story ever. It just shows how much you love her. That's one of the hallmarks of shifting to the endorphin stage of a relationship . . . sacrifice of one's pleasure for another's safety and/or comfort.

You hardly ever find that with norepinephrine or even dopamine."

David said something to Mindy in Mandarin and they both giggled.

"He wonders if you're, um, under the influence of something," Kris translated with a grin.

"Influence of intense research, tell them," Addie said, indignant.

"Yeah, I don't think this is the time." Kris went to the door. "We'll give you guys a few minutes to say goodbye, but you have to come with us tonight. Like David said, it will only make more trouble if you stay."

She nodded. "At least I know he still loves me."

"And think of this," Addie said. "Soon you'll be free and clear adults—because school doesn't last forever. Unfortunately."

"Isn't there anything you can do for her?" Kris asked as they slowly descended the stairs.

"Not unless she wants to end their relationship, in which case we're back to the same advice I gave her in Tess's room. Don't see him for the prescribed period. I don't think that system applies here, though."

"I feel really bad for them. They looked so pathetic and trapped." Kris pushed open the front door. "Why do parents do that to their kids?"

"It's a scary world out there. They're just doing what

they think is best. They want to guarantee that their kids will be okay."

"Hmm." Kris stepped outside. "Do you think it works?"

"I think they have no idea what they're up against. If they knew what I know about the potent effects of neuro-hormones on the adolescent brain, they would throw their children behind bars until the age of twenty-five." Addie followed him down to the yard. "Either that or wave the white flag and surrender."

Kris shoved his hands in his pockets and leaned against a lamppost as they waited for Mindy. "So, that explains Romeo and Juliet."

"Classic example. Romeo and Juliet meet in a high-risk setting. Their families are sworn enemies, yet he crashes the party, so right there the PEA is firing the epinephrine like mad."

"The what?"

"I'll explain later." She didn't want to give away too much before Kris had completed his own experiment. "They continue to engage in high-risk behavior that kicks their amygdalae into overdrive. A street fight. A battle with the parents. A ditched engagement. A one-night stand."

Kris grinned. "Not that risky."

"How about a secret marriage under penalty of death?"

"Okay. Got me there."

Addie wished she could have studied the real Romeo and Juliet in the flesh. Too bad they didn't cryogenically store blood samples in Verona back in the day. Because how awesome would it be to centrifuge their neurohormone levels, eh?

"The bottom line is that Juliet alone could be a public service announcement for what happens to a brain on boys," Addie said. "Poison? Dagger? Two dead? Any questions?"

Kris let out a loud laugh.

"Hey, you!" A girl stepped out of the shadows, weaving slightly and swinging a red bag. She was rail thin, with long legs and a short black dress. Her eyes were rimmed thickly in kohl. Streaks of crimson glowed on her otherwise straight black hair.

Addie let out a gasp.

Kris went, "Oh, crap."

"Condor! You came to the party after all!"

"Stay here," Kris said. "I'm going to talk to her. I'll be right back."

Kara. The girl who'd made her life hell.

Oh, and, how could she forget? Kris's girl*fiend*.

Kara fell into Kris's arms, resting her head on his shoulder. He wrapped his arms around her and whispered something in her ear, stroking her back.

Addie was suddenly smacked by waves of anger and

sadness, followed by a big glob of jealousy. Why had she let down her guard when she knew he had a girlfriend? After all the research she'd done, the case studies she'd read, the abstracts she'd collected, not to mention her own testing, somehow Addie Emerson had let herself become vulnerable to the same brain chemicals that had done in Juliet!

And like Juliet, in a matter of days, her own brain had reprogrammed itself to respond eagerly to his touch, his smell, even the mere sight of him. She would have to go through withdrawal and wait out the eleven weeks, two days, and three hours until she was back to normal.

If that was even possible.

She pulled out her phone and texted Ed.

Outside Hollis. Found Mindy. Kara is here and wasted. Come quick!

A half second later: *On my way!*

The door to Hollis opened and Mindy appeared. Under the light swarming with summer bugs, she looked so unstable that Addie rushed to help her.

"It's okay," Addie said, wrapping Mindy in a big hug. "Everything will be okay."

Mindy coughed back huge gulping sobs. "I love him, Addie. I love him."

No such thing as love, she thought bitterly. *At least, not for me.* Turning her back to the reunited boyfriend and girlfriend, she said, "Come on, Mindy. Let's go."

"But what about . . ."

"Don't worry about him." Addie cast one last glance at Kris, who was still in Kara's clutches. "He's with someone else."

"Addie, wait!" Kris shouted, pushing Kara off. "I'm coming with you."

She kept on walking. Forward, she told herself. Do. Not. Look. Back.

Then she heard Kara's loud, gleeful scream. "Wow. Is that Addie Emerson?" she cackled. "Is that who you've been putting me off for, Condor? *Her?*"

Addie winced and squeezed Mindy's hand.

"What's she talking about?" Mindy said. "I don't understand."

"Neither do I."

Footsteps came up from behind, stilettos on sidewalk, followed by heavier pounding.

"Come on, Kara," Kris pleaded. "Leave her alone."

Too late. Kara intercepted them and flung out her arms for a full body block. "Stop!" She checked Addie out from head to toe. "Got a makeover, did you? Adorable."

Addie let go of Mindy and shifted her eyes to Kris, who was mouthing, "I'm sorry."

"I don't like you," Addie said, squaring her shoulders.

"You are cruel and you reek of ethanol."

Kara burst out laughing. "Aren't you precious? Ethanol. Say, Miss Valedictorian, you still decapitating frogs?"

Addie blinked.

"No?" Kara pouted. "Twisting off the heads of gerbils, then?"

Kris gripped Kara's shoulder tightly. "That's enough."

She swiveled toward him tipsily. "Since when do you stick up for Addie Emerson?"

"Don't," Kris said, the muscles in his jaw flexing. "Look, let me take you home. You've had too much to drink and you don't know what you're saying."

She smacked at his hand. "Let go of me. You're not my boss. You don't tell me what to do."

Addie tensed.

"Please," Kris whispered. "Just leave it."

"Oh, don't act like you're so innocent, Condor." She rotated to Addie. "After all, we never would have gone down to the lab if it hadn't been for you. Brilliant idea, freeing all the animals."

Addie closed her eyes and wished she were back at school without any of them.

Kara touched her lips, pretending she'd made a faux pas. "Uh-oh. Did I let the cat out of the bag? I mean that metaphorically. Not the ones *you* dissect.'"

"That's it!" Kris yanked her so hard she stumbled.

"Hey," Kara protested. "You'll ruin my jacket."

Addie pushed Mindy through a cluster of students who'd come to check out the trouble.

She didn't care if Kris didn't have a ride back. She didn't care if he was rounded up by Harvard security and sent to jail. She didn't care if Foy banned him from campus forever.

Good. Freaking. Riddance.

So much for trusting someone and letting go. She wouldn't make that mistake again.

"Who was she?" Mindy asked as they reached the gates where Ed was parked with the flashers blinking.

"Who?" Addie asked, opening the door.

Mindy slid into the backseat. "That drunk girl."

"Oh, I have no idea." Addie got in the front and closed the door. "I've never seen her before in my life. She's no one, I guess."

TWENTY-ONE

The first Academy shuttle ran late on Sundays, leaving the Marblehead bus stop at ten a.m., arriving at the security gate at the Academy 355 causeway twenty minutes later. Aside from a few employees on that already-hot Sunday morning, one sheepish boy was slouched in the back, arms folded, head rested against the window, fast asleep.

"Do you have your ID?"

Kris cocked open one eye to see a dark-green-suited security guard scrutinizing him with suspicion.

"Oh, yeah, sure." He yawned and reached in his jeans pocket to produce the ID he'd been given almost a week before, when he'd hopped a ride with Ed and Tess and that strange girl, Addie Emerson. Eons ago, it seemed.

The guard frowned and handed it back to him. "This is temporary. It expired yesterday."

Now what was he going to do? He really needed to get back to his dorm. Not that he had any illusions of staying. If Foy hadn't already banned him from campus, he would once he had a chance to read Dexter's email.

"Can't you just let me get my things?" Kris said. "I'm leaving today."

The unsmiling guard whipped out a radio and called his office with as much urgency as if he'd caught a wanted terrorist trying to sneak into school. After a clipped discussion, he said, "There's a note for you to go to Administration. It's in Chisolm Hall, which is on the other side of the quad—"

"I know where it is." Kris got up and headed out to the quad.

A pack of students ran by, their sneakered feet pounding the road in rhythmic unison. They took one look at his rumpled shirt and unshaven face and laughed.

"Hard night?" asked one, chortling.

The proverbial Walk of Shame.

Not that he, technically, had anything to be ashamed about, aside from what he had done months before to Addie and the Whit, for which he would never, ever forgive himself.

He kept replaying that disastrous confrontation from the night before, the confusion, then disbelief, then shock on Addie's face, when she realized he was still with Kara. He could almost feel her disappointment like it was his, the heartbreaking, crushing shame that she'd ever let herself have anything to do with a creep like him.

And she was right. It was all his fault. He was the person who'd wronged her the most. How was that even possible?

"Oh, stop moping, Condor," Kara had said last night as he sulked on the couch of her parents' lavishly appointed Back Bay apartment. "Don't you get it? That's the thing about people like her. They don't care. They don't have *feelings.*"

He could have socked her then. If she'd been Mack—who certainly would have said something as obnoxious—he would have. But he just couldn't hit a girl. And he refused to let her drag him down further into the pit of moral decay by daring him to violate his one remaining shred of decency.

"Addie does have feelings. She's amazing. She's better. Smarter. Her brain . . ."

"Okay, okay. I get it. You have a thing for Addie Emerson," Kara interrupted. "You just should have told me instead of leading me on."

What? Incredible. He threw up his hands, exasperated. "Every time I tried to break up with you, you wouldn't listen or you'd threaten to do something crazy."

"I did not. Stop exaggerating." She rolled her eyes, got up, and staggered to her bedroom. "You can crash here, if you want, and dream about your precious little evil-scientist girlfriend. Don't wake me up in the morning, though, I need my beauty sleep. You can see yourself out."

There was no thank-you. No appreciation for how he'd guided her safely to the red and then the green lines of the T, keeping her steady as the trains lurched so she wouldn't barf over fellow passengers. Actually, Kara did vomit—right on his shoes—but not until they were a block away from the apartment.

He couldn't wait until he could leave Back Bay. If there was one highlight of that horrendous experience, it was the comfort he took in knowing he would never have to answer her hourly texts or listen to her rant and rave about poor, innocent gerbils.

The administration building was closed, of course, so Kris had to wait on the steps until Mr. Foy arrived, having been alerted by security that Kris had been on the shuttle.

Foy didn't even grace him with a glance as he bounded up the stone steps in his white shorts and shirt to unlock the massive front doors. "In my office. This won't take long."

Clearly, Kris's arrival had dragged the headmaster away from his regular Sunday morning tennis match, which meant he would be extra annoyed. Kris trudged up the stairs, each step leaden, wondering what was even the point. If Foy was going to kick him out, then just kick him out. Have security wait while he packed up his things and they could escort him to the gatehouse.

"Sit." Foy pulled out his own chair and sat at his imposing mahogany desk, where a green folder waited. Opening it, he removed a letter on Academy 355 letterhead and slid it to Kris.

It was one paragraph long.

It was his expulsion.

"I spoke to your parents last night. As you know, they're on the Cape, but they'll make arrangements for you to return to Connecticut this afternoon. They understand that you are to leave immediately."

Kris closed his eyes. This was even worse than he'd expected. Not that he cared about getting expelled or even having to go to the all-boys military school in Colorado. Both of those paled in comparison to the fact that he wouldn't even have a chance to apologize in person to Addie.

The letter required his signature of agreement. Kris picked up the pen and hesitated. If he signed this, there was no going back.

"You know what the real tragedy is here, Mr. Condos?" Foy asked. "It's that I had planned for you to meet me here tomorrow so that I could offer you another year at the Academy."

Kris clicked the pen. *Please stop,* he wanted to say. *Just don't.*

"You may be surprised to learn that I've been monitoring your progress. Every afternoon, I checked in with Buildings and Grounds, where your supervisor, Robert, had nothing but praise for your work ethic. You arrived on time, ready to put in a hard day's labor. You even woke before dawn to clean out the hornets' nest. But it was something Robert said to me that really gave me pause," Foy continued. "It was that he'd spoken to the security guard who caught you in the lab last spring with the can of spray paint. And the guard told him that you'd been trying to cover up the words, not write them. Is that true?"

"Yes," Kris whispered.

"Speak up, boy. I can't hear you."

Kris lifted his chin. "Yes, *sir.*"

Foy got up and went to the window, gazing toward the rec fields and tennis courts, where a group of middle-aged men were standing around talking, waiting for his return.

"Then why did you intentionally sabotage Dexter's experiment? Was it because of your animal rights stance?"

"I would like to say it was," Kris answered. "By now

you know my feelings on the use of lab animals. The way he kept shocking those crabs over and over was sick."

Foy nodded. "Much has been written on how the pursuit of science is often fraught with sacrifices."

Rhesus monkeys. "Yes, sir. But that's not why I took his crabs." Okay, that was a full-on admission. Point of no return. "I saw that Dex was doing everything he could to bad-mouth Addie Emerson's experiment, the one I'm in."

"Yes. Dr. Brooks has informed me that you've been diligent in this regard, too. Go on."

"The way I saw it, Dex couldn't get his act together by the award deadline. His crabs weren't trained or whatever. So he stuck with Addie until his crabs were ready and then he started bashing her project so you guys would substitute his instead. I just felt like that was unfair, so I evened the score, so to speak."

A silence settled over the room, the only sound coming from the *pfft pfft pfft* of the lawn sprinklers below the window.

"No matter the reason, you have committed a dishonest act, which school rules dictate requires immediate and permanent removal." Foy sighed. "Even if on some level I must admit I do sympathize."

Kris went back to the letter and was about to sign when he had a sudden thought. "Sir, is it possible for me to leave tomorrow?"

Foy pivoted from the window and this time regarded

Kris with a look that bordered on regret. "I'm afraid not. If you read the handbook . . ."

"I have, sir, but the last experiment is today. Lauren Lowes and I are supposed to have an overnight on Owl Island. It's a major part of Addie's project, and if I don't do it, she'll have no choice but to withdraw from the Athenian Award."

Foy considered this. "Let me call a quorum of the trustees and see if that's acceptable. In the meantime, you need to sign the letter and clean out your dorm room. I'll let security know what has been decided."

I, Kristopher John Condos, hereby admit that I have violated Rule #2 of the Academy 355 Student Code of Conduct by knowingly and intentionally committing an act of dishonesty, the penalty for which is immediate expulsion. By signing this letter, I agree not to appeal this decision. I acknowledge I must leave campus immediately and that I may not return unless specially invited by a member of the Administration and/or Faculty.

Kristopher J. Condos

It was done.

TWENTY-TWO

"Where is he? It's super-hot!" Lauren fanned herself with the brim of her white visor as she sat on Ed's boat, which bobbed off the Academy dock in the still, humid air.

Too still, as if the world was waiting.

Ed checked his phone for the zillionth time. "No word. We might have to cancel."

"We can't cancel. Addie already screwed things up by not letting me climb the rock wall the other day. The only way my Bio teacher is going to give me extra credit now is if I write up a report on this island doohickey thing whatever." She sighed petulantly. "What time are you coming for us tomorrow?"

"Depends on when we leave today. You guys have to make it a whole twenty-four hours without food or water, just surviving on what's there."

Lauren curled her lip. "Ew. There's nothing on Owl Island."

Ed shielded his eyes to see up the cliff. "There are a couple of fresh lakes with native perch to cook. There are no beaver out there, so no giardia that could make you sick. You won't die of thirst."

"Yippee! No beaver pee! Where do I fill up?"

A figure ran down the wooden stairs leading to the beach and Lauren said, "That's him."

Ed started the boat. Blue smoke puffed out the engine in the rear. "You made it."

Kris threw a leg over the side. "Sorry, man. How late am I?"

"An hour." Lauren tossed him a life jacket.

Much to Kris's disappointment, she was the only one on board. He'd been prepared for a cold shoulder or, more likely, a pair of red-rimmed eyes that seethed with hate. But for Addie not to put in an appearance at the grand finale of her own experiment? That was intense.

"What time you get in last night?" Ed asked, pulling away from the dock, one knee on the driver's seat as he chugged slowly through the harbor's no-wake area.

"Try this morning. Took the first shuttle."

Ed let out a low whistle. "So you and Kara are . . ."

"Never speaking again."

"Good. I heard she was pretty gross last night, and what she said to Addie . . ."

"Please." Kris slapped his hands over his ears. "I'm trying to forget it."

"Hey, what are you two talking about?" Lauren called from the back. "Who was gross?"

"No one!" Ed said, opening the throttle and letting the boat rip on the open water.

Kris leaned on the prow, relishing the fresh air and spray of seawater on his face as he kept his focus on Owl Island, where he hoped Addie was waiting. This was his final chance to look into those mesmerizing gray eyes and beg for her forgiveness.

Or say good-bye forever.

Big gray clouds hung on the horizon. In the back of his mind, an alarm went off, something about the air and the heat, the portentous quiet of the atmosphere. Owl Island came into view, a cluster of dark silver oak and green pine trees and rocks. Ed slowed the boat as they neared the beach. Not a single sign of life.

"Where's Addie?" Kris asked.

Ed didn't reply.

Kris turned. "I said . . ."

"Heard you." Ed killed the engine and went past

Lauren to the back, depressing the automatic winch that lowered the anchor.

Wow. Kris had no idea that Ed was so pissed at him. Made sense, he guessed. After all, Addie was his close friend, and Ed probably didn't appreciate that Kris had left her to take Kara home.

"We're stopping here? But how are we expected to get there?" Lauren pointed to the beach.

"Swim," Ed said. "The water's waist deep. You won't drown."

"Yeah, but." She peered over the edge of the boat. "Are those jellyfish?"

Kris jumped in and held out his arms. "Come on, Lauren. I'll carry you."

She slipped off her sandals and held them with one hand as she gingerly stepped over the edge into Kris's grasp. "It's noon," she called out to Ed, clinging to Kris's neck. "So be back the same time tomorrow and not a minute later!"

Ed gave her the thumbs-up and hauled in the anchor.

Kris turned toward the beach and saw the terns and seagulls not running along the water's edge as usual, but gathered together in a cluster, hunkering down. At the time, he didn't give it another thought.

Big mistake.

* * *

The island was dead silent, especially since there were surprisingly few motorboats on the water today, and even the birds were strangely muted.

On the bay side, which faced Academy 355, a sandy shore led to a salt marsh teeming with tide pools full of minnows, fiddler crabs, clams, and snails. It was a completely different story on the ocean side, where waves crashed against huge boulders leading to a high meadow of short, dense grass. In winter, the wind was so fierce it whittled the oaks to toothpicks.

Kris hadn't been out here before, though Lauren had during orientation, which of course he'd missed as a midyear student. She showed him the rustic cabin, where they found the cooler of water bottles someone had conveniently left.

Then they headed out to explore the middle of the island in search of the freshwater ponds Ed had described. It had to be over ninety degrees with 90 percent humidity. Even with the ocean breeze, they were hot and sticky and growing slightly bored.

"When's Addie going to get here?" Kris tried to ask as casually as possible, though he suspected that Lauren was savvy enough to see right through his act.

"I don't think she's coming." She led the way on a rocky path covered with pale green lichens. "Ed gave me a notebook from her where we're each supposed to write our before-and-after lists and journal our thoughts and feelings, et cetera. So that tells me she's off doing something else."

Kris was instantly deflated. The realization that his hopes were mere pipe dreams, that there would be no Addie, that he was stranded here with Lauren, was unbearable. They were only two hours in and already he was ready to flee. Swim back to the Academy if he had to. He was a mess. He was hungry and exhausted from tossing and turning on Kara's couch, worried about Addie, and at the moment he was under attack by a swarm of mosquitoes.

He smacked one on his arm. "Can you figure out the point of this experiment?"

Lauren ducked under a low-hanging branch. "Didn't Addie and Dex say at the beginning that they were trying to chart how males versus females responded to different situations?" She shrugged. "I don't get it, but I don't care, either. All I have to do is write a five-page paper on what it was like to be a guinea pig and my B+ in Bio is moved to an A-." They went down a slight hill. "Why are *you* doing this?"

He told her about the trouble he'd gotten into that spring.

"You were part of that?" If Lauren was faking disbelief, she was an excellent actress. "But I thought they were kicked out as soon as they were busted."

"Not me. I came clean. Confessed to everything." He could never bring himself to explain about trying to paint over the damage; it sounded like such a lame lie.

Lauren stood aside to let him go first. They were at a swampy part riddled with even more mosquitoes and probably she wanted to see if he got stuck before she did. "Does Addie know?"

He found a dead log and dumped it on the sodden ground as a makeshift bridge. "Yeah."

Lauren took his hand as she crossed. "You told her."

"Actually, she figured it out. Except that part about me being the one to come up with the idea of going down to the lab. She learned that last night."

Lauren hopped off the log and spun around, hands on hips. "And that's why you keep asking about her."

"Yup."

"So how long have you two been going out?"

He laughed. "Who says we're going out?"

"It's written all over your face. You look like a puppy licking his wounds." She stuck out her lower lip, pouty.

"We're not together," he said honestly. "Addie didn't want to while I was in her experiment and, well, after last night I think I blew any chances of us happening."

"Too bad for her!" Lauren said blithely. "Hey, I think I see water."

They stumbled down a sandy path to a tranquil pond. Kris ripped off his shirt and dove in, Lauren running after. The water was incredible, almost silky soft and clean. A glacial pond with no vegetation.

Lauren threw off her shirt and stepped out of her shorts to reveal a bright-yellow bikini. "This is awesome." She dipped her head back to wet her hair, and when she stood, pinching her nose, she reminded him of one of those *Sports Illustrated* models—beautiful, athletic, and totally airbrushed. Except she was real.

He must have been staring, because she lowered her eyes coyly and then swam to him with graceful strokes.

"This is wild, huh?" Her eyelashes were spikes that made her eyes mesmerizing. "Kind of funny that the school would be okay allowing the two of us on an island. Alone." She lifted and lowered one bare shoulder. "Not that I'm complaining."

It hit him then.

She had a crush.

He should have known at the dance, when Lauren kept whispering in his ear stuff he couldn't even hear because the music was so loud. She'd been sending other signals, too. Stupid, girly things like twirling her hair and running a toe along his leg under the table during those experiments. He was always the last to know when a girl liked him.

He barely noticed the gust of wind that rippled across the water. Or how the leaves were turning inside out.

She took one step forward, the dappled sunlight sparkling on her skin.

"You know," she purred, "I bet this *is* the experiment."

"What?"

"I'm guessing the reason they paired me up with two guys was because they wanted me to choose. And you know who I chose?"

At last an out. "Alex? I saw you guys in the gym and you were tight. He seems like an awesome guy."

"Alex is nice and everything, but . . . he's kind of vanilla."

Another gust of wind and the sky went dark. Kris looked up to see gray clouds amassing overhead. "Sudden shift in the weather. A storm's coming."

The pond water lapped the shore in gradually increasing waves. The small hairs on the back of his neck rose from atmospheric electricity and he felt a flicker of alarm.

Not just a storm, his instincts told him. A *monster*.

Lauren remained oblivious. She was swimming on her back like a siren, ankles crossed mermaid style. "For example, the rock wall? He'd never have done that. He told me so."

It took Kris a second to remember what they were talking about. Oh, yeah. Alex.

"But you went right up it without a rope. My pulse actually started racing when you did that."

She knew he didn't have a girlfriend. He'd admitted as much by fessing up about Addie. So he could scrap that as an excuse. Lauren knew he was a free agent and she was circling for the kill, just like the mechanical shark.

"No one will know what we do out here," she said, flipping around so her head bobbed by his chest. "What happens on Owl Island stays on Owl Island."

Something crashed in the woods and Kris jumped.

"Relax. It's just a branch. There are no big animals out here." Lauren stood and rubbed her bare wet arms. "Is it me, or did it just get colder?"

A lot colder, as a matter of fact. "We need to go." He ran out of the water, taking Lauren's hand to get her to move. She squeezed it playfully.

On shore, they threw on their clothes, which minutes before had been hot and oppressive and now were insufficient against the breeze and faint drizzle. A bolt of lightning cracked across the sky.

How far to the shelter? They were sitting ducks with all this exposure, and it was suddenly so dark he couldn't see the path. He would have to negotiate by memory and they would have to run.

"Hey, wait up," Lauren shouted, wriggling her foot into a sandal.

Kris impatiently waited for her to get ready. Finally, she joined him, panting in panic. "This is bad, isn't it?"

"It's not good." He wished he had his cell to call the mainland. There was still a chance Ed could pick them up before the storm got out of control. After a certain point, however, it wouldn't be safe for anyone to be on the water and they would have to hunker down.

Lauren stumbled and cried out in pain. "Damn tree roots. I think I twisted it." She was bent over, clutching her ankle.

"Are you okay?" A meaningless question. He just wanted her to say yes.

She tried taking a step and winced. "No. Hurts like hell. I can't walk."

Through the trees ahead he could make out a dark sliver of ocean. The path was too narrow for her to lean on him, which left only one option. He would have to carry her.

"All right. This is what we're going to do." He knelt. "Hop on my back."

"What?"

"Please, Lauren, I want to get out of the woods before the lightning hits us. This is the fastest way."

She hobbled over, slid her arms around his neck, and leaned against him. As he lifted her legs, she whispered, "My knight in shining armor."

Good thing she couldn't see his eye roll.

They emerged from the woods to two revelations: the clouds had temporarily parted to reveal blue sky, and waiting on the shore for them was Ed.

"I turned around when I got the weather alert. Wicked storm rolling in." He helped Lauren slide off Kris's back. "What happened to you?"

"Twisted my ankle on a tree root. Kris had to carry me."

Ed arched an eyebrow at Kris, who responded with a neutral shrug.

"We barely have enough time to make it back," Ed said, heading to the moored boat.

Lauren groaned. "I can't believe it. Another experiment ruined. I'm never going to get that extra credit."

"Worry about that later. Be glad you're not stranded here. They're saying it's a nor'easter, which means you would have been socked in for three days." Ed gave her his arm so she could lean on it.

But at the water's edge, she refused to take another step. "I can't. Those jellyfish. I mean, I just can't."

So for the third time that day, Kris had to carry her. He had just managed to get her on board and was about to pull himself in when Ed said, "Did you see Addie?"

Kris dropped into the water, stunned. "She's here?"

"Supposed to be. It's her experiment, right? She was watching you guys."

Watching? So she must have seen him in the pond with Lauren when she was . . .

And then he thought of the crash in the woods. "I know where she is." He pushed off the edge of the boat and swam back to shore.

Lauren called after him. "Where are you going?"

"To find Addie. She's in the woods."

"I can't stay," Ed shouted. "The Coast Guard wants everyone in."

"And I can't leave her." Kris motioned for him to leave. "Go!"

Ed gave him a thumbs-up. "Good luck, man. I'll come back for you when the storm's over." He hoisted up the anchor, started the engine, and zoomed off, relieved that Kris couldn't see how wide he was grinning.

TWENTY-THREE

Well, this would mess up her schedule. Just went to show that all the planning in the world couldn't prevent the odd bout of misfortune.

She refused to call it bad luck.

Bad luck did not cause you to fall out of a tree while you were attempting a close-up photo. Sure, landing on the rock was unfortunate, as was the impact of a dead tree limb falling on top of said leg. Neither was a cause for celebration.

But they could be chalked up to gravity and, okay, her general physical awkwardness. Not for nothing was she forbidden from playing field hockey.

Addie spit out a mouthful of pine needles and craned

her neck to check over her shoulder, where the heavy log lay across her calf. Tentatively, she reached down to touch her shin, and was chagrined to find it sticky with blood, mostly likely due to scratches from the tree.

Super. Things were just getting better and better.

She had to get out of here and find the first-aid kit in the shelter. How she would get to the shelter was in itself a daunting prospect. A walking stick and a splint to secure the broken bone were essentials because, if the radiating pain was any indication, this was a fracture.

Summoning all her courage, she tried to squirm free, only to be rewarded with a sharp stabbing sensation in her femur, as if her leg was breaking all over again.

"Oww!" she cried, tears springing to her eyes.

Now what was she going to do? She was trapped. The wind was picking up, with gusts expected to reach over seventy miles per hour on the outlying island, according to the weather reports she'd read that morning, and Kris and Lauren had left.

Her phone and camera had landed on cushioning underbrush and might be okay if she could get them inside the shelter before it rained. Unfortunately, they had fallen right outside the range of her fingertips.

Did she mention that the pain was excruciating?

Ed probably assumed she was A-OK, waiting for Kris so they could be alone for a night. This he had agreed to reluctantly on the grounds that Kris, having ditched her for Kara, deserved to be stranded solo on the island, where he could hunker down in the shelter to be devoured by a nest of hidden black widows.

"You don't have to go through with it. You can't stay on the island in a deadly storm with that loser," Ed told her on the drive back from Harvard while Mindy slept in the backseat. "I'll come clean with Tess about what we've been up to and why and she'll let you use our case for the Athenian project. She'd do anything for you. You know that."

Addie was moved by his support. Ed had been a loyal friend to her from the beginning, setting up the whole kayaking rescue scenario with Emma and Shreya, dragging out the mechanical shark and steering it from his boat. By happy coincidence, Kris had already been down at the beach waiting for her, so there'd been no need to concoct some excuse to get him on the water.

However, Ed could take full credit for coming up with the idea of loosening the harness so it would detach from the rope while they were climbing the rock wall. And he spent his entire Saturday afternoon setting up the final experiment on this island, all because he was so grateful to Addie for Tess, who remained blissfully unaware of her boyfriend's hijinks.

Which was why she couldn't use their relationship as a

case study for the Athenian Award.

"Tess's mothers," Addie said last night. "You know how they are about privacy. They'd sue me if I mentioned their daughter at a national meeting of neuroscientists."

His lips twitched. "Don't take this the wrong way, but I wouldn't place the Athenian Committee on the same level as the Grammy Awards. Besides, you're going with aliases, right?"

That hadn't occurred to her, though she supposed she could. "Except when I get to the experiment with Kris and me. Then I will insist on full disclosure."

"And that won't get you disqualified, for running an experiment on yourself?"

"Was Werner Forssmann disqualified from winning a Nobel Prize?"

Ed stopped at a light. "Who was Werner Forssmann?"

Oh, how quickly our heroes fade into obscurity, she thought. "He developed a theory that you could open coronary arteries by running a catheter through them. So he did. On himself. Threaded a tube from a cut in his arm all the way to his own heart."

"Ouch!" Ed stepped on the gas. "I guess making Kris fall for you is a piece of cake in comparison."

"*Was*," she said. "After what just happened, I think I'd rather have cut my own flesh."

And now here she was with a broken bone. How did

the saying go? *Be careful what you wish for because it might come true.*

Now what she wanted more than anything was for Ed to sense that something was wrong and turn around to rescue her. But that wouldn't happen. Already, the storm had moved inland and he was transporting Lauren and Kris to safety.

She rested her head in the pine needles. One night. That's all she had to survive was one night, and then she'd be safe. She yawned, exhausted from lack of sleep and stress and no doubt shock. Rest would do her good and it would help pass the time and keep her mind off Kris.

If only she weren't so cold.

"Addie! Aaaaadeeeeee!"

Addie was having a dream. She was Snow White in a forest and a prince was coming to rescue her from a deep and deadly sleep. He was searching and searching, calling for her to no avail. She heard his footsteps. So close. But he couldn't see her because she was hidden among the pines. She would need to rouse herself to make a sound. Otherwise, the prince would give up, leaving her to die alone.

"Hello!" she cried feebly. Her eyelids were so heavy. If only she could open them a peek she could break through the fog. "Helloooooo."

The rustling stopped.

"Ed?" Consciousness proved too elusive. "I'm here, Ed," she mumbled.

The rustling resumed. Feet pounding through brush.

"Oh my god. Addie! Are you okay?"

Not Ed. Different prince.

Someone was slapping her cheeks. "Wake up, Addie. Come on. Open your eyes."

All right, she thought, just this once. Then I'm going back to sleep. She hoped he would be satisfied with a flutter of eyelashes. Mission accomplished. Back to snoozing.

"You're alive. Oh, thank god. You're alive. We've got to get you out of here. A huge storm's coming."

So tell me something I don't know, she thought, drifting off peacefully.

"Stay with me, Addie. Don't go back to sleep."

Why not? Sleep was easy. You didn't have to think when you were asleep and she was always thinking.

Thinking. Thinking. Thinking.

"You think too much," her father once said. Yeah. Right. As if.

A weight was lifted off her leg and a rush of fresh searing pain invaded her consciousness, startling her to alertness. Then she remembered the fall. The tree limb. The break.

"*Owwww!*"

She opened her eyes fully to see Kris there, examining her calf. She was mad at him, but she was thankful, too. Emotions were ridiculous. Never uniform or logical. Had no respect for a schedule. That's why they called them emotions, she supposed.

"What are you doing?" she whispered, her mouth so dry it was almost impossible to speak.

He opened a water bottle and brought it to her parched lips. Water had never tasted so good. "What happened?"

"I fell and a limb snapped off and landed on my leg."

"I got that. What were you doing in the tree?"

"Later. I broke this thing." She pointed toward her leg.

"I'll be right back," he said, getting up. "Have to find a splint."

The wind was crazy. Leaves and twigs were flying and thunder rumbled. In a daze, she watched him vanish and then return with a sturdy stick.

"Felled by a tree, saved by a tree." He took off his T-shirt, revealing a lean, tan chest lined with muscles.

Addie swallowed some more water. The pain was annoying. But Kris's body wasn't. "Aren't you going to be cold?"

"I could take off your shirt, if you're concerned." He winked.

Winking was a signal of intimacy. Or a speck of dust in the eye. In this wind, it could be either.

"Is it compound or simple?" she asked.

He bit the collar of his T-shirt and tore it in two. "Hard to tell. No bone poking out. Thank god for small blessings, right?"

"Very small."

"Okay, this won't be fun." He hesitated. "Not that any of this is a party. I'm going to roll you over onto this splint. Then I'm going to tie your leg to it with my T-shirt. I'll try to work fast. It would help if you didn't scream."

"I won't."

She did.

For a good ten minutes, she let out a howl louder than the gusts of wind. It was as if someone had taken a knife and was piercing it over and over into her shin. The pain ran up her leg and thigh and set her entire right side on fire.

Kris worked methodically, aligning the leg on the splint, tightly wrapping strips of cloth from his T-shirt.

"Where did you learn to do that?" she asked, panting.

"Nepal. They taught us basic first aid, though, honestly, this is something any Webelo should know."

"What is a Webelo?"

"A very small Boy Scout."

She giggled a little. The dopamine. Quite a dose, if her loopiness was any indication.

"Ready?" He slid one arm under her back and another under her knees.

"Where are we going?"

"I'm carrying you to the shelter. Then I'm calling the Coast Guard if we can. I found your phone but we're too far inland to get a signal."

He crouched down and lifted her from his knees, wobbling slightly to avoid a blowing branch. The pain in her leg was so brutal that Addie buried her face in his neck, taking comfort in his steady pulse, his strong sinews, the fresh smell of his skin.

"I'll try not to bash your leg on the way there," he said. "Hold on tight."

She wrapped her arms around him and tried to steady her breath. It would not help the situation if she passed out. They walked silently for a time, Kris swiveling sideways down the narrow path, being careful not to drop her on the downhills.

He said, "I'm sorry."

"That I got hurt?"

"No, well, yes, of course. But I'm talking about what Kara said last night."

"Oh."

"I don't expect you to forgive me, but I want to tell you how it happened." He ducked under a low-hanging branch. "Kara was really upset by the way animals were being treated in the lab. She complained about it constantly, even cried. And to be honest, Addie, it made me mad, too."

"I guess."

He let that lie and kept moving. "So one day, while we were sitting around listening to another of Kara's rants and raves, I said, 'We should do something. We should get all the frogs and the gerbils and set them free.' Only . . ." He massaged his brow as if the memory alone caused a headache. "Kara and Mack—*especially* Mack—took it to extremes. Mack showed up with a crowbar and spray paint and went ballistic."

Addie felt herself slipping and gripped him harder. "Dr. Brooks said the damage was in the thousands."

"Yeah, which is why I'm not getting paid this summer. Working my debt off one hour at a time."

She bounced along and thought about this, the pain in her leg so intense that thinking felt like an Olympic sport. "How come you weren't expelled when the others were?"

"I almost was. I tackled Mack . . . and stopped him from doing even more damage. And I came clean right away. I went to Foy that same day and took the blame for everything."

"But you didn't smash up the equipment."

"No, but Mack wouldn't have done that, either, if I hadn't come up with the bright idea to sneak into the lab in the first place." He lifted a leg over a fallen tree. "It really was my fault, Addie, no matter how you spin it."

The world was beginning to fade and Addie worried she might throw up. There was one last question she needed to ask. It lingered in the back of her mind, almost unreachable, until Kris stopped to see how she was doing.

"Oh, Addie," he said, frowning. "I'm really, really sorry."

She looked into those dark brown eyes, so familiar now, and felt a tug. "Kara. Is she . . . ? Are you two . . . ?"

Kris went back to walking. "Try to forget her. Kara will never come back to the Academy." He readjusted Addie on his back. "And I'll never go back to her."

Good enough, Addie thought dreamily before being startled by a new wave of crushing pressure on her shin.

"Almost there," Kris said softly, sensing her agony. "You've done great."

They arrived at the end of the path. Up ahead, she could make out the churning gray sea, the billows of black clouds. They were soaked. But they were going to be okay.

"But did you have to spray-paint the lab walls?" she asked.

Kris trudged across the wet sand to the shelter. "I didn't paint those. I'm sure you don't believe me, but I'm telling you the truth. I had the can in my hand because I was covering up the graffiti." He kicked in the door and laid her down gently on the floor. "You can ask security. They found me trying to cover it up."

The floor was hard and smelled like mildew, but they were dry.

"There are sleeping bags in the corner," Addie said. "Ed and I put them there yesterday, just in case."

He unrolled one sleeping bag and then folded another under her head. "How's that feel?" he asked, brushing back her hair with his fingers.

"Painful, but okay. Is there a signal?"

He checked his phone. "Nuh-uh. I'm going to walk along the beach and see if I can find one. Will you be okay by yourself? I'll prop open the door so it's not so dark."

She grimaced. Her leg had begun to throb, indicating the possibility of internal bleeding and swelling. "I'm good."

He stuck a piece of driftwood in the hinge and trudged off. One gust of wind and the door slammed shut, leaving her alone in the darkness to listen to the roar of the wind and waves.

She must have suffered a concussion, too, because her head ached and she was sleepy. *Soooooo* sleepy.

After minutes, or maybe hours, the door swung open and Kris stepped in, clapping his hands. "Wake up, Addie. Ed called the Coast Guard. They're on their way with

Foy. I told him about your leg and that you hit your head. We're going to get you to a hospital, okay?"

"Okay."

He knelt beside her. "Look, I don't know when I'm going to see you again."

"We'll see each other on the boat. And you'll come to the hospital, right?"

"I mean, alone." He exhaled deeply. "I've been kicked out, Addie. I'm done. I signed the letter of expulsion this morning."

A lump rose in her throat. Even in her emotional muddle of heartbreak and self-pity and anger about last night, she didn't want him to leave. "What did you do wrong *this* time?"

He smiled lopsidedly. "Dexter's crabs. I kind of set them free."

"*Again?*"

"And then I rigged the wiring to give him a shock when he put his hand in the water."

She gasped. That was truly horrible.

"Don't worry," he added quickly. "I installed a ground fault interrupter so he wouldn't be electrocuted and used enough resistors to keep the shock mild."

"You *should* have been expelled for that."

"Yeah. I know. But Dexter was trying to screw you over. Also, those crabs. How would you like to be them?

The way he kept shocking them was sick."

The image of Dexter stamping his foot as it dawned on him that his tortured crabs had been stolen caused her to experience the strangest of reactions. It was like a hiccup, except the spasm didn't affect just her diaphragm. Her whole body convulsed.

"You freed his crabs!" she blurted. "Where did you take them?"

"To the beach right by the docks. They zoomed straight down, shock free. Couldn't wait to get out of there."

"I bet." By now, she was in full hysterics. Wrenching, uncontrollable waves of laughter were overtaking her whole body.

"You're laughing!" Kris exclaimed.

"I know," she said, gulping for air. "I'm not a gelotologist . . ."

"Jell-O-tologist?"

"Gelotology is the science of laughter." She took a breath. "But that fall must have destabilized my left superior frontal gyrus, because now I can't stop. And also, before Mr. Foy rescues me, I have something to confess."

"Wait. Is this some concussion thing?"

"Nope." Her chest heaved as she tried to regain composure. "I got you back for trashing the lab. And I got you back good, so we're even. Shake?"

He took her hand but didn't shake. "Hmm. Definitely a brain injury. You don't believe in revenge, remember? You told me that once."

"You'll see at my Athenian Award presentation. I'm going to reserve you a front-row seat." Then she pulled him to her, with a deep long kiss, because this time it was her turn to call the shots.

As she'd been doing all along.

EPILOGUE

The Brain Adrenaline, Dopamine, and Amine
Synthesis System (B.A.D.A.S.S.)
by Adelaide Emerson
as delivered to the Athenian Award Committee
on October 14 at Cornell University, Ithaca, New York

"Ladies and gentlemen of the Athenian Committee, it is an honor and privilege to be standing before you today as a nominee for the very prestigious Athenian Award. As each of you has been provided with a copy of my research as well as video footage of the interacting couples from my three experiments, it is inefficient to restate what has already been stated.

"Instead, I would like to use this opportunity to update you on the couples' progress since the submission deadline, starting with the first couple, who, for the sake of anonymity, I have labeled Ted and Bess. Although Ted was informed of the experiment shortly after implementation, Bess was not. Or so we both assumed.

"Apparently, Bess did deduce that her attraction to Ted was spurred by artificially stimulated neurohormones, but chose to not reveal her discovery for fear that this would harm their relationship. This perfectly comports with my thesis that artificially stimulated PEA release can still lead to the production of long-term 'love' hormones such as endorphins and oxytocin. They are still involved and committed, though not completely certain until Thanksgiving, when they will meet each other in person for the first time since Ted left for college. That he attends a school whose unofficial motto is Where Fun Goes to Die is definitely in Bess's favor.

"Unlike Bess and Ted, Kris, Lauren, and Alex understood they were joining an experiment when they volunteered as participants in exchange for extra credit and other nonmonetary compensation. Although it seemed initially that Lauren was more attracted to Alex—despite their low-adrenaline sessions—as my thesis accurately predicted, she developed what in layman's terms is called a 'crush' on Kris after she witnessed him engaging in high-risk activities. Photos and video of them interacting at a school dance and, subsequently, in an isolated pond are attached. Lauren was unable to pursue this relationship with Kris, as he was otherwise engaged.

"Which brings me to the third and more controversial of my experiments, which is already the topic of heated debate in the neurological academic community. Colleagues have asked me when I decided to include Kris in my own personal experiment, and the truth is that I immediately saw an opportunity on our flight to Boston. He possessed many desirable qualities that made him an outstanding candidate: he reacted viscerally to adrenaline stimulation, as evidenced by his hyperventilation during turbulence, and he was kind to a strange child, thereby displaying empathy.

"Finally, Kris was—is—attractive, and I was not averse to the prospect of engaging him in close physical contact.

"Was it wrong of me, a scientist, to mislead this unsuspecting guinea pig for my own personal gain? As my former lab partner once said so eloquently, the pursuit of science is not pretty. I need not remind you of the animals who have been bled, poisoned, drugged, infected, and, ultimately, killed on the road to better medicine. They were never informed, nor did they give consent, to such experiments.

"Are we humans that much different?

"But the real reason I chose to apply my theory to practice on Kris was far more primal: I liked him. I really liked him, and I wanted to see how far we could go. After all, what would be the purpose of my research if only to understand how one might fall in love when I could actually be motivating the cutest boy in the school to fall in love with me?

"If that violates the scientific method, then so be it. I am happier now than I have ever been, and not merely because I nabbed a perfect score on my SATs last month and have been invited by the dean of admissions to apply to my dream school, Harvard. (Pause for applause.)

"I am happy because my brain is bathed in endorphins as part of a long-term relationship, a luxury I did not imagine possible when I was informed that Kris had been expelled.

"Fortunately, our headmaster wisely reasoned that Kris's personal sacrifice to stay on the island in a dangerous electrical storm to rescue me far outweighed whatever actions he may or may not have committed months before during an especially transitive period in his own brain chemistry. Also, in the spirit of transparency, a couple of very prominent actors with a daughter who attends Academy 355 threatened to terminate their generous annual contributions to the capital fund if he was not readmitted to the Academy.

"In summary, I present to you a multidimensional project that I hope furthers our knowledge of how the brain creates the illusion of love by implementing the most powerful and dangerous natural drugs available to humanity, drugs that aren't manufactured in a lab, but by our own brains.

"Thank you for your consideration."

ACKNOWLEDGMENTS

It doesn't take a brain scientist to figure out that I'm not a brain scientist, so I would like to thank the following source of information: *My Stroke of Insight: A Brain Scientist's Personal Journey*, by Jill Bolte Taylor, PhD. It was my launching pad for imagining the powers of the brain, especially in adolescents, when so much wiring is still being connected. Taylor's memoir is a fascinating, inspiring, and easy read.

I am also grateful to articles published by or quoting: Semir Zeki, PhD, a neurobiologist at the University College of London; Martha Bridge Denckla, MD, a research scientist at the Kennedy Krieger Institute; David C. Geary, PhD, a professor of psychological sciences at the

University of Missouri; Anne Marie Helmenstine, PhD, a science writer; and *Brain Architecture* by Larry W. Swanson, which gave me the basics.

That said, I do not recommend using this book as the basis for any science paper in which the sought grade exceeds a C+. Instead of measuring neuron reception, for the most part my brain is pretty much distracted by boys.